PICTURE PERFECT

Summer of Adventures 4

Alex Silver

CONTENTS

COPYRIGHT

SYNOPSIS

Is it too much to ask for a whirlwind romance that sweeps me off my feet?

I'm fed up with one-off scenes at the club. Online dating has become an endless conveyor belt of rejection. Enter Jax, the picture perfect friend with all the benefits I crave, and none of the drama I can't stand.

I'm used to fading into the background. Growing up as the middle child of seven siblings and now being the quiet one in my friend group, it's easy to accept being overlooked. Never quite fitting in and never rocking the boat by demanding more than others care to give. But lately, I've been wanting more. More time with the family I love. Both the people that raised me and the folks I found at Adventures. More balance with my dream job before I find myself burnt out by thirty. More of everything, but I'd settle for a once in a lifetime romance.

I want to be loved and cherished by a partner who can be both a tender caregiver for my little side, and a devious dom. One who leaves me filthy and debauched. I might be asking too much. Maybe the best I can hope for is getting all my kinky needs met with Jax. Should I hold out for a love connection when being in his bed makes me feel like I'm on top of the world, or will it all come crashing down when I can't help but fall for him and his adorable dog?

Picture Perfect is a kinky M/M romance between Jax, a genderqueer kink photographer who is *not* a daddy and Connor, a pierced trans boy who works for a nonprofit and just wants someone to love him. It includes sensation play, e-stim, figging, wax play, mild caregiver kink with a little who loves to get messy (sploshing), tentacle roleplay CNC, and oviposition.

CHAPTER 1

Jax

ite not found. I click the refresh button frantically. The same error message loads again. Here I sit at my desk on a sunny Monday morning, staring down an incomprehensible error code and trying to figure out what I did wrong. Moments like this, I envy Gia, my golden retriever. She's snoring in her plush dog bed without a care in the world while I try to curtail a stress spiral.

I had the best of intentions to tackle one of those annoying tasks that I always swear I'll get around to. Well, wedding season is just around the corner and I know I won't get to it if I put this off much longer. It's been six months since I last updated my website with new images. And the restricted access section of my site, where I keep my kinky boudoir portfolio, desperately needs new material to reflect my latest offerings.

When I first needed a website, I got lucky in that one of my close friends, Kylee, agreed to barter with me. I offered photo sessions for her and her pup in exchange for building my website. I might have to see about offering those two another shoot with the deluxe print package thrown in to update it. Kylee gave me easy instructions for updating the gallery, and a foolproof tutorial for the password locked section of the site for my racier photos. The update process still intimidates me.

I hit refresh again, since clearly the photos I tried to upload aren't doing what I wanted. The error message persists. I tap at the keys some more, trying various combinations to undo whatever it is I did to the site. Or refresh away the ominous error code. When that approach fails, I try the history tab and click on every option that seems like it might undo this mess.

Nothing works. I try pulling up my site on my phone, just to reassure myself that it's still there. The home page loads just fine. But the restricted access section is gone. I groan in frustration, then resign myself to the fact that I can't fix the issue on my own. I still click around a bit more, just to be sure.

This situation could be worse. Like, if I somehow stripped away whatever code Kylee used to render the password protected portion of the site semi-private. The models and clients who agreed to be showcased behind a password signed release forms authorizing me to use their images on my site. But there were caveats, like limiting access to prospective clients.

Kylee set it up to make saving high res copies of those images difficult, too. The last thing I want to do is put my subjects' kinkiest moments on blast to the internet at large without their consent. I don't think I did that, but I'm not messing around with guessing how to fix whatever I broke, if that's even a possibility.

I need to call Kylee and work out a deal to get this fixed. With another heartfelt sigh, I scrub my fingers through my hair and dial.

"Kylee's cell, Quent speaking. What can we do you for?" Quent, her long-time partner, answers on the second ring. I can hear Kylee in the background, but not clear enough to make out what she is saying. It sounds like the two of them are in a car. When Quent replies, their voice sounds muffled and I'm pretty sure they are talking to Kylee, not me. "I know you use it for work, Mommy, but it's just Jax."

I laugh at that. "Just Jax, huh? I see how it is, you impertinent pup," I tease.

"Sorry, Jax. Mommy says 'hello'. She's driving, so she can't talk right now."

"Ah, are you two headed somewhere fun?"

"Eh, not really? Doctor appointment, blargh," Quent says. I can picture the grossed out face they're probably pulling as they speak and it makes me grin. Quent is fun to photograph, always expressive and willing to try anything. Hopefully Kylee will trade more pics for fixing whatever I did to my website. "Can I take a message or do you want to call back later?"

"Is everything okay with you both? It's not an emergency or anything, but I did something to my website when I was trying to update the photos in the private gallery. Any chance she'd be able to fix whatever I messed up?"

"Oh, yeah, we're both fine, just some routine stuff. And she will definitely fit you in. Hold on one sec." Quent holds the phone away from their mouth as they relay what I said, with several embellishments, and then speaks back into the receiver. "Mommy says you can swing by later tonight with your laptop and the files you wanted to add, and she'll squeeze you into her schedule. She says around four, if that works for you?"

"That would be amazing. I'll owe you two another photo session, alright?"

"Sweet. I might be in the market for one of your packages soon. Probably. I think. Shifty eyes."

I stifle a snort. Only Q would say the emoji aloud. For all their lack of enthusiasm about going to their appointment, they seem to be in a particularly excitable mood. "Great. Well, I won't keep you. Good luck at the appointment."

"Thanks, see you later."

We hang up and I fritter away the rest of my allotted administrative hours sorting through my most recent photos to find the best ones for my website. I'm already mentally making a wishlist of the photos I'd like to add if I had my pick of subjects. I've photographed several kinky workshops and done private shoots at Adventures, the kink club where I'm a member. But several items remain on my kinky wishlist that I haven't gotten an opportunity to shoot yet.

A growing chunk of my clientele is part of the local BDSM community. So having more examples of what I can do to make their kinks shine to show off in the gallery is a legit work expense. And I can take tamer, safe for work, shots for stock sites at the same time.

I can afford to hire a model. That just leaves finding willing models with a variety of kinks and body types. That, and dreaming up my wishlist. Is it any wonder creating the wishlist beats out dealing with my website and tackling the pile of notices I need to send out over unpaid invoices?

The rest of the morning goes to formalizing my wishlist and checking my stock photo sales to see what's already selling well and note what's trending. Not exactly what I had on the agenda, but it is still technically admin stuff I've been putting off, so it counts. I even make a sizable chunk of progress before Gia interrupts me with her broad head shoved into my lap and a plea in her big brown eyes.

It would take a stronger will than mine to deny my sweet girl anything, so we walk to a dog friendly cafe for lunch on the outdoor patio. We're the only ones braving the cold winter weather to eat outside, but it's worth sitting under the heated awning to bring my girl along with me. After our walk, I get in a few more hours of work before I have to drop Gia off at home. Once she's settled, I head over to Kylee and Quent's place to deal with my website.

CHAPTER 2

Connor

My latest match shows up to our first date late. Not a deal breaker. Most folks around here act laid back about being on time. Except for a few stuffy suits I've dated, but the less said about them, the better.

If it weren't for my parents drumming punctuality into all of us kids, I wouldn't care much. Then again, with seven kids to keep track of, we had to stick to a schedule. Otherwise, no one would have ever been where they were supposed to be on time.

This date is not looking all that promising. Even after Lorence sits at the table and smiles that million watt grin that made me take a chance on him on the app. His profile didn't give me much to go on, so I gave that winning smile the benefit of the doubt.

"Hey, Connor, right? Have you been waiting for long?" He leans forward and makes intense eye contact.

"That's me." I glance at the mostly empty soda in front of me. Yeah, it's been a solid twenty minutes since I sat. And that isn't including the time I waited to get a table before he texted to say he was close and to 'go ahead and order drinks.' I don't say that. Instead, I give him a bland smile and let him off the hook; I want this date to be different. "Not too long, Lorence."

"Cool. Have you ordered?" He picks up a menu and peruses the options.

"Nope, I was waiting on you." Does that sound passive aggressive? If it does, Lorence must not notice, engrossed in the menu as he is.

"Awesome, I'm starving. I think I'll grab a burger. Want to split some fries?" More of that intense eye contact.

"Sure." I agree. Considering he picked a burger place, the burger seemed like a foregone conclusion.

I'm fine with ordering a veggie burger. All the other options come slathered in cheese. I'm not in the mood to figure out the intricacies of what menu items might be kosher. Like Modaddy always says when Pop waxes philosophical about different rabbinical interpretations, because he's a nerd like that, you can't go wrong with assuming veggies are safe. It's not like I'm super religious, but you spend enough years with certain customs and some of them are bound to stick. Keeping to the broad strokes makes me feel connected to my family.

Lorence and I make small talk about our jobs until the server comes to take our order. Nothing too groundbreaking there. He's in marketing for a finance firm. My civil engineer title seems to interest him; until I tell him I work for a social housing nonprofit. That makes him lose interest real quick. Not promising, but I let it go.

I let a lot of petty annoyances pass unremarked. Until we order and Lorence gives me a side-eye that seems entirely uncalled for, since I didn't order a burger crafted from the finest of human infant meat.

"You're a vegetarian?" Lorence sneers as soon as our server is out of earshot.

"Um, no." I force a smile that I am *so* not feeling. So what if I was? Ugh, some people. At this point, I'm done. I doubt explaining that my family is culturally Jewish because my pop is religious will win him over. Since I include my dietary restrictions in my dating profile to save myself this exact conversation, I know this dude didn't even bother to read my profile. Which means he probably also thinks I'm cis. Big sigh. "I just felt like a veggie burger."

Lorence grunts and pulls out his phone.

Yeah, I'm not even going to bother with the whole disclosure thing at this point. He showed his true colors. If I didn't have another difference for him to reject, I'd consider sticking out the shitty date in favor of getting laid. But I doubt he'll take my lack of a cis dick any better than he's taking my food preferences or my job. I don't need to deal with any more rejection tonight. Rather than let him leave and stick me with the bill, I stand to find our server. "You know what? I don't think this is going to work."

"We could just skip dinner and fuck." Lorence grips my hand on the table and I tense. I doubt he'll make a scene, but his eyes drift to where my nipple piercings press against the thin fabric of my nice shirt. Yeah, not happening. I wrench my hand free and step back.

"I don't fuck on the first date," I lie through clenched teeth.

"That's too bad." Lorence frowns, but he lets it go, leaning back in his seat with a parting shot about not paying for my food.

Works for me. Our terse exchange draws the server's attention. So I get my meal changed to a to-go order and leave the burger place with my less than exciting meal in a takeout container. I don't hate veggie burgers, but the bun is going to be all soggy by the time I get to eat it now. Before I even make it to my bus stop, I call my best friend to vent. Quent will get it.

I know another crappy date isn't exactly the end of the world, but would it seriously kill a person to read my profile before messaging me? I agonized over whether to disclose I'm trans on there just to avoid this sort of train wreck situation. If I didn't have to worry about whether he knew, I might have taken Lorence up on his invitation for a quick fuck, but I'm not in the mood now.

Making it public means that I have to slog through way too many shitty hot takes about my anatomy in my DMs. Or potential matches who have questions they seem to think I'm obligated to answer, ranging from the basic to the deeply personal.

At first, I didn't mind educating people, but a dating app really isn't the place for it. I just want to find a compatible partner, not provide free emotional labor. If they want to know what it means when I say I'm a trans man, they can google that.

I don't mind discussing details that are specific to me with a partner once we establish a connection, or have plans to jump in bed. But it's frustrating to have to explain or justify my existence to satisfy strangers' curiosity when most of them don't actually seem interested in dating me.

"How was the date?" Quent answers without preamble.

"Guess." I shoot back.

"Hm, from the hour I'm guessing dude either hit a home run and you are calling to let me know his deets so I can bring the wrath of god down on his ass if anything happens to you, or he struck out and you're calling to vent?"

"The latter."

"Ugh, sorry, Connor. I swear the right guy is out there somewhere. Do you want to come over and veg on the couch? I'm about to order Thai, so you can share my noodles." My bestie laces their tone with enough innuendo to sink a ship on that last line. They perk up with the invitation, so I'm pretty sure they're bored and their Mommy is busy with work.

"Share your noodles, huh?" I tease. "I know how much you like to keep your mouth busy. Too bad I've already got a burger. Think your Mommy would mind if I crash at yours tonight?"

"You're always welcome here. She's got a client over for an emergency website fix, but I'm sure she'll be fine with us taking the guest room if you need a cuddle buddy."

"That would be nice. Thanks, Q."

"Not a problem. Text when you get here?"

"Yep." I hang up to grab a bus and use the ride out to the burbs where Kylee and Quent live to catch up on the family text thread.

There's several dozen texts waiting unread. Modaddy's wake up message wishing us all a great day. Pop chiming in to remind us to caffeinate. My oldest brother, Prescott, griping about his six-year-old, Carl, making it a not so very good morning when he puked up his breakfast all over his little sister.

Our next youngest brother, Cameron, replied to that with a line of barf emojis followed by another line of laughing emojis. The two of them bickered about kids for a while until Pop told Cam to be nice. Then our sister, Viv, offered to watch the kids if Prescott or his husband can't stay home. She's on mat leave with her youngest anyway and she's pretty sure her older kid is the one who gave Carl the stomach bug. Prescott took her up on the offer.

The chat was silent again until the twins both messaged to remind everyone about Marietta's travel team soccer game. Eli asked who is picking them up to go to the game instead of taking the bus home. Modaddy sent back a message that they aren't supposed to have their phones on at school. Pop reminded them he would be there to get them and not to dawdle with their friends if they wanted to get to the game on time.

More silence with the occasional photo of my niblings from

my sister to my brother. The thread came back to life not too long ago with a burst of congratulatory texts aimed toward Marietta. She apparently scored a tie-breaking goal near the end of the game. And even more texts when that goal turned out to give her team the win.

From there, the talk turned to celebrating the game. Gretchen, Viv's wife, asks for Prescott and Matt to bring a to-go order for their family when they pick up their sick kid. Since Viv and her wife are both home with all four of my niblings, they won't be at the family dinner tonight either. I wish I was going with them. Or staying with Viv, Gretch, and the kids. But I'm also looking forward to seeing Quent tonight, having someone to hold me.

Where to go for their celebratory meal still appears to be an ongoing decision among the rest of my family. Judging from the incoming messages lighting up my phone, the debate is getting fierce. Even though I swear there's only about three local restaurants that can accommodate the entire boisterous group of us. Them.

So, yeah, reading the family chat makes me feel like I'm peeking in at their lives. Somewhere between a voyeur and a virtual participant in their day-to-day routines. I hate being so far from home on days like this. I send Marietta a congrats GIF and a bunch of emojis. Then I message Viv that I'm sorry she's stuck with a passel of puking kids and offer to babysit next time I'm in town. In the group thread, I joke they should grab a helping of the sticky coconut tofu I love from the Chinese buffet in my honor and tell them all I miss them.

Modaddy sends me a separate message asking how my date was and I fill them in that it was a bust. I don't mention just how bad of a bust because they'd get upset for me. I don't want to upset them when they are celebrating Marietta's sports victory with the rest of the family. So I let it go, tucking away my phone and ignoring the hollow ache of loneliness.

CHAPTER 3

Connor

By the time I get to Q's place, I'm in a full-blown melancholy over missing my family. It feels like I'll never find someone to make a family of my own with. As I'm walking from the bus stop having a pity party for one, I get another text on the group chat. It's a photo attachment that opens up to reveal the coconut tofu and the caption, 'just for you, with love.' It's from Pop's phone.

I thank my parents and make the obligatory joke about actually sending food through the interwebs, and then I text Q that I've arrived.

They meet me at the door and wrap me in an enthusiastic embrace that reminds me why I've stayed in Vancouver, aside from my job. Q and Kylee, along with my other friends at Adventures, are my chosen family. They watch out for me and make the city home. With them, I have room to explore my kinks. Even if I'm pretty sure my prospects of finding a long-term partner at the club aren't much better than for finding what I want on some dating app.

"Do you want to talk about it?" Quent tows me toward the den, grabbing their partially eaten food from the kitchen counter along the way.

"Not really. Just sucked. Dude would've saved us both a crappy night if he bothered to read my profile." I sigh. Q winces sympathetically, because they know the type.

"Want to follow up dinner with a pint of ice cream? I've got some mint chip on standby and a *Supergirl* marathon ready to stream."

"Sounds like a plan. It's almost like you know me," I tease. My light tone doesn't hide how much their sweet gesture, geared perfectly for me, warms my heart. They don't make a big deal of it, though.

"Almost." Quent hugs me again, this time just a quick squeeze around my shoulders and a gentle hip check. We set up our respective takeout meals on TV trays and they hit play on our show.

Quent steals my fries whenever I'm not paying attention. When I only pick at the soggy, lukewarm bean burger, they insist on splitting their noodles with me. We scooch close to share and being with someone who cares helps me relax.

My earlier sense of isolation from my family ebbs as I'm folded into Quent's warmth. I'm not alone, even if I am lonely sometimes. And I can visit my family whenever I want. They're only a few hours' drive from the city in the same little town where I grew up.

When our meals are gone, Q pauses the show to swap our takeout boxes for the pint of ice cream and two spoons. We curl up together to share directly out of the carton. Which is how Kylee finds us several episodes into our TV binge when she and her client emerge from her office.

The approaching footsteps alert me to a vaguely familiar voice talking with Kylee. She pokes her head into the den and turns on the light.

"Oh, hello there Connor, were we expecting you tonight?" Kylee smiles at me, her maternal warmth shining through.

"No. Had a bad day." I lick my spoon guiltily. I know Quent has rules about asking permission for treats. And we didn't ask.

"Sorry to hear it. Are you two going to be taking the guest room tonight, Q?"

Quent pushes the ice cream toward me, which only draws Kylee's attention to the treat. "Mhm."

"Did you eat already, pup?" Kylee asks, her eyes narrowing in on the half-eaten pint. Q freezes with the spoon in their mouth and nods.

"Mhm." Quent slurps their spoon clean.

"And are you supposed to be eating all the ice cream?" Kylee tilts her head toward them.

"No, Mommy." Quent admits, pushing the ice cream container toward me again. I cradle the pint to my chest and eat another bite.

"What are the rules?" Kylee asks.

"Use a bowl and ask permission." Quent sets their spoon on the TV tray.

"And did you?" Kylee folds her arms together and taps her toe.

"No." Quent admits.

"Why not?" Kylee presses.

Quent hunches their shoulders and wriggles against me. "I was trying to cheer Con up."

"Are you blaming your friend for you breaking your rules, pup?" Kylee gives Q a narrow-eyed look, offering them a chance to reword their reply.

Quent sighs. "No, Mommy. Can Con and I have ice cream and a sleepover, please?"

"You may." She steps into the room to kiss the top of Quent's head. "You know I'm always happy for you to have friends over."

"So, no punishment and I can have all the ice cream?" Q ventures. They give a happy little wiggle as they peer hopefully up at their Mommy.

Kylee snorts an amused laugh. She cups Q's cheek. "Oh, my sweet puppy, you know better than that. We'll discuss this upstairs."

Quent huffs. "It was worth a shot." They heave themself up from the couch with an over-dramatic sigh.

"We'll be back shortly, Connor. Will you wait to restart the show?"

"Yes, Miss Kylee." I nod. Quent slinks out of the room.

"Are you okay with waiting, or shall I deal with them after you've gone home?"

Most of the time, I'm fine with watching Kylee punish Q. Chastity is so not my thing. Unlike me, Q needs it to anchor them sometimes, and I suspect that's what they're going to be dealing with upstairs.

They both enjoy the game and Q is cute and even more cuddly when they go into their pup-space. Which they almost always do with punishments like this. Honestly, cuddling up on the couch with pup Q sounds like a good way to spend the rest of my night. I don't want to watch the intimate moment between Domme and pup when I'm still raw over my prospects of finding a relationship like they have, though. So waiting in the den while they do their thing works for me.

"It's fine, Miss Kylee. I'll be good while you're busy."

"You're always a good boy, Con." She cups my cheek and presses a kiss to the crown of my head. It's nice. I'm not really little right now. But I still like that Kylee accepts that part of me and makes her home a safe place to be little when I need it.

CHAPTER 4

Connor

Kylee follows Quent upstairs. I watch them go. My eyes drift to Kylee's client, who is still standing in the hallway with his laptop. It's someone I know. Jackson.

We've got plenty of mutual friends.I've chatted with him at parties and at the club, but I don't know him well. He's always nice to me when I'm little, but there's a difference between playing a role for a scene and really getting to know a person.

"Oh, hey, Conman, I didn't realize Kylee and Q had company. How are you tonight?" Jackson seems so earnest, I'm tempted to spill about my crappy date.

"Better after a few episodes of *Supergirl*. We skipped to season four, because Nia Nal is badass. Something about young people saving the city makes my troubles seem trivial by comparison. You know?"

"Sure, but they have superpowers, so really..." Jackson exaggerates a shrug, trailing off to let me infer his meaning.

I chuckle. "Fair point. I guess I'm letting work stress get to me and feeling like I'm missing out on my siblings and niblings' lives."

"Big family?"

"You could say that. I've got six siblings, and between them they've got four kids so far."

"Wow! Seven kids? That's a lot. No wonder you like superheroes; your mom must be one to wrangle all that chaos." He's joking. I know he is, but the comment still rubs against old wounds from years of disparaging comments about the size of my family.

"Um. Not quite." This is also far from the first time I've had to correct hetero-normative assumptions about my family. At least Jackson will probably think it's cool that my folks are queer. "I have a non-binary parent and a step-dad, not a mom. My parent goes by Modaddy. Like, a portmanteau of mom and daddy."

"Sorry, my bad. That's super cool that you had queer role models like that."

"It was just my normal, you know?" I shrug off his apology, because I won't say it's okay, but I don't want to make a big deal out of an honest mistake, either. "And I actually started my social transition years before Modaddy figured out their identity and came out to us, so they sometimes joke that I was their queer role model." I chuckle and Jackson joins in.

"Nice. They sound supportive."

"Yeah, my family is great. Both my parents always made room for us to be ourselves. They let me socially transition before I even started school and helped me get on puberty blockers when the time came. Then Pop was Modaddy's best advocate when they decided to transition, and seeing that made me believe I could have the same sort of supportive relationship someday, too. And they definitely helped make our hometown a better place for me and my queer siblings to live. Most of my sibs are some sort of queer, too."

"That's great. No wonder you miss them." Jackson commiserates. I nod, and before the silence that follows can grow awkward, he asks, "Modaddy is an interesting name; is there a story there, or just combining mom and dad?"

"Noa, my youngest sister, used to just call both our parents mama-dada instead of differentiating which one she wanted. And then her twin, Eli, picked up on it, too. It ended up getting shortened to Modaddy when they got a little older. Modaddy thought it was awesome, Pop, not so much. But, I think that was one of the early clues for them they might be non-binary. Having a neutral title felt better than either gendered one. Anyway, TL;DR: when they came out as non-binary, the name became official. But also, my folks wanted a large family. I can't imagine growing up without a single one of my siblings. So it sucks when people act like it's weird or bad, or utter chaos, you know?"

"You're right, that was rude of me to joke about it. I didn't mean to imply there's anything wrong with having a large family. Only child here, so I can't imagine having that many kids in the house all the time."

"See, I can't imagine life without them. It's always loud and there's always something going on or someone to talk to if you need it." I can't hide the longing in my voice when I talk about them. If it were as simple as going home, I might move closer, but I've never felt like I could be myself in the town where I grew up. Even with Prescott and Viv in same-sex marriages, it just doesn't feel like home anymore. Not the way the city has become my home.

"Ah. Hence needing to come be around people after a bad day?" Jackson guesses.

"Pretty much." I shrug and stab my spoon into the ice cream. "I've got three housemates, but that isn't really the same."

"And Q is a good cuddler," Jackson says, tone knowing. "Want me to keep you company while you wait for them?"

We both glance toward the stairs. I pat the couch where Q was sitting. Jackson sits beside me and picks up Q's abandoned spoon.

"Share?" He holds it up toward the carton in supplication.

"Sure." I offer him the melty ice cream and we both have a few bites.

"So. Want to tell me about your crappy day or try to distract you?" Jackson licks his spoon and I catch myself staring at his tongue as it swirls over the glob of sweetness.

"Uh, just the usual crap at work, and then I had a crappy date."

"Sorry to hear it. Anyone I know?"

"Nah, random internet stranger from a dating app." I gesture with my spoon before going in for another bite.

"Ah. I didn't know you were looking to date. I'd have thought you would look for a match who shares your kinks."

I shrug. "Yeah. Well, dating apps have a slightly larger pool than the singles at Aventures, you know? And with the right guy, I can still get my needs met at the club."

Jackson grunts noncommittally and takes another bite of ice cream. "Sure." He sounds skeptical, but I don't want to hear why my plans are flawed, so I change the subject.

"So, what about you?" I ask.

"What about me?" he asks.

"Do you date?"

Jackson snorts. "Nope."

"Not interested?" I press.

"You could say that. Like you said, I can get my needs met at the club. My most recent ex had insecurities that made it impossible for me to do my job. It's easier not to bother."

"Sounds like you deserved better." I bump my knee into his, trying to convey sympathy.

"We weren't a good match." Jackson shrugs. "He wanted me to stop shooting kink and boudoir sessions, but those are my favorite parts of the job. And I get it. I take photos of people when they are naked and vulnerable. It takes a lot of trust for a partner to accept I'm not there to be a part of the scene; I'm there to make the subjects of my photos shine. It gives them something to see their strength and beauty through an outsider's lens, you know?"

"Yeah. You take awesome pictures."

"Right? Thanks, Connor. But my ex couldn't handle the jealousy so we parted ways since I didn't want to stop and I also didn't want to keep hurting him. Ever since, it just seems like a lot of hassle. I can find a partner to scene with at the club when I get the itch to play. And there are hookup apps for everything else."

I grimace. "I hate hookup apps. It's always so hit or miss."

Jackson eyes me skeptically. "You're telling me a hot young stud like you has trouble hooking up?"

"Yeah, well," I gesture toward my crotch. "Some assembly required, you know? Not everybody gets it and I'm never sure if the people who message me are safe to tell. It's stressful."

Jackson looks at my lap and then my face and he gets this mortified expression. "Oh. Right. I can see where that might complicate matters."

"Yeah, not having a cis dick on the dick market tends to do that." I shrug it off. Jackson has known I'm trans for ages, so I'm not sure if he forgot or just didn't realize that it might make casual sex more of a challenge. I don't really mind that much. I'm not big on casual sex when my toys do a better job of getting me off, anyway.

"Sorry." Jackson says sheepishly.

"Don't be. I don't have a problem with my body, and if other people do, I don't particularly want to fuck 'em, you know?"

"Here's to that, don't fuck 'em. They don't deserve you anyway." Jackson taps his spoon against mine in a weird pseudo-toast.

"Pretty much." I lick my spoon again to get my mind off the thought that his spoon was just in his mouth. What would it be like to have his mouth on me the way he's slurping his ice cream? "So, what's your favorite kink to photograph?"

"I can't pick just one. I think regardless of kink, it's that moment when the sub finds the headspace they need. Whether it's a deeper connection with their partner or flying high on endorphins. I've got one where Q is wearing nothing but fuzzy ears and their collar and gazing up at Kylee. Kylee has her hand on Q's head and it's that quintessential moment of unconditional love between them. Or another of my favorites is of Angel in suspension with the ropes cradling their body and you can tell their mind is a million miles away, just floating."

"I can see why you wouldn't want to give up that kind of passion." I lean closer to him as he talks. The joy he finds in his job lights him up like a beacon. And I really don't need to be crushing on the person who just told me he doesn't date, but maybe that makes him safe, in a convoluted way. If nothing can ever come of wanting him, he can't break my heart, right? I study his face surreptitiously. He's got ruggedly handsome features, and I think he might have accentuated his eyes with a hint of makeup. Seriously sexy.

"Yeah. It means a lot to me to capture those moments for my clients. There are tons of photographers who will do the usual vanilla stuff, but there aren't as many who will treat a kink scene with the same care, you know? I had a wax play shoot recently that was awesome. One of my regulars came out as trans and their partner set up a session to do a twist on a gender reveal with the different colors of candle wax. It was so cool, partly because of the visual appeal of the colors and partly because it was so meaningful for them both."

"That sounds fun. I never really had a big coming out moment. Or, if I did, I don't remember it."

"Oh?"

"Yeah, Modaddy says I was one of those kids who always knew and told them I was a boy from the time I was old enough to talk. And I got lucky enough to have a family who believed me and advocated for me."

"No wonder you're close with them." Jackson smiles.

"Yep, my family is pretty great. Other than the whole living in a tiny town where I don't fit in and would have a hard time finding work in my chosen field."

"That's awesome, Connor. What do you do again?"

"So, I'm technically a civil engineer, but I'm working with a social housing NGO to improve urban housing affordability. We work with other groups to create new cooperative housing, help clients access housing, and all sorts of other stuff. Our emphasis is on underserved communities and the LGBTQ+ community in particular."

"Oh. Wow." Jackson looks impressed. "So you really are a superhero saving the city?" He gestures at me with his spoon. "You're the whole package, huh?"

I laugh. "Sure, saving the city one grant proposal at a time. It's not nearly as glamorous as it sounds."

"I think you're being modest, but agree to disagree."

"Yeah, enough about my job."

"Fair enough. Can I get your opinion on something as a little, then?"

"Like what?"

"So, I want to offer smash cake sessions for littles. Think there's a market for that?"

"Like, where parents have a special cake for a first birthday party so the baby can destroy it and smear frosting all over themself?" My older niece, Camile, loved her smash cake and tried to feed me fistfuls of slobbery cake on her first birthday. It was adorable. Matt sent me the photos afterward. I missed Carl's first birthday because of finals. Chuck pretty much ignored his cake. Edie will be getting her turn in the fall, though, and that kid is already a mess monster with her baby cereal, so I'm sure it will be cake carnage.

"Exactly. I think it might be fun for littles, and I could get some really cute birthday pics. I could totally offer it as a kinky gender reveal too."

"Sounds messy." I smile at the thought of having a cake to destroy with my face and a partner to share the mess with.

"It is." Jackson agrees with a grin. "That's half the fun."

"What's the other half?" Our eyes lock. I have a half-second of wondering what it would be like if he was the one kissing gobs of frosting off my face before I shake off the impulse.

"Helping them get cleaned up, of course. Preferably in the filthiest manner possible." Jackson winks at me, like he's reading my mind or something. I flash to the way he's been licking up his ice cream. Oh, heck yes, sign me up for some of that action.

"Well, in that case, I'm in." I knock elbows with him, just as he's lifting his spoon from the pint and it dribbles onto my lap. The cold splat makes me jerk my arms back. I tip the container, spilling more ice cream down my chest. "Heck, that's cold," I whine, trying to wriggle away from the chill. My squirming makes the trail of cold, melted ice cream run further down my thighs, threatening the cushions under me. I hold still, squeezing my legs together to stop the spillage from migrating further.

Jackson takes the ice cream carton and sets it aside on the TV tray Quent and I used earlier. Then he assesses the mess. "Better get you cleaned up before you drip on the couch."

"Yeah." I nod, still squirming as the cold wetness seeps into my shirt and pants.

"Hold tight; I'll be right back with a napkin." He goes into the kitchen and returns with a roll of paper towels held triumphantly aloft. "Found it."

"Give it here, this is icky." I make grabby hands and his eyes light up at my whiny tone. Jackson dangles the roll in front of me.

"You want me to take care of it for you, doll?" He crouches in front of me.

I nod. "Yeah. Like if you were doing messy pictures for a scene."

"If this was a scene, I'd lick you clean. Suck the sweet, sugary goodness right out of your lap. Bet you taste sweet as candy, don't you?" He tears off a bit of the roll and pats at my lap.

"Would you suck me, after?" I ask, spreading my thighs for him. Jackson smiles at the blatant invite to touch me more. I'm a little disappointed when he only pats away the last of his spilled ice cream instead of taking advantage of my none too subtle offer. He shifts to sit beside me on the couch again. I turn to face him, drawing up my damp leg onto the cushion with my ankle tucked under my other knee.

"If you wanted." Jackson runs his fingers along my thigh, stroking over the wet patch from the spill, and then higher, brushing against my packer. It's not nearly enough pressure to

26

be anything but a tease. "I'd strip you out of your messy clothes and warm up your poor cold skin. Lick you until you're all slick with spit for me."

"Yeah? What about my shirt? It's messy, too." I gesture to the second spill and draw my shoulders back. Jackson meets my gaze, leans in close, and pauses inches from my chest. There's a question in his eyes and I nod my permission.

Jackson's mouth is hot through my soft cotton shirt, and I shudder at the sudden sensation of his mouth on me. He slurps up the gooey ice cream blob, then keeps licking. His tongue lathing my skin through the fabric is strange, but wonderful. Raspy licks like a cat's tongue, except way sexier. And then he finds my nipple and latches onto the sensitive nub and my metal piercing with a wet, openmouthed kiss. His mouth has me arching into him and reaching for his head to hold him there. Jackson moans and the vibrations send tingles right to my groin.

"Oh, yeah. Pinch the other one," I encourage him. Jackson sucks and licks the nipple in his mouth while his hand slides under the hem of my shirt. His fingers skim over my belly and up to twiddle with the barbell in my other nipple. He gives it a gentle twist that has me leaning into him and wishing for more.

Jackson keeps up the stimulation for a moment longer, grazing me with his teeth and pinching the sensitive flesh. It's like he's pushing to find the line where it crosses from exquisite to too much. Before he gets there, I try to pull him into my lap. I want to grind against him until we both get off, and then return the favor by cleaning up the mess in his pants. I can lick up spilled cream just as well as he can. The silly joke makes me snort.

Jackson pulls back before I can get him on top of me. "I should spill ice cream on cute boys more often. You're better than any cone." He licks his lips, like he's savoring me.

"There's still a bit more in there." I jut my chin toward the carton in a blatant plea for more.

Jackson chuckles as he shakes his head ruefully. "Much as Kylee and Q are generous about people fucking at their house during play parties, that would be rude. I don't know how much they would appreciate walking in on me licking ice cream off every inch of you on their nice couch."

"Q would just want to join in." That, or be grumpy about missing the fun and ice cream. Kylee might not appreciate the mess, though. And Jackson is right. It's probably not good etiquette to fuck a friend on my other friends' furniture. In their den. Even if said friends are upstairs for Q to take a punishment. And Q has sucked me off on this couch more than once in the past while Miss Kylee offered instruction from the sidelines.

"Be that as it may, how about a rain check?" Jackson stands and tidies away the used paper towel and the mostly empty ice cream container.

"For real?" I pluck at my damp shirt. The wet patch over my pec is not nearly as exciting now that it's cooling. I enjoy playing with Jackson when our social groups intersect. He's a nice guy. I'd consider him a friend in the broadest sense. But I've never specifically sought him out for any sort of one-on-one time.

Do I want to make plans to hook up with him? Is he proposing a friends with benefits arrangement or a pity fuck since I as much as told him I have zero game? Or just letting me down easy with a throwaway line he has no intention of following through on? I'm not sure about any of that, but I am pretty sure I'm overthinking this.

"Yeah." Jackson shrugs. "You're hot and I'm all for having you laid out for my enjoyment. We can see how you like other types of sensation play, since the ice cream got you all hot and bothered." His eyes slide to the damp spots on my clothing. The lust in his gaze makes me shiver with the memory of his mouth on me.

"Like ice cubes?" I try to distract myself from sex thoughts by planning out this hypothetical scene, or hook up, or whatever it is.

"Among other options. I already told you I enjoy capturing wax play."

"I'd be down for trying that. Um. Is sex on the table?"

"I prefer it in my bed," he teases, "but I could fuck you on the table after licking various foods off of you, if that's something you're into?"

I grimace. "So long as none of the food actually goes inside orifices other than mouths. Like I said, original factory parts, so I'm not keen on getting an infection down below."

"Duly noted." Jackson stifles a smile. "I'll be sure to get us both nice and squeaky clean before I put anything inside you."

"What a gentleman."

Jackson tips an imaginary hat to me. "I aim to please." His intense focus leaves no doubt in my mind that he wants to be inside me and I like the idea of that happening. Sex with him would be easy. A known quantity in that he knows what I'm packing below the belt and he's still into me.

"Well, it would please me to get together sometime." I aim for flirty and hope I don't come across as clingy.

"How about this weekend?" Jackson suggests.

"Sounds good. I'm usually down for a bit of no strings kinky fun. Even better if there's something new to try involved." I try to sound casual about it, but the arrangement he is proposing sounds like all the pros of dating without having to slog through all the messy cons. In short, a perfect friends with benefits solution to my dating woes. And none of the risk of hooking up with randos. I give him my number and he punches it into his phone. Ball's in his court.

"Then you should absolutely stick with me and we can get into all kinds of mischief together. Between the props I've gathered for the studio and the tops I work with for stock photos, I've got so many fun toys to try. I will totally be your casual lay so you don't have to brave the wilds of online dating and hook up apps as a value added service."

"Value added, huh? And what are you getting out of this arrangement?"

"Hmm, I get regular sex with a hot guy, a partner to play with. And if you're up for it, a ready and willing victim—er, I mean, model—to try some new shots I'm interested in messing around with."

"What kind of shots?" I ask, just as Q and Kylee's voices in the hallway remind me that Jackson and I aren't here alone. We jerk apart as they reenter the room. As if we're getting caught at something we shouldn't be doing even though the shameless nipple play part of the evening is already long over.

"Oh, I've got so many ideas for the new site update Kylee was helping me with tonight, but I should get home. We can discuss more this weekend. I've got your number, so I'll text with the details." Jackson gives my thigh a proprietary pat. I savor his touch more than I should from a friend. Then he takes the trash out to the kitchen. He greets Q and Kylee with a smile and I stare after him, feeling weirdly let down that he's just going to walk out the door.

"Hey, sorry to leave you hanging. I'm all yours for the rest of the evening." Q flounces back into the room to rejoin me. "Mostly." they add with a slight wince when they sit, confirming my suspicions that they're now wearing something kinky under their clothing. Kylee sits in the armchair.

"Everything alright?" Kylee asks me.

"Yeah. Thanks for having me over." I hope I don't appear as disheveled as I feel after Jackson left me hanging. Q and Kylee both look freshly fucked, but I can hardly begrudge them getting frisky in their own home. Not when I'm sitting on their couch with a hard-on pressing against my packer as I fantasize about having Jackson's mouth all over me. I glance toward where Jackson is still puttering around in the kitchen.

"How about some popcorn?" Kylee offers, catching my longing gaze.

"Yes, please." I agree.

"Score!" Q wraps an arm around me and snuggles in close.

"I'm taking off, thanks again, Kylee." Jackson pokes his head into the den.

"Not a problem. We are always happy to have you over, Jax." Kylee waves at him.

"Aren't you two cozy? Have fun tonight. I'll be in touch." He winks at me. At least I'm pretty sure it's at me. And then he leaves. I spend the rest of the night cuddling with Q. First on the couch where they clutch me close and we share snacks with Kylee. And later in the guest bed, where Q and I don't fool around for once. We just spoon until I fall asleep. They must sneak away to their Mommy's bed for the rest of the night after I zonk out. The spot beside me is already cool to the touch when I wake up the next morning.

CHAPTER 5

Jax

The day after we talked at Kylee's, Connor texts to see if I want to meet him at Adventures to play this weekend. I counter by inviting him to my place. It's our first time doing anything one-on-one, but I've known him for ages now. And he knows me, at least enough to agree to hooking up.

I explain I want to make the sort of mess that isn't really feasible at the club. He agrees with a joke that's not really a joke about how Q will end me if anything happens to him. I play along, but I get the idea he actually worries about his safety around hook ups.

We text off and on through the rest of the week. Nothing too deep. We discuss favorite cake flavors and he sends me a pic of the decimated remains of his niece's smash cake, sans niece. Saturday evening, he messages me a picture of a cupcake with a note that it made him think of me and my smash cakes. He ends the message with a wink emoji.

I message back that the frosting would look even better on him. He replies with a photo of his finger covered in frosting. That's totally not what I meant, but it's still hot. I can imagine sucking the sugar from his fingers. From there, it's not much of a leap to call up the memories of his response to my mouth on him.

The other night when I teased his nipples, Connor's entire

body arched as he moaned. Would he have the same reaction with my lips around his knuckles? I bet he would. I want to find out in person. When I tell him as much, he says I better get a cake before he comes over, then.

So, once Connor and I hammer out the details of him coming over tonight, I swing by the bakery for a cheap cake. I place it inside the oven, out of doggy reach, as soon as I get home. Then I take Gia for a jog to the dog park to tucker my girl out before my playdate. Otherwise, being shut out of the bedroom will make her antsy. I split the day fussing over Gia and getting everything set up for Connor.

Gia is contentedly munching on her favorite chew toy when he arrives a few minutes early. She perks up at the visitor, tail already wagging in anticipation of a new friend. She woofs quietly, giving me a questioning tilt of her head. As if to say, 'aren't you going to get that?'

"I know. I'm excited to see him too, girl. Come on." I scruff her ears and she brings her toy down the hallway to the door, trailing at my heels as I let our guest inside.

Connor grins when he sees me. "Hey. Hope I'm not too early?"

"Right on time." I gesture for him to come inside. He does, and when his eyes land on Gia, he drops into a crouch to greet her.

"Aw, hello doggo, your daddy didn't tell me he had a beautiful pupper at home. What's your name?" He coos to her and Gia's whole body wags with excitement as she crowds into his space and licks his face. Lucky girl. I cringe at being called her daddy, but I don't correct him because I don't want to get into anything too personal. Best to keep things casual if we're doing this.

"This is Gia." I nudge her shoulder to get her to calm down, though Connor seems thrilled with her attention. "She thinks she's a lapdog."

"Aw, do you like cuddles, Gia?" Connor keeps scratching

behind her ears and doting on her. She licks his cheek, then glances up at me for approval. "Don't you let your mean daddy crush your dreams. You can be anything you want to be."

"She does. And I'd rather crush her dreams than deal with crushed balls when she inevitably stomps on them, the big galoot. You can be the one she squishes with her overzealous snuggles if you want to let her chase her doggy dreams, boy." Guess it looks like I might have to say something about the daddy thing after all. The title just never sits right with me on a visceral level.

Connor sticks his tongue out at me. "That's easy. I don't have balls for her to crush." He says it lightly, like it's not something that bothers him, but I wince internally at the thought I might have said something dysphoria inducing to him.

"Sorry."

Connor shrugs, his smile still in full force. "It's fine. I'm happy with my body. Just don't like the way other people react to it sometimes." He keeps petting Gia, rubbing along her neck and back, much to her delight. She's shedding again, so tufts of golden fur float to the floor and I'm going to have to sweep again soon.

"Okay. Cool. I guess this is as good a time as any to discuss what language you want me to use while we're fucking." I make the segue.

"Yeah, so, you might have already surmised that I've got sensitive nipples and I enjoy having them played with. Hence the piercings. Calling them my nips or pecs is fine, tits is a no-go term. I call my junk my dick. And the stuff under that my sac, the hardware is a Guiche ladder. No balls, but treat that bit like a ballsac and you won't go wrong. And uh, the piercings might give you a hint since they block access, but ignore the innie. Oh, and you can call my packer my dick, too. Usually context works to make it clear which dick we're talking about. If not, ask. And

I do have a couple of dick options for topping, but that's not my usual preference."

"Noted. So, my turn. I don't know if you've heard through the grapevine, but I don't use masc titles or honorifics."

"Oh, shit. I'm sorry. Are you Gia's human then?" Connor asks, immediately picking up on his faux pas.

"Yeah. That's a better fit, thanks." I smile at him.

"I guess I just assumed you're cis. Are you?"

"Genderqueer. I use he/him pronouns, but I'm not, you know, a cis man." I pull a face. "More like a demiguy."

Connor nods like he gets it. "Gotcha. My bad. So, no gendered titles. How about compliments and anatomy stuff?"

"I'm good with masc coded terms for that. It's really just titles that bother me. I guess it feels like those are calling me a man, whereas calling me handsome or referring to my dick are just acknowledging how I present?"

"Makes sense." Connor nods, and I think he really does get the distinction, unlike a lot of people I've told in the past. That's why I don't tell everyone; it's not worth the headache. Now I'm glad I told him, though. "How didn't I know this?" He gives me an apologetic glance. "Sorry, that sounded wrong. I mean, are you out as genderqueer?"

"Ish." I wobble my hand in the air. "My close friends and play partners know I'm trans. But I'm comfortable with the pronouns I got assigned at birth." I shrug. "Not much to tell, I guess."

"Q always calls you Jax." Connor says it like that detail is just now dawning on him. And he smacks his forehead with the heel of his hand. "I feel like an asshole for not noticing."

"I go by Jackson, too. Especially at work. Personal and professional lines can get blurry, considering my job. It's fine. If

I wanted you to call me Jax, I'd have asked. But yeah, since you brought it up, Jax is more me."

"Got it, Jax. During our scene, what should I call you?"

"Mx works for me, in place of Sir or Ma'am. You like to be addressed as 'boy', right?" I've noticed how much he lights up when other tops use that diminutive with him, so asking is more about confirming I've got his consent. Connor nods eagerly, as I expect. "Good. So, I think that's enough sharing to get us started, yeah? Want to take off your shoes and we can get Gia settled?"

"Sure." Connor gives my dog one last pat, then stands to take off his shoes and gestures for me to lead the way. Connor and Gia trail me back to my kitchen, where I grab a Kong full of Gia's favorite wet food from the freezer to keep her occupied. She dances in place and whines as I carry the toy to her bowl. I know she's going to eat it on the dog bed in the living room while Connor and I are busy, but that's fine. It washes well.

"Wait." I set the treat in the bowl, wash my hands and grab the cake from the oven. Connor's eyes widen and he claps his hands together with glee. So now I've got two sets of wide pleading eyes trained my way. I chuckle as I remove the packaging from Con's cake. Gia licks her chops and whines.

"I'm with you, girl." Connor laughs, then he copies her whining noises. "Give us our treats already, Mx."

"Go ahead, Gia." I give her the release command and she's on her toy in a flash, trotting off to the living room with it in her mouth.

"My turn?" Connor asks hopefully.

"Soon. Come with me." I lead him to my bedroom. The rubber sheets I use for messy play are already in place. As are the under the bed restraints. I'm not sure if we'll use those tonight, but Connor said he's into that. I've got several dozen electric candles, leftovers from various romantic photo shoots, laid out on every surface for mood lighting.

"Oh. Fancy. What are we doing?" Connor takes in the room, his gaze appreciative.

"Shut the door, so Gia doesn't give us an audience, boy."

Connor obeys. "Is it cake time? What are we doing?"

"You said you wanted to try the smash cake, right?" I check.

"Yeah." He nods, eyes drawn to my mouth. He licks his lips and I'm pretty sure we're both remembering the other night with the ice cream.

"That's the plan. You are going to be a good little boy and let me get some cake smashing photos of you, and then I'm going to help you get thoroughly messy."

"Mhm. And then you're going to help me get unmessy after, right?" He levels me with a pleading look again.

"That's more than half the fun, doll."

"Well, then." He looks good enough to eat with his hands on his hips, just begging me to dominate him. "What are we waiting for?"

Excellent question. I set the cake down in the middle of the bed. "Are you up for a costume?"

"Sure." Connor glances around, like he expects it to be laid out for him already. I go to my closet. The two outfits are front and center. I have a couple of options in his size, which he texted me with only a little begging for hints as to why I wanted to know. Both are skimpy bits of glittery cloth and straps meant to mimic the outfits for boys in all the prettily staged smash cake photos online. Instead of neutral tones, or shades of blue, these suspenders are neon rainbow stripes and the skimpy underwear attached to them is a pair of sexy white lace manties. The other option I pull out for him is a sexier take on a jumpsuit in gold lamé. Both outfits leave little to the imagination.

"Oh, I like the shiny one, please." He reaches for it.

"Want to change in here or the washroom?" I ask as I hand over his chosen outfit and put the other one away.

Connor gives me a look like he finds the offer of privacy absurd. "You're gonna see me naked when we fuck, right? Like, the benefits we discussed include penetration and orgasms?" He's already pulling his shirt over his head as he talks.

"Yes. But naked to fuck and naked to change are a little different." I shrug.

"Eh, not that different. I want you to see me, Jax." Connor shoves his pants and boxers down, exposing the packer he's wearing underneath in some sort of strap. I can't argue with his logic, and more to the point, I want to see him.

Despite his brazen words, the boy doesn't give me nearly long enough to stare my fill at his body. He steps into the gold jumpsuit, tucking his cock into the front so the bulge lies at a natural angle. He shrugs into the arm straps and poses for me. "How do I look?" Connor teases, puffing out his chest.

He looks amazing. The thin straps frame his pierced nipples. The open 'V' of the outfit draws my eyes down his toned abs to the sparse trail of hair leading to his dick. I want to trace that same path with my tongue. If he responds to my mouth on his pecs the way he did during our last encounter, I can't wait to get his dick in my mouth.

"Well? Like what you see, Mx?" From his smug little smile, I think he knows the answer to that. Connor shifts his weight to show off the stretchy fabric hugging the curve of his ass. Yeah, he knows.

"You're damn hot, boy. And you know it. Get up on the bed with the cake in front of you and we'll get a few shots before you start the smashing part of the evening." I position myself so that Connor is framed in front of the backdrop I pinned over my headboard to prepare for tonight.

"Oh, are we going to play naughty photographer? Are you going to seduce me as your naïve young model?" He flutters his lashes at me.

"We can discuss consensual nonconsent later, boy. It's a bit edge to spring in the middle of things." I don't hate the idea of trying a scene like that with him another time, though.

Connor pouts but nods. "I guess. So. You want me to be little for this, or what?"

"That's up to you. Are you okay with me taking pictures of our scene?"

"Yeah. Nothing that shows my junk and my face together, though, please."

"Fair enough. I might want to sell some of these pictures as stock or use them on my website as an example for potential clients. Are you good with that?"

"Yeah. I can sign a release or whatever. So long as you stick with SFW images. No genitals or anything out for sale? And let me see them first?"

"Absolutely. I'll let you review the contract I use with my models before you sign anything. And if you sign off on commercial use, I'll compensate you. Sound good? I don't want you to feel like I'm springing anything on you. Or taking advantage."

"Yep." He gives me a cheeky grin. "I kinda figured you'd want pics of this, since that was the whole idea behind the scene."

"Still, always better to ask than assume." I take my camera out of its case and adjust the settings for the lower lighting in the room. "Now, why don't you get nice and cozy with that cake, boy?"

Connor's grin turns wicked as he picks up the little cake that I covered in rainbow confetti sprinkles, and tips it toward the camera as he beams at me. I snap a few photos.

"Good. Now, spread your legs and set it down and try gazing down at it." I suggest. Con does as I direct. We cycle through a few more excited poses with the cake intact.

"Smash it now, Mx?" Con asks after a while. The longer I make him wait, the more he seems to get into the role of a boy begging for his dessert. And as he gets more comfortable with me, he hams it up for the camera more, too.

"Taste it first." I urge him.

"With my face?" He points to his mouth.

"Or grab a fistful of cake. Don't be shy about it, either way. I want you to commit. Don't worry about the camera. If you want to get into that 'kid on a sugar rush' headspace, that's what I want to capture. Okay?"

"Okay. Cake now!" Con drives both of his fists into the frosting, so I get a shot of him wrist deep in the cake. The genuine smile on his face as he goes to town on it is perfect. He grins and makes eye contact with the camera lens as he takes a bite from the hunk of smashed cake covering his hands. Con giggles as he continues to destroy the confection. There's something taboo about just mashing your face into an entire cake and the experience seems to delight him.

It's easy to snap dozens of photos as he lets himself go and gets into our scene. He's a joy to photograph, and I love the rush of pleasure at his easy obedience to my every suggestion. It's obvious from the way he smiles at me that he enjoys our session, too. I haven't had this much fun with a partner in a while, and I'm glad to be sharing this moment with a sweet boy like Con.

CHAPTER 6

Connor

I'm covered in frosting and giggling like a little kid by the time Jax puts away his camera and comes to join me on the frosting covered bed. I giggle and reach for his face with my sticky fingers. He grabs my wrist, stopping me from sharing my mess.

Before I can so much as pout about it, Jax guides my thumb to his mouth and sucks. He licks me clean, then pops the next digit into his mouth until all my fingers are frosting free.

The suction goes right to my t-dick, so I'm squirming in my ridiculous gold jumper. I want to push his mouth down there, but sugar. So instead, I pull his face to mine and kiss him, sharing the sweet taste of cake between us. I'm a sticky mess, but there is just something about breaking free of norms and demolishing an entire cake, mostly with my face. I have crumbs and globs of frosting all over me, and I just don't care. It's a rush to throw away social mores and just act on impulse.

Jax must get that same thrill, to some extent. He makes out with me, his hands painting more frosting across my chest in swirling patterns across my pecs. He ends with a daub on each of my exposed nipples.

I shiver at the sensation of cold and the grittiness of the sugar. I pull my mouth from his. "Clean me up, Mx?" I ask. His mouth is heaven. Last week on the couch at Q's has been playing on a loop in my brain—Jax slurping ice cream off my body. It's been an age since anyone touched me with this level of sexual charge, drawing it out instead of just getting off. This is already the best sex I've had in months and neither of us is even fully naked yet.

I almost chickened out on coming tonight and I'm so glad I didn't. That I texted him, even though a huge part of me still believes not asking him for this was the only path that didn't lead to Jax eventually rejecting me. Sometimes my brain is an asshole, telling me I'm not worth caring about. Especially when I'm anxious. And Jax makes me anxious.

At least it's the excited type of nerves that comes with meeting a new love interest. Or, I guess, lust interest in this case. The kind where I want to share everything about myself with him, and get to know him and be friends. I want him to like me. I want him to want more than the few minutes of fondling on Quent's couch that I've blown up into this huge *thing* in my head.

Rolling the dice on some random guy from my dating app doesn't compare to the memory of Jax sucking my nipples through my shirt. His voice a breathy purr as he tells me all the things he wants to do to my body when he has me at his mercy. I just can't seem to make myself get excited to settle for plain old vanilla dating when there are so many things I haven't gotten to try yet.

He's the one whose lips I've been imagining wrapped around my cock when I tease myself with my dick pump for the past few nights. How many times did I fantasize that the hot suction could be Jax's mouth instead of a machine? And now it is this close to becoming a reality and my fantasies didn't begin to do his mouth justice.

Jax swipes some frosting off my nose with his tongue, then feeds it to me with another languid kiss. "You want me to lick you clean, boy?"

I nod vigorously.

"Lay back, and let me kiss you all over then, doll."

"Literally." I giggle as he pushes me onto my back. Jax follows me to the bed, kneeling over me on all fours. His body hems me in and I shiver at the heat in his gaze as he kisses and licks his way over my face, down my neck to my chest. He lathes away the frosting he painted there, paying special attention to my over-sensitized nipples.

I arch up under him when he takes the barbell in his teeth and tugs at it, licking more. He shifts his focus back to my face, leaning over me. His groin brushes my belly as he feeds me another mouthful of frosting that he's licked off my body. I shiver at the contact.

It's like I'm a sugary buffet laid out for him to feast upon and he wants to share the bounty with me. I don't have words to describe the weird sense of being objectified, and at the same time, honored. It's a trippy headspace and I enjoy every minute of his mouth on my body. He takes a long time to clean me up, feeding me more of the cake every so often. Until I'm so horny I could get off just from the pressure of my packer whenever he leans over me and presses our bulges together.

Jax lowers himself onto me further as he gets into this. Eventually he's laying on top of me, his hard dick pressed between my thighs, jamming my packer into my junk. I writhe under him.

"Fuck me," I whine, pulling him closer. Jax grinds his dick against me and I shudder at the thrill of pleasure the motion causes. "Yeah, just like that." I grab his ass, massaging and trying to encourage him to thrust harder. Jax reaches for my legs. He urges me to wrap them around him, opening myself up to him as he thrusts to find just the right angle. I want to shove my packer out of the way to let the hard ridge of his dick slide along mine skin-to-skin. Too bad there's too much clothing in the way.

I hump up off the bed, hoping to get enough friction despite the layers. Jax catches my intent, and he shifts up to push his lounge pants down enough to free his throbbing erection. I want to lick it, and get it inside me, but for now, I'll settle for having him rub against my junk until we both come.

"That's it, doll; open up and let Mx take care of you." Jax croons as he drives his dick against me harder. I squeeze tight with my legs to keep him in the spot that's doing it for me. He splays me open, just to where the stretch in my hips and thighs burns.

Jax reaches under me to pull my ass snug against him as we rock together. "There, yes, there, more." I moan, rocking into his every movement on top of me.

I love the weight of him pressing me into the mattress. The heat and friction of our bodies moving as one. His hungry kisses as he devours me. His lips crash into mine. I chase every trace of sugar in his mouth even as his cock on mine makes me soar off into a climax almost as hot as him.

"Oh, fuck," I groan as my orgasm rockets through me, tensing my entire body. My toes curl as I gasp for breath and cling to him, hoping that it will never stop. I can ride the tide of pleasure for an eternity, trapped under his bulk. The warm pulse of his jizz painting my groin tips me off that he's come too as he rocks more slowly, and then stops. Jax rests on top of me while we both catch our breaths.

When he eventually rolls off, I'm shivery and cold in a puddle of sticky slop. Mushed cake and saliva and cum still coat my belly. I grimace at the cooling mess.

"This was way sexier when you were licking every inch of me." I complain, running a hand through the goo.

Jax laughs and lifts my sticky hand to his mouth, licking a stripe across my palm. "You still taste sweet to me." He turns my palm and kisses the back of it. "Why don't we get cleaned up?

There's still one part of you I haven't gotten to taste." He palms my oversensitive bulge suggestively.

"Hey, I'm nowhere near ready for another round yet. You fucked me silly." I bat his hand away with a laugh.

"And here I thought you were already silly, boy." Jax boops my nose playfully. "So, no to showering?"

"No, I want a shower." I gather myself and roll out of the bed, trying to ignore the squish of more frosting under me as I move.

"Here, let me wipe off the worst of the mess first." Jax gets a towel and chafes it over my body while I sit on the edge of his bed. I survey the thorough mess we've made of each other and the sheets.

"Rubber sheets for the win," Jax observes, following my gaze. "I'll change them out after the shower. Did you like that?"

"Yeah. By the end, it sort of seemed like you were eating me. Just devouring me and making my essence a part of you. I loved making an unapologetic mess of us both. And your mouth on me is…" I shiver, at a loss for words. I love his mouth on my body. Jax finishes the vigorous toweling by wiping my feet so I don't track frosting across his carpets.

"Anything you'd change for next time?"

"Hm. Less sugar, so we can frot, skin-to-skin."

"Good to know. Um, we should probably have discussed this before, but what about condoms?"

I shrug. "Yeah, so, I know it's potentially risky, but I enjoy getting messy." I hold up my sticky hand and wiggle my fingers at him for added emphasis. "Anyway, I'm on PrEP and I get STI panels done every few months. And I had my gametes removed first thing when I was old enough to sign the consent. My folks helped find a doctor who would actually do it. So no oops babies. Anyway, frot, oral or letting you jerk it onto my skin is lower risk, just not directly on my junk? We can use condoms for anal if you want, though. What we did tonight was fine with me."

"Good to know. I get regular testing, too, so condoms for anal works for me." Jax sets aside the towel and offers me his hand. I let him haul me to my feet and guide me into his washroom. While he gets out clean towels for us both, I take in the room.

There is a bottle of makeup remover and a couple tubes of mascara or eye liner on his counter. So, he does use cosmetics like I thought. It looks good, accentuating his expressive warm brown eyes. I squirm out of my messy clothes. I also remove my packing strap and packer because damp straps chafe. If Jax and I are going to do the casual sex friends thing, he's going to see my dick. And it might be small, but I'm still proud of the little guy; I want him to see it. I want him to like it.

Jax doesn't look at me right away, grabbing towels from the linen closet for us, so I investigate the shower. It's one of those walk-in tiled surrounds that could easily fit several adults. "Swanky." I saunter up to the spigot as he turns the knobs to adjust the temperature. "Big enough for a party." I spin with my arms outstretched and my fingers only graze the walls. It really is nice.

Jax snorts. "Sure. Is group sex on your kinky wishlist? And how's the water?"

"Eh? Been there, done that." I wink at him as the tepid water cools my back. "I want to try more sensation play. Like wax and a Violet Wand. And crank up the heat a bit more?" He does. I turn to test it on my hands, the hot water pelting down on me in a heavenly spray that has the air around me clouding with steam. "Perfect."

"That can be arranged." Jax walks up behind me and tugs my back to his front, reaching around me to check the temperature. He snatches his hand back. "Ah, you're one of *those* people who likes it scalding, I see." He shakes off his hand. Looks like we lack shower compatibility, but that just means more hot water for me.

"Sorry, but I'm not sorry. I've got three housemates, not to mention their assorted significant others, so the hot water is a joke if I don't get to the shower first before work. This is a luxury." I step out of his arms and under the pummeling spray, letting it wash away the sticky residue of our play session in a cascade.

Jax steps back. When I glance over my shoulder at him, he's just watching me. I wink at him. "Want to soap my back, or just keep staring?"

"I've got you. So, are we making this a regular thing?" Jax grabs a bar of soap, lathering it between his hands, then smoothing the suds over my shoulders and back. I suppress a moan at his touch.

I'm no Q, turning to putty in the hands of anyone who touches me, but I like this. His attention and focus. Which might not be the most conducive to keeping this arrangement a friendship only. I'll have to set boundaries. No sleeping over for sure. Probably shouldn't shower together after tonight, either. There's a reason Monty, Tate, and Q are all swoony about bath time with a caregiver. Jax washing my body is too intimate if I want to keep him at a distance.

"I do." The benefits are already killer, even without the post-coital pampering in the epic shower. Next time, I'll suggest we take it solo. Incompatible water temperatures and all.

When I turn to rinse my back, Jax holds the soap out to me. "Want to get your own front?"

I nod, surreptitiously watching for his reaction to my body on full display. Jax's eyes drift to my junk, catching on the shiny metal rings of my Guiche ladder. He licks his lips and the heat in his gaze doesn't dim at all. If anything, he looks like he wants to devour me all over again. That reaction is such a turn on. Jax likes my body. "So, yeah, you cool with all this?" I stroke soap over the area in question.

I told him the truth when I said I'm happy with my body. My bits work for me. My t-dick and the piercings that shape my labia into something that resembles a sac, even insofar as they create a weight dangling between my legs, are enough of a physical transition for me. But I'm still wary of how my partners react to seeing me naked. Jax looks more focused on the piercings than anything else.

"You've got a very pretty cock, Connor. And your piercings are hot." Jax pulls his gaze away and turns to fuss with the shampoo bottle on its tidy little shelf. "No need to fish for compliments. Next time, we'll leave the sugar at the door so I can show you just how much I like it. I want to play with your sac while I suck you."

"Sounds perfect. Same time next Sunday?" I scrub soap over my belly, since it's still a little sticky.

"Sunday works for me. In the meantime, I'll send you the pics from this week to see what you think. Sound good?"

"Yep. You send me the contract and the release forms and I'll fill them out." I grimace as I scrub more frosting out of my hair. "Next time, no sugar. I like it messy, but I really don't need an infection down below."

"Sure thing. I've got some ideas. Want me to surprise you again?"

"Yes, please. But give me hints like this time?"

"You want me to tease you?" He grins at that, and I return his smile.

"Yes, Mx. The anticipation is half the fun." I finish rinsing off and step out of the water. "Well. Guess I should get going. It's been real."

"Yep. See you next week?" Jax sounds vaguely disappointed, but he doesn't try to talk me out of leaving.

"For sure."

Jax leans in to give me a peck on the cheek. His thumb and forefinger rest on my chin for a second, as though he wants more than that quick goodbye. "Good night, Connor."

"Night." I step out of the tiled surround, and towel off. Jax turns down the temperature before taking his place under the water. I hang my damp towel on a hook on the door, gather up my packer, then leave him to it. My clothes are where I left them, outside the splash zone for our messy play earlier. I dress hastily so as not to deal with more awkward goodbyes. I waffle over whether to just leave the mess on the bed. In the end, I ignore it. I don't know where he keeps his cleaning supplies, and I want to be gone before he gets out of the shower. Next time I'll help.

Gia is still gnawing on her rubber toy when I ease Jax's bedroom door shut behind me. I make sure it latches so Jax doesn't emerge from his bath to find his dog eating what's left of the cake. Ironically enough, it's vanilla, so I don't think it would be too bad for her, not like chocolate, but still.

"Hi, Gia." I go over to her and pat her head. Her tail thumps the ground agreeably. "It was nice to meet you." Getting to pet her is another tick in the benefits column for this whole arrangement. Apparently, I lucked out with a premium platinum level friend with benefits. Kink, orgasms, and a good doggo.

CHAPTER 7

Connor

J ax and I text throughout the week between our scheduled scenes. He sends me the photos of our cake smash. They came out great. I can totally picture my friends wanting to do similar sessions. Minus the hot frottage afterward. I send photos to our group. Q forwards them to their Mommy, as expected.

Jax really captured my playful side as I destroyed his cake. I particularly like the one where I've got a giant goofy grin, eyes crinkled almost shut as I laugh at something he said to me. There are cake crumbs smeared over my face and my frosting covered hands raised in a triumphant pose.

I read over his modeling contract, make a few adjustments that we discussed. Mainly, I specify the style of photos I'm comfortable with him using, then return it to him with my signature. Jax asks if I'd want to model for him again. I agree, but we don't make any concrete plans about that.

We exchange kinky memes and discuss our preferences in and out of bed. We don't get personal. I mean, beyond the inherently personal nature of learning each other's sexual and kinky preferences and boundaries, that is. It's not the same as knowing him. Asking how his dog is doing. Sharing about my family's daily drama. With so many of us to keep track of, there is always some new bit of family gossip to share, but that isn't the sort of friendship we're forging.

I don't tell Jax about Marietta's latest game. Or Viv's late night pro and con list for whether to have baby number three now or wait a few years. And how Cameron, our second oldest brother, opened the file and made a bunch of ridiculous changes to Viv's lists as a prank. I don't bring up the stakeholder meeting I have to present at work later this week. Nor do I mention the policy changes I've discussed with my boss that we're hoping to implement to make the organization more responsive to the needs of our community. I don't discuss work or family with him at all.

Jax doesn't tell me about his work days either, unless it overlaps with our kink talk. He mentions doing a photo shoot with a couple who liked the proofs of our cake smash session and requested something similar.

He brings up a Dom he knows who has a Violet Wand, if I'd be interested in modeling for some e-stim photos he has planned. That brings up the pros and cons of boxes versus wands and the sensations each produces. It's an area I've been interested in for a while, but the entry costs are prohibitive for something I'm not even sure I'll like.

I've also held off because even if I can use a wand solo, more than half the fun is playing with a partner. The tease, the buildup, the not knowing where the sensation is going to land. As far as I'm concerned, most of the time, solo play is like trying to tickle myself—a self-defeating exercise in frustration. But I've got Jax to play with now, and I'm excited about all the experiences we can explore during our, hopefully regular, play dates.

I screencapped the bit of our conversation where he teased me with possibilities to revisit it when I'm spinning out fantasies about what we're doing this weekend.

Connor: I guess, as an only child, you had more practice playing alone than me. :P

Jax: I'm sure you're more than adept at *amusing* yourself.

Connor: Orgasms are like presents...they're more exciting when someone else gives them to you, even if they aren't always exactly what you'd have gotten for yourself.

Jax: LOL. Are you impatient to visit me again? Is this a booty call? Or would that be a booty text?

Connor: I wish. Is it a sad indictment upon my youthful vitality that I've reached the age where sex has become a scheduled event?

Jax: I'm gonna go with nah. You're just getting old and adulting is a scam.

Connor: Rude! If we were in person, I'd be blowing a raspberry at you. Where is the *pbbbt* face emoji when you need it?

Jax: So sorry, my bad. What is your favorite thing about playing with a partner versus solo?

Connor: Uh, only everything?

Jax: Really? Be more specific. For me, I love the way my bottom reacts to what I'm doing. I like to tease and see how far I can push them. How close to the edge we can fly without falling. I mean, within their limits and boundaries and all.

Connor: You like teasing? *shocked Pikachu face*

Jax: You are such a brat. Here I thought you were a shy, sweet boy.

Connor: I am a shy, sweet boy...who is also a mouthy brat once I get to know a person. ;P

Jax: Answer the question.

Connor: Fine. Bossypants.

I had let the dots bounce as I tried to articulate my response, typing and erasing a dozen attempts. But Jax didn't push for me to hurry. I appreciate that about him more every time I re-read the exchange. He has a knack for knowing when to push and when to let me sit with something and process it when we chat.

Connor: Okay. Promise not to judge? My favorite part is when my top screws with my head during a scene. I like to play with people I know have a solid reputation. Or at Adventures in the public area, so I have a built in safety net because I like the rush of halfway wondering if they'll really *hurt* me.

I held my breath while I waited for him to respond.

Jax: And you trust me to take you up to that line without crossing it?

Connor: Yeah. Quent says you're a good Dom.

And Quent would never steer me toward someone who would do me real harm. Not on purpose, anyway. Jax replied to that with a string of devil face emojis interspersed with the typical sexual emojis.

Jax: Remember you said that this weekend, boy. ;)

After that conversation, I can't stop thinking about what he's got in store for me. On Friday, I ask him for pup pics when I'm hitting a wall with my ability to concentrate on work. Jax sends snapshots of Gia lounging around his house and studio. Chewing on her Kong, dining with him on a pet friendly patio, running around the dog park, and all over town. It's clear she's a huge part of his life.

We keep mostly to the relevant topics, though. Aside from floof pics. I don't know what Jax likes to eat, but I know he likes to give oral. It makes this flow of conversation easy. Quick lines dropped into the chat whenever one of us isn't busy. No pressure for it to be more than it is or to respond right away. We're just fuck buddies, so it's easy to drop all pretenses with him.

I don't know his favorite color, but I know that one of his

favorite things about kink is creatively repurposing everyday objects for play. That jibes with both our sensual encounters so far. I tease him about how we haven't so much as had a meal together, even though both our physical get-togethers involved food. He jokes back that he fully intends to keep the streak going strong, then refuses to elaborate on the hint, reminding me I said I want to be teased.

Jax makes good on his promise to give me vague hints about his plans for us. I'm not sure what to expect on Sunday when I arrive at his place. Too fidgety to wait around my apartment, I hit the gym and still end up arriving at Jax's almost an hour earlier than we planned. I hesitate to knock. I don't want to seem overeager.

There's a cafe on the corner across the street where I could grab a cookie or something to pass the time. Might not be a bad idea to eat something light before a scene. I could also wander the area, since his apartment is just around the corner from a strip of independent businesses. I passed several interesting looking restaurants and a cute little bookshop between his place and the bus stop. Before I can decide, Jax's front door opens, and he leads Gia outside.

"Oh! Didn't realize you were here." Jax greets me with a smile. Gia's tail wags and she crowds in close to me, nosing at my hands for pats. I oblige her.

"Just got here. I was running a bit early, sorry to interrupt your walk." I try to read Jax's expression, but he doesn't seem put off at me being here early. If anything, he looks happy to see me.

"Not at all. Want to come along? She's already been to the dog park this morning, but I wanted to give her a potty break. And a chance to stretch her legs before your visit." Jax gives the briefest hesitation before the last word. That pause imbues it with shades of meaning that have lust pooling low in my gut. Memories of our last two encounters run through my mind.

"Yeah, I'm excited about my, uh, visit, too." I glance down at Gia, trying to hide just how much I want back into Jax's bed. Jax gives Gia a command, and she licks my hand once more before falling into step beside her human. I move to walk on Jax's other side so I won't get in her way. We stroll around the block at a leisurely pace.

"So, how was your day?" Jax asks me.

"Good. Went to the gym. Since the weather's been cold and I've been all cooped up inside at work."

"Do you get outside more in the summer?" Jax asks.

"Yeah, our office is near a walking trail, so I like to jog on my lunch breaks. But it's been icy lately."

"Ah. Too bad." Jax says awkwardly. "I take Gia on the public trails in the summer, too. She likes to sniff all the trees." Jax jokes as Gia snuffles around the trunk of a decorative tree set into the sidewalk. Jax lets her sniff around for a spot to pee.

I chuckle. "I'm not in it for the tree sniffing. But it's nice to get outside. Fresh air and not a building in sight in places. It's kind of amazing to think about those same trees being here before there was even a blip of what became the city, you know? Some trees on the North Shore are over a thousand years old."

"That is pretty cool," Jax agrees. We continue on our meandering path around his neighborhood. Jax points out his favorite places to eat and the dark storefront that houses the physical studio for his photography business. "That's where the magic happens. I started the entire enterprise working out of my home, but now that it's established, having a professional studio space with dedicated lighting setup, props, and backdrops helps. Especially in the colder months. I still do a lot of shoots at locations, too, but the studio gives me more options."

"I bet. Will you take my pictures there? For your kinky stock photos?"

"Sure, if that's the best location for the shoot." Jax glances around to be sure no one is close enough to be listening in on our conversation. He leans closer and lowers his voice as he says, "but for tonight, let's just say I've broken out the rubber sheets again." Jax gives me a flirty wink.

"Mhm, you already told me it's going to be messy. I'm curious to see what you've got up your evil sleeves for me today." I pout.

Jax chuckles. "Soon," he teases me as we approach an intersection. "Should we go another few blocks? Maybe stop for dinner first?"

I scowl at him. "You're not funny."

Jax laughs harder. "Is that so? Did you want to go back to my place already, Conman?"

"Yes. Gia does, too. We both want you to get us some t-r-e-a-t-s." I spell out the last word. If Gia is anything like the dogs I grew up with, she'll recognize it. I don't want to tease her if she isn't actually getting something. I reach for Jax's hand and tug him to turn around. Gia picks up on my mood and whines, nudging Jax with her nose.

"Fine." He turns toward home. "You're an impatient boy today."

"I've been very patient all week," I protest, crossing my arms over my chest.

That gets another chuckle out of Jax. "You have," he concedes. "I guess I'll have to reward you when we get back to my place, won't I?"

"Yes, please." I agree, all but skipping along at his side as he meanders back the way we came. Gia's panting, so I guess she's probably tired from the run he mentioned taking her on earlier. If not for that, I'd swear he's taking his time on purpose. He ends up grabbing my hand and tucking it into the crook of his elbow to get me to match his more sedate pace. I scowl at him and grumble about wanting my surprise, but I secretly like it.

Jax linking our arms reminds me of being little and cared for, but in a 'friends' way. Q, Tate, and Monty would walk arm in arm like this with me. With our heads tipped together to share inside jokes. Or my siblings when we were younger. Just another of those friendly benefits, getting to connect with another person without all the messy baggage of a romantic relationship label.

When we get back to his place, Jax gives Gia another of those frozen Kong treats, like last week, and sends me into his bedroom. There's a large Ikea bag on his counter that I want to poke around in. That's got to be related to whatever we're doing tonight, right?

Jax smirks when he catches me looking. "Go wait for me, naked on my bed. No camera tonight, just you, me and my bag of tricks." He gestures toward the bag. When I dawdle to try sneaking a peek instead of obeying, Jax gives my ass a playful swat. "As in, now, boy. Scoot."

I jump in surprise at the suddenness and noise more than the actual smack. I told him I'm good with corporal punishments and corrections like that in our texts. It shouldn't be a surprise that he corrected me. I like the spreading sting, so I wiggle my ass at him to give him a tempting target before darting toward his room. Gia gives me a startled look and a tail wag before deciding to ignore my antics in favor of her treat. "Don't take too long," I call out from his doorway.

"Or what?" Jax challenges me.

"I might get started without you," I tease him with a nonchalant shrug. My dick is already raring to go, so it wouldn't take much.

"You can do that," Jax says calmly. His acceptance of my

brattiness is oddly disappointing. I don't want him to let me walk all over his authority. "If you want to finish without me, too. I can sit in the chair and watch you show me how you top yourself all night long if you want to run the show, boy."

I grin at him. That's much more like it. "Yes, Mx." I duck my head. "I'll be good and listen to you."

"Yes, I think you will. It would be a shame if all the surprises I prepared to fill your tight little hole had to go to waste."

I lick my lips. "No, I'll be good. You don't have to waste anything, Mx Jax."

"We'll see. Show me you're a good boy who deserves his rewards. Naked. On my bed. No touching yourself without permission, got it?"

"Do you want my packer on or off?" I ask.

"You might want to take it off," Jax says. "I don't want to damage the silicone, but that is always up to your discretion if you're more comfortable with it on, Connor."

"Off is fine. Thank you, Mx." I blow him a kiss and shut his door behind me. His room is lit with all his electric candles again. I wonder if that's special for sexy times or if he just likes the mood lighting all the time. The rubber sheets are bare, offering no further clues to Jax's plans. I strip naked and arrange myself on the bed so I won't give into my impulse to snoop around for clues.

Jax keeps me waiting. I have plenty of time to reflect that he might not have taken quite so long if I hadn't gotten mouthy. I'm not usually one for bratting, but Jax makes me comfortable enough to say whatever's on my mind. He's safe to be myself around. Safe to bare my body in front of. I fidget, cycling through several poses that he might find alluring. I scan the room for hints again. There's a stack of towels and a couple of bottles that look like lube on the side table.

I already know we're going to get messy and he wants to penetrate me, though. And for all I know, the lube is always there for his personal use. My hand drifts unconsciously toward my hard dick at the thought of Jax touching himself, right here in this bed. Nope. I will not risk my surprise by breaking his rules. I can imagine it, though. Or well, no. It's hard to imagine anyone sleeping on the bare waterproof sheet he's covered the bed in. With no pillows and no blankets.

I distract myself from fantasies of Jax jerking off by trying to guess what sort of bed linens he uses when he isn't getting me all kinds of messy. Not boring white. I can't picture him using default neutral colors. The curtains are a sage green, a few shades darker than the paint on the walls. The carpet is beige, though I doubt he chose it. I'm guessing his bedding is a bold geometric pattern. I can picture him having a quilt or something homey like that. Or I'm reading too much into his style. Still, someone who doesn't care about the aesthetics of his space wouldn't have candles on every flat surface for ambiance.

My sheets are purple. Have been since I was a little kid and Modaddy married my step-dad. Keeping up with laundry for all of us kids meant getting creative with keeping track of chores. We each had linens and towels in our favorite colors and it was our responsibility to make sure our stuff got washed on our assigned laundry days. The habit stuck and even years into adulthood, all of my sheets and towels are still in shades of lavender.

Ugh. I squirm; rubbing my thighs together to get friction on my dick doesn't really count as starting without him. I snort at myself. Good luck convincing Jax of that if he catches me. I spread my legs to avoid the temptation. Adjust the piercings dangling from my groin, surreptitiously giving them a good tug. Mm. I could maybe—the door opens.

Jax sweeps his gaze over my body, taking in everything. "Did I say you could play with your sac, boy?" He latches the door, then sets his bag on the floor next to the bed. His expression is more amused than disappointed in me.

"No, Mx." I fold my hands behind my back so he can see I'm not touching myself.

"And yet..." Jax lilts.

"I was just—" I start to explain, but he presses a finger to my lips. There's a pungent aroma I can't place. I'm tempted to move. Lick him, or take his finger into my mouth or something. I settle for pressing into his touch, almost kissing the finger he's using to silence me. Slow heat builds where he's touching me. A tingle that grows with every passing second.

"No excuses. Since you appear to be giving in to your naughty streak tonight, we'll start with something that has a little bite." He pulls his finger away from my mouth, leaving a hot pulse where he touched. I'm not sure if I'm imagining things or if he had something on his fingers. He dips his hand into his pocket for a moment, fiddling with something I can't see. Still, I watch his every move, entranced by him. "I'm going to blindfold you and you're going to present your ass for me to stuff full of whatever I want to put in it. Is that acceptable, boy?"

I swallow hard at the edge of cheerful menace in his tone. Jax wouldn't hurt me, but the implication that I'm here for him to stuff and use according to his whims is hot. "Including your dick?" I ask, unsure what I want the answer to be.

"We'll see." He runs his eyes over my body, then reaches out to tweak my nipple. The burn starts out faint as he rubs whatever is on his fingers into the sensitive flesh. It might just be the friction from him rubbing, pinching, squeezing and rolling the tender nub. "I'm going to make you feel. Make you guess what's going inside of you. Think you can do that?"

"I can try, Mx." I arch into the warmth building between his fingers. It's not just friction, and it's getting more intense the longer he touches me. Is it capsaicin? Did he cut open some peppers in the kitchen after he sent me in here? I whimper at the thought of this tingling ache ballooning into the throbbing, pulsing burn I've experienced after various culinary forays at Q's place. Will the places he's touching continue to ache for hours after our session? Then I imagine the same fire in my ass and I shudder.

"Good boy. Are you ready to begin? All clean and stretched for me like I asked?"

"Yes, Mx." I nod. "I prepped after the gym."

Jax lifts the bag onto the bed beside me and pulls out a silky length of dark fabric. He offers it to me. "Kneel facing away from me and wrap that around your eyes, nice and snug."

I obey. My nipple pulses and throbs and I want to touch it to soothe away the ache. Or press it and make the dull thud of the sensation blossom into real, vibrant pain. I'm not sure which. Right now, it's an annoying hum of noise in the periphery of my attention.

Jax takes the ends of the blindfold from me and knots the cloth behind my head. He makes it snug without digging in too hard. "How's that? Can you see?" Jax asks. His arm brushes my shoulder, so I think he's waving in front of my face. There's some light seeping in around the edges, but I don't really want to worm around his restrictions on my senses. I want to play by his rules. So I close my eyes behind the soft fabric.

"It's comfy. Can't see, Mx."

"Good." He squeezes my shoulders. "Assume the position, then. Ass up, face down, get comfy." He nudges me down and I go willingly, presenting him with my ass. He nudges my legs apart, fingers groping at my genitals briefly, like he wants to be sure he can access all my sensitive areas. Or he's letting me know that my sac and dick are fair game, too. I tense at his touch, but he handles me the way I told him I like. Squeezing my sac and stroking the length of my dick using a firm hold on my foreskin. I relax into my pose, jutting the relevant bits closer to him.

Jax withdraws his hand. "Ready for your first guess?"

"Mhm." I wiggle my ass.

Jax swats me, gently. "Hold still, boy."

I hear him rummaging in his bag. The distinctive sound of a lighter. I tense, expecting heat. Is he lighting a candle? Can I smell the hot wick? Something drips onto my ass cheek. A searing drop of...it runs right off my skin. Water. He dripped water on me. Cold water, but I expected fire, so it burned. This is going to be good. I lick my lips and wait for whatever he does next.

Oh slippery burning cold pressing between my cheeks. More water as the ice cube melts against my skin. Jax traces the ice along my crack to my hole.

"Bear down. Tell me what I'm putting inside of you, boy."

"Ice." I obey. The wet cube presses inside, burning cold as it stretches my rim. Jax teases me with it, until at last, the ice slips inside, all smooth edges and intense cold. I fixate on it wedged inside, a lump of confusing sensation that my brain wants to interpret as burning. I squeeze and water leaks out even as I shiver at the cold.

"That's right." Jax runs another cube over my skin, distracting from the one he shoved inside of me. He fingers my hole, shifting the ice around so it doesn't sit in the same spot and get too cold. Despite his efforts, as he adds another cube, it saps the warmth out of me. Leaves my hole almost numb. His fingers are a warm contrast to the melting ice as he pushes inside of me. The chill is less intense once the ice slips past my rim.

Jax's other hand moves another cube along my crack, up past my sac until he's tracing moisture over my dick. He teases me with the frigid touch, pressing it against my foreskin until I buck away from it. The shivery sensations from the one he inserted ebbs away as it finishes melting. Warmth tingles back as he pulls out his fingers.

Another drop of—something—splashes on my skin. Cold that turns hot as my nerves scramble trying to decide what Jax is doing to me. I squirm and it dribbles down my back a bit except this drip sticks instead of cascading off of me. Wax. The candle I thought he lit earlier.

"Wax?"

"That's right. And this?" A pin pricks me, and then another beside it and another, a roll of somethings picking at my skin in rapid succession.

"One of those pinwheel things." I guess.

"A Wartenberg wheel, good boy." Jax dribbles more wax onto my skin. The heat lands in sharp little zings that fade to a pleasant warm glow in the time it takes me to inhale sharply.

"Wax." And then more hot that's actually cold as he lets the ice drip onto my skin. "Ice." I guess. He rubs a slick finger over my hole, massaging my rim.

"Lift up." Jax urges me to move, but I'm not sure what he wants, exactly.

"Huh?"

"I want you a little higher," Jax clarifies. Well, okay then. I curl my toes under me and lift. Jax parts my cheeks and runs more ice along my crack. Then he blows over the moisture it leaves behind and I twitch at the rapid shift in temperature.

"Jax," I groan his name.

"How are you liking this so far, boy? Ready for more?" He taps his finger against my hole and I push up into him, craving more. Jax slaps my ass layering on another variation in the wash of conflicting sensations. "Yes. More please, Mx." I lean into his touch. Jax rubs and massages me, then scrapes his nails over my smooth skin, peeling off the dried wax. Everything is a mixed up jumble by the time he presses something smooth and round against my rim, working it in a tiny bit before pulling it back.

"Give me your hand." Jax reaches under me and I offer him my palm. He presses something small into it.

I explore the object. A smooth narrowly tapered cylinder. About the width of his thumb and the length of a pencil. "A candle?"

"That's right." Jax agrees. "I need you to hold very still for me now boy, we wouldn't want to lose anything in that greedy hole of yours."

He wouldn't. I *know* he wouldn't actually shove a lit candle into my ass and risk a trip to the ER to extract it. And yet...I clench my fists and hold as still as possible as he pushes the blunt tip into me. I tremble with the effort of not moving as I hear another click of his lighter. The scent of a burning wick. When the first drip hits my ass, I jerk and more splashes onto me. It's not as hot as I'd expect.

"Am I your new candleholder?" I ask in a breathy whisper. "I know we said no pictures, but if you've got a lit candle in my ass, I want to see it."

"Nervous?" Jax huffs out a laugh and fucks the rest of the object's length inside of me. The base of the narrow butt plug rests nestles between my cheeks.

"What about the wax?" I fidget.

"Melted paraffin. Is the temperature alright?"

"Yeah. I can do it hotter. Just, watch you don't get it on my piercings." That would be a pain to clean up.

"I know. I've got you, boy. Are you ready for something a little more intense?"

"Yeah."

Jax stretches me with the plug, using it to open me up for whatever he has planned. I listen for any hints of what's coming next. A wet sloshing noise. He withdraws the plug. Something smooth and almost slimy presses at my hole. I bear down and the new plug, much wider than the first, slides home. It feels weird. The material has some give, but it isn't quite like any other plug I've used.

Jax pushes it inside slowly, easing me up to the widest girth. I take the entire thing, the base once more resting against my ass. At first, this doesn't seem like much more than an average sized plug stretching me.

"Is it a dud?"

"Just wait." Jax taps the base. "Give it a little squeeze. Gently." Before I can clench, the familiar tingle from his fingers earlier sets in. Oh fuck. The heat ramps up. My nerves scream that this is going to get very bad, very fast, and I made a terrible mistake in trusting that Jax knows what he's doing.

"Hot peppers? Or some sort of chili oil? Jax? Oh hell, no. Fuck, it burns." I whimper. It's not the burn itself that gets me. It's the knowing how much worse capsaicin gets once it's applied and how long it lasts. I whine as the pain increases. My eyes tear at the thought of it. "Take it out. Please? Yellow." I'm tempted to call red. If he really did what I suspect from the growing ache, then I should. I should call off everything with him. Tears burn my eyes, hotter than the flame in my ass at the thought I might have misjudged him so badly. It takes all my trust and self-control not to just rip out whatever he's stuck inside me for myself.

Jax rests a palm on my lower back and gently eases the plug out of my hole. I whine at the rush of cool air against hot abused flesh. The burn is still multiplying even with the source removed. I moan at the thought of how much worse it's going to get, biting down on my fist to distract from the ache. How long will I have to endure this fiery burning as it grows exponentially in intensity?

"Hey, relax, Con. It's not chili oil. You're okay." Jax rubs a soothing circle low on my back. "Are you scared or hurt?"

"Both." I'm trembling with adrenaline now. But objectively, the low burn isn't getting any worse. It's bearable. Somewhere between pleasant warmth and the dull ache of a mild sunburn.

"Okay. I've got some lube I can shoot inside of you to dilute the effect." Jax offers, still rubbing my back. It's comforting despite my fear.

"You can't just make it stop." I growl at him. His response goes a long way to soothing my anger. I'm even grudgingly impressed at the mind fuck he just pulled. I'll probably be more impressed when I'm not still shaking with the dump of adrenaline and the emotional whiplash of thinking he betrayed my trust for a second there.

"No, but if it's too much, I can make it better. *Is* it too much or are you scared because of what you think I put in you?"

"Fuck you." I say with no heat. All my heat remains centered on my ass at the moment, but the ache is actually getting pretty nice now. My fear notwithstanding, it's almost a glowy quality. A radiating warmth that makes my bits extra sensitive. "Tell me?"

"It's ginger, carved into a plug with a nice wide base. The effects should wear off in about thirty minutes. And the lube really will dilute it, promise. I didn't expect it to scare you that bad. Are you okay?" Jax asks.

"Figging?" I echo what he just told me.

"Yep. Do you hate it?" he sounds sheepish.

"No. You got me fucking good, though."

"Yeah. At the risk of having to turn in my sadistic Dom card, I really didn't mean for it to freak you out that much. Do you want to stop?"

"Well, first, you absolutely need to turn in the sadist card, I'm telling. And second, I'm okay now. If it doesn't last too long and it doesn't get too much more intense than this, I can take more."

"Sure. Tell me if you need me to take it out again."

"Yeah. I will."

Jax eases the plug back into place, going slow. This time the burn creeps up on me faster, building on the lingering effects from the first time he inserted it. It climbs to a peak and then plateaus. Everything is a hazy blanket of heat concentrated around my hole. It's exquisite and I want more. "Mm, like it." I wiggle a bit, and the heightened sensitivity from the ginger makes the plug feel really good in a weird way.

"I'm glad. Would you like to dial it up a notch?" Jax offers.

"How?"

"I've got a tawse here. You can either relax and take your lashes, or clench up to ease the blow and squeeze more juice out of the ginger."

"Yeah. Fine, you can keep your Domly-Dom card."

"Is that a yes to smacking this pretty ass?" Jax caresses me. His hand brushes the plug's base, jostling it inside me. My dick aches with arousal that matches the steady throb of warmth inside me.

"Yes. Make me feel it."

Jax takes a minute to get what he needs. I relax through the first few slaps of the strap against the meat of my ass. Easy peasy with the wax from earlier blunting his strikes. Feeling it flake off adds another dimension to the sensations. By the ninth blow, the outside of my ass burns as hot as my hole, though. I tense as the tenth strike lands.

"Ungh," I groan at the spark of heat the ginger sends through my insides.

Jax rubs my sore cheeks, gently, and then with more force, until I clench again with a low groan. "Oh, fuck, it's so sensitive, Jax. More. Make me come like this."

"By strapping your ass like a naughty Victorian schoolboy?"

"Is that a thing? Sounds oddly specific."

Jax snorts. "Look up figging sometime. Apparently, it's one of those weird Victorian things."

"Ok, well, I guess I'm a naughty Victorian lad then. Spank me headmxter. Is that who doled out the punishments?" I tease, barely remembering to swap in a neutral title so I don't take him out of the scene.

Jax snorts as he lays into me with the strap again. "Count out your punishment, boy."

I get to fifteen before I'm a blubbering mess from the dual sensations. Jax sets aside the tawse. "On your back, so I can show you some real head mastery."

I let him roll me over; the motion shifts the plug still lodged inside me, awakening my nerves anew. At the same time, Jax pushes my thighs open and takes my cock into his mouth. Engulfing me in wet heat that seems to blend with the burning ginger and the strapping he gave me, and just, everything.

It's a symphony of pain and pleasure and tangled up

sensations melding into an arousal so potent I never want it to stop. I want to bury myself inside Jax and never come up for air. I'm so unbelievably sensitive right now. The fact I still can't see anything he's doing to me only intensifies things. I'm helpless on my back, spread open, skewered on his plug and utterly at his mercy.

Jax's mouth is full of said mercy and he lavishes it on me until I see stars and the orgasm rolls through me like it's going to launch me into space. Each pulsing involuntary clench of my muscles milks more sparks from the ginger root. And I'm a melted spent puddle of goo by the time Jax eases the plug out of my hole. He gently fills me up with something that dulls the pulsing burn significantly. If I wasn't wrung the fuck out, I might swoon at the way he prioritizes my needs as the scene ends. My new fuck buddy is the total package.

"Hey, Jax?" I reach for him, pawing at the air where I think he is since I still can't see.

"Yeah, Conman?" Jax captures my questing hand and squeezes it briefly. I waggle my finger at him.

"You know we said friends with benefits? Well, you, my friend, are knocking the bennies out of the park."

"Good to know," he says with the rumble of a suppressed chuckle. "Rest now, and I'll get you cleaned up. Sound good?" He pats my hand.

"Mhm." I lay my head back onto the mattress.

Jax is as good as his word about taking care of me. He leaves the blindfold in place and murmurs sweet nothings to me about what a good boy I am for him while he cleans me up. Once more, I ended the session in his bed as a sloppy mess. I'm all floaty, with no urge to come down. It's perfect bliss. Even the pulse of heat that's still thrumming through me after he removes the ginger. Jax is, without a doubt, the most creative guy I've done this with. I hope he doesn't get sick of our arrangement anytime soon.

CHAPTER 8

Jax

I roll Connor onto his belly to clean the remaining wax residue off his ass. The strap did a decent job of removing most of what was still there. I use the last of the melting ice cubes to stiffen what little remains, and scratch it away. Connor reacts to the cold, tensing with a sharp intake of breath.

"Sorry, just using it to make this easier." I scratch the flakes of wax away. Connor lifts into my touch, making a contented hum in his throat. Fuck, I want him to make that sound with my dick in his mouth. I haven't gotten off yet, but that's fine. Tonight was about exploring his reactions. My goal going into the evening was more of a mind fuck than actually fucking him. That went a little further than I'd intended when I planned this scene. Not outside the bounds of what we've discussed he likes. At least, I don't think I crossed any lines. Maybe if I'd actually stuck a hot pepper up his ass. That thought makes me flinch.

I wanted to make him second-guess everything he experienced tonight. But I didn't want to truly scare him. Even if I had planned to come tonight, I couldn't have kept it up at the genuine anguish in his voice when he begged me to make it stop. A sadist I am not. Although it wasn't the pain so much as the perceived betrayal that got to me. Every minute he's spent in my bed is a minute he's trusting me to take care of him. I can't take that trust lightly. Especially not if we're going to be doing more scenes together. I hope he still wants to after tonight.

Connor seems very relaxed as I scrape my nails over every inch of his butt. I stretch out the process far longer than necessary since we're both enjoying the touching. If his periodic little moans and the way he angles himself toward me are anything to go by. He lifts his ass into every touch like a cat arching into a particularly satisfying scratch.

Once he's free of every fleck of paraffin, I wipe him down, then rub aloe into his skin to further dull the burn. I double check that his piercings are all clean and wax free, and if touching him there leads to tickling, teasing brushes along his cock, well, he doesn't complain. Far from it. Connor humps my bed as I fondle his sac. The piercings hold the flesh there together in a way that resembles cis balls. He seems to like when I play with it the same way I'd fondle a cis guy.

"Hm, you like that, Connor?" I tug experimentally on one of his piercings.

"Yeah." Connor agrees. He lifts his ass and gives a little shimmy. "You can fuck me. If you want to get off."

I snort. "Are you offering because you want me to fuck you?"

"Yep. These benefits go both ways, right?"

"You don't have to put out for that to be the case."

Connor shrugs languidly, which I wouldn't have thought he could actually do with the angle he's laid out on my bed. He gets the idea across though, and the motion presses his junk against my hand more firmly. "Mm. Well, if you don't want to, you can still jerk me off. I won't complain."

"No, it's cool. I'll fuck you and you can come again on my cock or not at all." I tug on his sac and he groans.

"Mm, yeah." He pulls away, increasing the tension. "That won't work for me. I enjoy getting fucked from behind, but that's not enough stimulation to get me off again so soon."

"Let me grab something." I release my grip on him and dig into my side table for condoms and a bullet vibe for him to use. "Give me your hand?"

Connor reaches between his legs, and I press the vibrator into his palm. "More candles?" he jokes.

I guide his thumb to the power button at the toy's base. "Not quite."

He presses the button, and it vibrates. "Lube?"

"I've got you." I squirt a generous glob out and smear it over his dick and sac. Connor squirms. I smear more of the lube over his hole. "You want my cock inside you, Connor?"

"Yes, please." He runs the vibe around the base of his shaft.

I roll on the condom, then position him closer to the edge of the bed. Connor moves willingly, spreading his legs to grant me better access. I ease into him slowly, mindful that he's probably already tender from our play. "You okay?" I ask, rubbing gentle circles in the small of his back, since he seemed to find that soothing earlier.

"Yeah." His voice is tight, though. "Just go slow, I'm still all warm and glowy from the ginger."

I give him time to adjust. The low buzz of the vibrator fills the silence. Connor rocks back toward me. "I said slow down, not stop."

"Okay, Mister Bossypants." I press inside. Connor bears down on me, squirming as I bottom out inside of him.

"Ooh. Stings a bit." Connor wiggles again, clenching around me.

"Want me to pull out?" I offer again.

"Nah, just a second." He raises his chest up off the bed and rocks into me, fucking himself slow and gentle. I stop rubbing his back and grip his flanks, squeezing hard to resist the urge to thrust into him harder. Connor sets the pace, and I clench my hands hard as he draws out every movement. Each stroke along my length seems to take an eternity, and he keeps shifting around like he's trying to find just the right angle. "Sorry, it's super sensitive right now, but your dick feels really fucking good stretching me."

"Take your time, then." I encourage him. The glacially slow fuck isn't my typical, but it's enough to be inside him. Connor makes the most gorgeous noises during sex. Hisses of breath, the cut-off rumble of a moan, gasps of pleasure. Like everything inside him is dialed up to an eleven and even the slightest friction as he fucks himself in slow motion is lighting him up.

If we ever decide to ditch condoms, I want to try figging him bare. I want the residual burn to spread from his hole to my dick, warming us both. Earlier, I tried rubbing a bit of the ginger peeling on myself while I prepared for tonight. So I have an idea just how intense the burn gets. I understand why he freaked out when he didn't know what it was. But I also get why he seems so enamored with the lingering heat, too. I want to burn with him, join in his euphoria.

Instead, I hold myself still and let him use my dick however he sees fit. He picks up the pace, so gradually that I can't pinpoint when it goes from easing into having a dick up his tender ass to full-on fucking. The squelch of lube as he strokes his dick with one hand and takes me deep with his entire body moving to meet me picks up the tempo.

"C'mon, Jax, fuck me like you mean it." Connor taunts. I don't have to be asked twice. I'm horny as hell. He's been playing with my dick for long enough that I plow into him at his invitation. I squeeze his waist and pound his ass hard, taking my pleasure as he gasps out hoarse cries for more.

"Fuck, yes. That. There. Oh, hells. Mhm." Noise pours out of him. I'm pretty sure he's coming again. Good, I'm close too. The rhythmic squeeze of his muscles as he orgasms wrings my climax out of me.

If we were face-to-face, I'd stop his incoherent sex babble with a kiss. It might be just as well that he's on all fours under me. I'm pretty sure our benefits only extend so far. Kissing to feed him a mouthful of cake as part of a scene is not the same as kissing him while I spill my load buried deep inside of him. I thrust a few more times, chasing the last dregs of pleasure, and then pull out to deal with the condom.

Staring at the puffy and engorged rim of his hole makes me long to touch him. Prod him until he makes more of those sweet sounds. He looks utterly debauched. I'm tempted to take a picture of him for my personal spank bank. But we agreed on no photos tonight, so I just stare, trying to memorize my marks on his body. Nothing that's likely to be obvious for long upon visual inspection, but he'll carry the deep ache with him tomorrow. I hope.

"Ah, are you trying to earn your sadist card back by admiring your handiwork?" Connor breaks into my reverie. "Because your poor neglected bottom needs to get cleaned up. And to have this blindfold off, if we're done."

"I thought you were supposed to be a sweet, shy boy?"

"Pft." Connor snorts. "I'm shy with strangers. Pretty sure that ship sailed for us when I started letting you put random household objects up my ass."

"Did it?" I give his reddened ass a gentle squeeze.

"Ah." His breath hisses between his teeth. "Yeah."

"Arnica?"

"You just want an excuse to squeeze my ass more." Connor

75

snort-laughs. "I swear every top at the club buys that shit in bulk."

"Hey, it's not my fault that you have a very sexy ass. Is that a yes?"

"Can't hurt. Guess it's my fault for spending all those hours at the gym making my body irresistible, huh?" He grins as he presents himself to me with another wiggle.

I get the cream and apply a thick layer to Connor's ass cheeks, even if the red marks from the tawse are already fading. He waits for me to pull his underwear back onto his body and guide him up to sit on the edge of the bed. I can't deny enjoying his slight wince, further evidence that he'll have a physical reminder of this session after he leaves.

He could have easily removed the blindfold himself at any point, but he waits for me to do it. The visual proof of his willing and ongoing submission to me makes this even better. I have to pick at the knot a bit to get it loose. When it falls away, he squints into the dim light of the room and blinks at me a few times. Connor rubs his eyes.

"What did you think of that?" I ask.

"Loved it." He bounces on the mattress, legs swinging, then winces.

"Anything you'd change for next time?" I try to hide my smug satisfaction at knowing I did that. I made him feel, and he's going to keep remembering me in that visceral way for a while after he leaves here.

"Nope. I mean, you got me good. But if you ever think you want to shove actual hot peppers up my ass, I will call red. And we will be done with this arrangement, but the figging is a definite yes, would try again. And I like how you fucked with my head a bit. Makes things more interesting."

"What did you like about that part, tonight specifically?"

Connor considers. "I think it was the adrenaline rush of not knowing. The fear. Not just of the pain, but the fear of—" he hesitates, eyes darting to my face and then to the floor, "—well, fear of you, I guess. Or of my judgment being shit. Which, by the way, is a bit of a thing with me, so you definitely triggered a more extreme emotional response there, but not in a bad way. I don't think."

"If it helps, I'll only play head games with you on purpose during a scene."

Connor nods. "Yes. That. That's good to hear you confirm. Thanks."

"Is that why you like CNC, too?" I ask.

Connor taps his fingers on his thighs. "I mean, I don't think there has to be a reason. But yeah, I like the idea of playing with the fear of my partner. Like I can take control of that legit abstract fear that you can never really *know* what's in another person's head by making it into a game. I dunno. It just gets me hot to fantasize about it."

"You don't have to tell me now, but if we decide to explore that kind of play, I'd like to know if you've ever had similar real-life experiences. Anything that might be triggering during that kind of scene, okay?"

"Okay. Same applies to you." There's a beat of silence where we both are watching each other. Then Connor stands with another slight wince, stretches, and grabs for the rest of his clothing. "I should probably head out. Thanks for the awesome scene. Was there anything you want me to do to help you clean up before I go?"

"Are you sure you're okay to leave?"

"Yeah. I told Q we were playing tonight, and they offered to let me spend the night for cuddles."

"Do you need cuddles after a scene?" I should have asked about that earlier, but he didn't request anything specific and he seemed to want to leave once we dealt with the mess last time.

"Only the really good ones." He winks at me. "Q is my go-to person for that, if I need it."

"For future reference, I can cuddle, too." I offer. I get the between-the-lines implication that he's used to taking care of himself after scenes. What he's mentioned about his dating history makes that unsurprising. He says he wants a relationship, but he's clearly wary about opening up outside of a scene. That's not really my business, though. We're just kinky fuck buddies.

"Noted." He nods in acknowledgment. "But I wanted to see them, anyway. If that's okay with you?"

"Of course. Want me to drive you there?" I'm not entirely comfortable sending him home on the bus right away. I'd rather be the one snuggling him and making sure he comes down from the scene alright, but I don't want to overstep. This is casual, and the offer is on the table for next time.

Connor bites his lip like he wants to refuse me out of hand, but then he nods and flashes me a grateful smile. "That would be nice. Bet your car has softer seats than the bus."

"That it does. And I'll even throw in extra doggy cuddles if you want to sit in the back with Gia."

"Oh, yes, please. See, you've got all the best benefits. We should have become better friends ages ago. Now I get bio puppy snuggles and Q puppy snuggles." He considers my room for a minute. "Don't suppose you have a clean sheet or blanket or something? Q's allergic to dogs."

"Yep, I'll grab you something to wrap up with. Might be good to hop in the shower when you get to Q's anyway, though. Or use a lint brush, the backseat is Gia's domain, and she's a shedder."

"Yeah. I will." Connor bites his lip and looks at me, his gaze sharp. "Will you be okay?"

"Yeah. I've got arrangements for puppy snuggles with my bestie, too." I wink at him and he laughs. "Text me later?"

"Duh. How else will you tease me about whatever we're doing next week?" Connor pulls on his shirt and pants. I dunk the used candle tapers into the bowl of melted ice to be sure they are completely extinguished. The bowl of water, with a few sad ice chips still clinging to existence, I dump in the washroom sink. Then I gather up the rest of the detritus of our evening and stuff it all into the Ikea bag to deal with later. I hang the bag from a hook on the back of my door to keep it out of Gia's inquisitive reach and the three of us leave.

CHAPTER 9

Connor

Jax and I meet up for kinky sex once a week through the rest of the winter and into spring. The weekend after Valentine's Day, he ties me spreadeagled to his bed, blindfolds me again, and paints me in melted chocolate. He edges me for hours as he licks me clean and starts the process over.

Jax narrows my entire world to warm gooey chocolate, his hot breath, and eager mouth. The cool breeze of an oscillating fan makes me shiver every time it sweeps over an area he's finished licking. That, and a top of the line massage wand. He tapes the vibrating wand in place, angled to just barely stimulate my junk no matter how much I writhe to get it where I need it. I'm a sobbing, pleading mess by the time the chocolate runs dry.

Jax loosens the restraints on my ankles to lift my ass onto his lap so he can fuck into me. Time has already lost all meaning as he rocks his cock inside of me, then fucks me hard enough to pull on my restraints with every thrust. Hard enough to feel it tomorrow. So hard I might come apart at the seams if I can't find release.

Just when I don't think I can handle another second of his sweet torture, Jax presses the wand against me. It's fucking magic as every muscle in my core contracts and I could swear this is what it's like to bust a nut as a cis guy. The sudden geysering release of pent up pressure through my cock. Jax pulls out to finish on my belly, adding to the sticky mess we've already made.

Basically, Jax is a devious genius, and I keep coming back for more. He's kind of perfect. I mean, with a few glaring incompatibilities. But if I'm honest with myself, I've already all but abandoned hope of meeting a kinky Daddy who wants a boy like me. So really, a Dom who fits all my other kinks is better than I'd hoped to find.

And, well, sure, Jax isn't actually into relationships, but he's got me thinking I can live with that, too. If he keeps making me come my brains out, I don't need the relationship trappings. Besides, if I eventually find a boyfriend who agrees to me getting my kink on with other people, Jax and I can keep up our arrangement indefinitely.

It's possible I don't even really need a relationship when I've got Jax to fulfill my every kinky wish and friends who love me. Quent and Kylee make me feel like I've got a home and family in the city. I've even put my dating apps on hiatus lately. The aching void doesn't seem as bad when I have my nights with Jax to look forward to. Our texts are fun to scroll through when I need fapping fodder. The message thread between us is replete with the pictures he takes of me while he's driving me wild.

I hope I'm not being foolish to think that this can last and I can have it all. But I don't want to give up my access to regular, mind-blowing sex with Jax. I still want the sort of relationship Q and Kylee have, though. Or what my parents and older siblings have. Someone they come home to and build a life with. That isn't Jax and me. But what we have is legit good enough that I considered skipping the visit home I had planned for Purim so I could see him at our usual time.

Except, I went home, because getting to dress up in costumes and bake cookies with Pop is one of my favorite family traditions. I haven't missed another Sunday with Jax since my trip home for Purim, though. Not until this weekend, anyway. It's May, and I'm home visiting my folks again this weekend instead of fucking Jax, because I miss my siblings and my folks if I stay away for too long. Seeing Prescott, Cameron, and Viv all settled and happy and raising families of their own awakens the familiar ache in my chest. The loneliness, the sense of not quite fitting in with them.

Despite that, I miss all my rambunctious siblings and niblings. Quent finds the chaos and noise in my childhood home overwhelming when they come with me, but to me, it's familiar. It's the sound of family and being surrounded by people who love me. I love my job and my found family at Adventures. It would be harder to find people who share my kinks out in rural BC, but part of me wants to be around more. I want to come back for the big development team soccer tournament Marietta excitedly talks about wanting to win before starting highschool in the fall. And the art show the twins are having at their school this weekends. Eli's dance recital and Noa's spring concert with the school band.

I want to babysit my niblings. Be in the audience at every game and recital now that my three youngest siblings are growing up and honing in on their interests. All of them are growing up way too fast. It seems like I blinked and my oldest nibling, Carl, transformed from a chubby-cheeked infant into a grade one student. The time I get to spend with them all is precious, yet here I am, sulking by myself because I need a minute to breathe.

While I've been soaking up the family time, I ignored a text from Q for too long. It's like they've got Spidey senses about when I'm being morose. They call me while I'm hiding in the den from the board game that my folks and the little siblings who still live at home are all playing. Noa, Eli, and Marietta asked me to join them, but they didn't press when I said I wanted a nap instead. The sunlight is already getting dim when my phone rings, so Shabbat is over, or near enough. They'll put away the board games and get back to the hustle and bustle of life again soon.

"Hey, Quent." I answer the call.

"Hey, yourself. I thought you said you're allowed to text on Shabbat?"

"Yeah, it's a gray area. But the little kids aren't allowed on their phones so that we can actually have family time, so it's a solidarity thing? Plus, the whole point of visiting is to see them."

"Mhm. And yet...you answered on the first ring."

I sigh. "Got a little overwhelmed, I guess. Spent last night with all the siblings."

"And they all have what you want? With the partners and living within a short drive of the rest of the family?"

"Pretty much." I pick at the seam of my pants. "I mean, I'm happy to be the cool big city uncle. But I guess I envy them for being able to fit the defaults without sacrificing their happiness. Does that make me a terrible brother?"

"Nah. They know you love them, but it's hard when you don't quite fit. No matter how much they love you back, it's not the same as being with people who get what it's like."

"I mean, my folks are queer, too. And Viv and Prescott are happy living here."

"Sure. But your folks also figured that out after they had established a life there. They had a partner to lean on. And Viv and Prescott are settled with their partners, too. It's harder when there isn't a clear roadmap marked out for what a happy queer life might look like for you. Heteronormativity is baked into every scrap of media you consume before you're even conscious of what you're consuming, and we don't get to have that as much. Your feelings are totally valid, babe. It's fine to want what you want. I'm here for you, okay?"

"Yeah. You're right. Thanks." I hug my knees to my chest, but Quent's words are comforting.

"Other than the melancholy, are you having a pleasant visit?" They press.

"Yeah. Noa and Eli have a school art show going on, so we're supposed to check that out in a little while."

"Nice. Oh!" Rustling sounds alert me that Quent is moving around, probably changing positions to go along with the shift in topics. "Did I tell you I got my first AF this week?"

It takes me a minute to make the connection. "Your period's back?"

"Yep. Sorry I've been poking around fertility forums too much. It makes me giggle every time they write AF, because I read it as 'as fuck', but apparently the 'Aunt Flo' lingo rubbed off on me. So, 'Operation Brothers' Baby' is a go. All systems ready."

I wrinkle my nose. "You seriously have the worst way with words, Q."

"Right?" They agree with evident glee. "I mean, I have to joke about it because otherwise the idea of getting knocked up with Logan's baby batter is kind of gross. He's practically my brother too, at this point. They've been together for years."

"I can't even imagine carrying a kid for my siblings. Sure, I love them all. I'd die for any of them, but surrogacy is where I draw the line." I play it off as a joke, even though the idea of a pregnancy scare is legit the stuff of nightmares for me. Hence, I got my hysto as soon as my doctor would sign off on the procedure.

"Good thing they've got so many other siblings to volunteer for the honor then, huh?" Quent teases.

"Pretty much. I bet Viv would offer for any of the rest of us who might need to borrow a uterus. She actually likes being preggers."

"What a weirdo." Quent's dry tone makes me smile.

"Hey, you said it, you big weirdo. Are you nervous about it?"

"Yeah. But also excited? I mean, I'm really excited about the scene Mommy agreed to try for the actual insemination. Breeding kink is *so* my jam, and it's kind of hot to know it will be real. At least the 'trying to knock me up' part of the role play. It makes me super horny to think about it."

I chuckle, because I know all about Quent's favorite fantasy playlist. "And the actual pregnancy part?"

"Oh, yeah, that part I'm nervous as hell about. I mean, I don't think it will be too bad physically? It's not like most people gender me correctly as it is. But for now I get a decently even mix of pronouns, and I'm sure a big preggo belly will skew everything more femme for a while. So that will suck. Plus, doctor visits are the worst. Ugh...why am I doing this again?"

"Because you're the most generous person I know, and you love your brother a ridiculous amount? And you want a nibling?"

"Hm, yeah. True. Tell me more about how awesome I am?"

"You are totally awesome, Q. And once you get some niblings like me, you can join the cool folks club."

"Hey! I don't think that was nearly effusive enough. I am the best best friend ever, too, remember?"

"You are. And you'll be an awesome nibling haver. Um, what title are you going to use for the kid?"

"Oh! That's the best part of being the surrogate. I saw some shirts and stuff, and I'm totally going to make the kid call me their stork. Fun, right?"

"That is very you, pupper." I laugh. Q blows a raspberry into the phone. "Ew. I almost forgot to tell you how mature you are." I tease through my laughter.

"Yes, I am. Thank you for noticing." They retort primly. We both chuckle at that. "Miss your face...and speaking of missing things..."

"What?"

"Are you missing your playtime with Jax?"

I roll my eyes. "We rescheduled."

"Oh?"

"Yeah, he's got a photo session lined up for me to play with a friend of his who has a Violet Wand. I'm psyched."

"Do I know the Dom?"

"Brian. He's brought his toys to the club before. I just was too much of a wuss to ask for a chance to play."

"Oh. Yeah. Okay. I know of him. I thought it might be Cedric." Q makes a yuck sound.

"What's wrong with Cedric?"

"Nothing. I mean, except that he's a pompous asshole who thinks he's better than everyone else. He only brings his expensive toys to the club because he'd never be able to find a play partner without the lure of getting to play with his things."

"Wow, tell me how you really feel, Q." I chuckle.

"Hmph." Quent grumbles, voice low, probably so their Mommy won't overhear them gossiping. "He might have made some remarks about puppy play being for cis men and everyone else should stay out of *his* space. Even though he isn't even *into* puppy play. At all. Like, the guy came to a mosh and had no clue what he was doing and no respect for the rules of our group."

"That sucks." I sympathize.

"Yeah. But Brian is fine. Not your usual type, but he'll show you a good time. Give me a full report. I know you've wanted to try e-stim."

"I will. Might come by for snuggles after, if you're free?"

"I'd love to have you over, babe, but this week might cut it close with my ovaries. Check if Jax or Brian can handle it?"

"Yeah. Of course. No worries." I try not to let the rejection get to me. Quent's life doesn't revolve around me. That wouldn't be healthy for either of us. And Jax has offered to snuggle with me as part of our aftercare. No big deal.

"Or check in with Tate and Monty?" Q offers, picking up on the hurt in my voice that I can't quite hide. It's not a bad idea, but Quent is my favorite snuggle buddy.

"It's fine. Jax said he's available for cuddles." I assure them. Something squeezes inside me at the idea of taking him up on the offer, though. Even after a couple months of getting off together and letting him take me apart emotionally, physically, and sexually, I'm not ready for him to hold me afterward. If I let him put me back together after the scene, I might not ever be able to let him go.

Oh well. It's one night of snuggles after sex. That won't change anything. It would be silly to think it could. I mean, really, I let Jax tie me up, smack me around and cover me with various questionable substances; drawing the line at post-coital cuddles is beyond ridiculous, right? Right.

"Perfect. Okay, so I've got game night with Mommy and Jared and Logan, but I wanted to check in since we haven't talked in a few days. See you soon?"

"Yep. Have fun, Q."

"Uh huh, you too. Go hang with your family while you've got the weekend with them, Con."

I hang up, knowing Quent is right. I'll regret hiding out in the den if I don't go back out there soon. It was good to talk to Quent, though. And it might be ideal to let things cool off between Jax and me. At least for one weekend. I can go an entire weekend without getting off with him. It's just kinky sex, nothing more meaningful than that. Fun, sure. Some of the best orgasms of my life, unquestionably. But nothing more than that. Nothing like the lasting love between my parents.

They're in the living room, still playing their game with my little siblings. Marietta seizes on my rejoining them to insist on starting a new game. A sure sign that she's losing. That kid has a competitive streak a mile wide. Noa protests the loudest, and a glance at the board confirms that she's currently in the lead.

Pop offers to let me take over for him so he can go get dinner started, and that mollifies Noa, though Marietta continues to protest that it's not fair. Eli stays out of the fight between our sisters, going to get himself a soda while they bicker. They're still at it when he gets back, and he kicks my feet under the table out of boredom. I nudge him back and we end up in a fight to see who can pin the others' toes to the ground first. Like a larger scale thumb war.

Modaddy eventually gives us a quelling look to stop when we bump the table with our knees. Then they cut Marietta a side deal using house rules that allow for future trading during other players' turns. Noa grumbles, but lets it pass and I've missed this. All the loudness and squabbling and love. It's nice to be home with them all, to feel like a part of them again. Even if it's just for a few days before I have to get back to my job and the family I've made for myself in the city.

CHAPTER 10
Connor

When Jax first asked me to model for him, I figured it was a flimsy pretext to play. Not that I even needed a pretext to be all over that action. I agreed to it, more because I'd been craving a scene than because I fancy myself the sort of person he'd actually want to advertise his business with. The default photo frame images don't look like me.

Not that I look bad, I've got decent muscle definition. I picked up the habit of working out my anxiety at the gym from my eldest brother, Prescott. But I'm not exactly a blue-eyed blonde cis guy with a chiseled jaw or anything. I look a lot like my bio dad, which is weirdly affirming for me. I wish I'd known him, but he died when I was two. So I don't remember the man in my baby photos who has my smile and my wavy dark hair.

When I get off the bus to meet up with Jax and Brian, I almost walk right up to Jax's apartment by default. It's like my feet know where to go when I'm about to get the really good dicking. Except we aren't meeting up for sex tonight. I'm here to play with Brian.

Jax is just taking pictures of the scene. My first scene with someone else since we started playing. That has butterflies dancing in my belly. I know where the studio is, a modest storefront that's usually dark when we walk by with Gia. Not that I have routines outside of the bedroom with Jax. Sometimes I just show up early and we walk his dog together. No big deal.

When I step inside the studio for the first time, the door chimes. Jax's warm voice greets me right away. "You made it! Come on back and let me show you what I've got for us to use today."

Jax beams at me from the reception desk and I get the strangest impression that if he weren't at work, he'd have hugged me. I brush that image aside as wishful thinking. Just because the man likes to put his mouth on me until I come during our hookups doesn't mean he's as eager as I am for any scrap of affection. No matter how much I read into his hooded gaze.

When I follow him through a door to the actual studio, there's another person waiting inside.

"Connor, this is Brian. He's letting us play with his Violet Wand today." Jax introduces the other person.

Oh, yeah. I am so here for this. I look between Jax and Brian. "Nice to meet you, Sir. I'm Connor." I offer my hand to Brian, and he gives me a firm shake.

"Good to meet you, Connor. Jax has told me a lot about you."

"He has?" I try not to sound skeptical as I look between them, but how much does Jax really know about me to tell this guy? Unless he means they discussed my kinks? I don't think Jax would share anything too personal without my permission, though.

"Don't look so shocked, boy. I pay attention when you talk." Jax winks at me. He fingers his camera like he's nervous about my response, though.

Brian chuckles at my reaction. "Relax, all good things. Our friend here says you're an obedient boy, eager to please, and open to trying new things. Is that wrong?"

"No. Jax is right. I told him I always wanted to play with one of those." I point at the device nestled in its carrying case with several attachments laid out next to it.

"You can touch it," Brian says. I shiver at the filthy mental images that his low rumbling voice giving me permission to touch sends tumbling through my brain. I can well imagine him using that same coaxing tone as he offers me his cock. Only it's Jax's cock that I picture him ordering me to touch, not Brian's. I shake the unwanted mental image away.

I reach out a finger to stroke along the smooth glass curve of the largest attachment. Brian's intent stare as I examine his toys only reinforces my initial reaction that there's a subtext here. I pull my hand back. "How do you want me?"

"You wore what I suggested under the street clothes?" Jax asks.

I nod.

"You can change in the washroom or here. We'll get started when you're ready." He gestures to a small door next to his office. The fact he offered me that added privacy makes me more comfortable shucking off my t-shirt and jeans there in the studio. In front of Brian. I've been naked in front of Jax enough times not to be self-conscious around him anymore. And honestly, I don't care what Brian thinks of my body. Jax likes what he sees, and so do I.

Underneath, I've got on my favorite harness and a jock that does a pretty good job of covering my junk without making it obvious that I'm packing. I fold my clothing and try not to shiver at the two pairs of eyes on my mostly naked body. I'm not ashamed of how I look, but I get shy with new people.

"Here, I'll put your clothes in a cubby." Jax gestures to a shelving unit on the far wall. Most of it seems to be stuffed with props or costumes. I hand Jax my clothing. The brush of his fingers against my hand makes me all warm inside. It's silly to be hung up on the memory of his hands wiping the gooey aftermath of our various play sessions off my lap, but that's where my mind goes. To his mouth on my bare skin as I stare after him like a lovestruck fool. I shake off those thoughts, turning toward Brian when he talks.

"I can see why you want to photograph him," Brian says to Jax. Over my head, like I'm not even there.

Objectification isn't usually my thing, but I kind of like that Brian looks at me and just sees a sexy submissive boy. Someone desirable. And a part of me likes how he defaulted to treating me like I'm Jax's with the way he worded that. I stand straighter, pull back my shoulders and flex a little, wanting to reflect well on Jax. It almost feels like he's sharing me tonight, the way a full-time Dom might. What good is all my gym time if I can't show off my muscles a bit, right? And Jax wanted me to have this scene. He wants to capture it with his camera. He's the reason I'm here, waiting to try something new.. That shouldn't make me as happy as it does.

"Very nice." Brian circles around me, inspecting his canvas for our session. His gaze locks on the barbells through my nipples. He reaches toward them, pausing before he makes contact with my body. "May I?"

I nod, and he flicks the end of one of my piercings. I tense up at the jarring sensation.

"What are these made of?" Brian doesn't look away from his examination of my chest.

"Surgical steel, Sir."

"Any other piercings?" He sweeps his gaze over me, as if searching for them.

"Yeah." I brush a hand over the two in my left ear.

"Is that all of them?" Brian asks.

"Nope." I smirk and dart my eyes down to his junk. Brian has an impressive bulge in his tight jeans. Jax makes a choking sound, since he's intimately familiar with all my jewelry.

Brian flicks my barbell piercing. "Is that how you address a Dom you want to play with, boy?"

"No, Sir. Sorry, Sir." I lower my gaze to the ground. I don't know how seriously he takes protocol and I don't want to fuck things up before we even get started.

"Not a problem, I prefer to be addressed with respect, if you want to scene with me; do you?"

"Yes, Sir." I lick my lips.

"That's much better. Thank you, boy. Are any of the piercings new?"

"No, Sir. I've had them for years."

He nods, eyeing me like a toy he can't wait to play with. That look sends shivers up my spine. This sense of being wanted is a heady thing. "And do I have your permission to touch you?"

"Yes, Sir. Um, nothing sexual, though. Sir."

"That's fine. Does that include getting you out of that jock? Nipple play?" Brian clarifies.

"Jock stays on. I'd prefer nothing below the belt. Nipples are fine."

"Okay." He circles me, eyeing my entire body. "Hm, well, seeing as I'm not spotting any other visible piercings, would I be correct in assuming the other one is through your genitals and thus off limits?"

"It's a Guiche ladder. And you can touch it with toys, but not your hands." That's not what the parlor called it. They used anatomical words that I don't. Not maliciously, just enough to

93

clarify exactly what I wanted and whether they could do what I asked them for.

Those piercings took me ages to work up the courage to get for that reason. Three simple silver hoops give my sac shape and heft. The euphoria those three affirming piercings create has more than made up for the anxiety and discomfort getting them caused me, physical and otherwise. The rings' weight makes me feel like I've got dangly bits, like any cis guy. I like when guys play with them. But I don't want to go there with Brian. Especially not with Jax watching us. I refuse to think too hard about what that implies.

"Hm. We agreed nothing below the belt, boy. Besides, I'd prefer to have a visual on what I'm working with so I don't do any damage to the skin, especially since you've got a conductive piercing in the area. Perhaps another time, when you're more comfortable with me."

"Yes, Sir." I try to hide my disappointment and not be too angry that dysphoria might steal a huge part of the fun of yet another experience from me. It's not even dysphoria really, it's just knowing I don't look the way he expects me to and fearing his reaction. That's the main reason I'm not taking off my pants.

"Don't be sad, boy, we can still have plenty of fun while respecting your limits." Brian palms my abs. I tense under his touch. Brian doesn't move his hand until I relax again.

"Yes, Sir." I swallow my bitterness.

Brian's hand moves up to the straps of my harness, tugging and dancing along the leather to the metal studs. "Metal?"

"Yes, Sir."

He runs his hand over my chest, getting me used to his touch, I suppose. As he strokes me, he asks what I'm looking for from him. If I have any health conditions or heart problems, a pacemaker, anything that might impact our scene.

He mentions pregnancy is a no-no with e-stim, but chuckles, like it's a foregone conclusion that we don't have to worry about that particular issue. It's weirdly affirming that the possibility that might not be as impossible as he assumes never seems to cross his mind. If I think about it too hard, it will make me sad later. That it would never occur to him that someone like me exists.

Would he be as excited to play with me, if he knew? Should I tell him? Before I can, the conversation moves on and it doesn't matter. He isn't getting in my pants. And I don't think Jax would have me model with a transphobe. I should be safe here. With Jax.

We go through the standard safety questions, stoplight safewords, my limits and Brian's for the session. Then he turns away from me and assembles his tools. Since we're not going below the belt, he tucks the e-stim box with its wires and pads back into his gear bag. He mentioned it's probably not as exciting for Jax to photograph, anyway. Since the pads would conduct right into my body instead of the more visually impressive glow and shooting sparks the Violet Wand creates.

Jax steps closer to me. "You ready for me to take your picture?"

"Yes, Mx." I agree, practically using the title he prefers by rote after my chat with Brian. I enjoy saying it to him, though. I want him to look at me with the same heat using a title puts in Brian's expression every time I say it.

Jax claps me on the back. "You don't have to call me that tonight, Connor. I'm here to be a fly on the wall."

"Sure. Sorry." I duck my head to hide my disappointment about that. I like playing with him.

"It's fine, I like when you call me that, boy, but I don't require it." Jax's warm smile leaves no doubt he really does like hearing his title on my lips.

"Look here, boy," Brian calls to me, and I glance up to see him attaching a broad mushroom head attachment to his wand. The purple glow inside the glass dances hypnotically. I want to touch it.

"You want to touch, boy?" Brian asks, correctly reading my avid expression.

I nod, then recall his rules. "Yes, Sir."

"Good boy, come here." He beckons me closer.

I step onto the cushy dark mat with a brick wall backdrop set up behind me, stopping in front of Brian.

"Good. Stand on the tape. Don't move from that spot until I give you permission." Brian points to the tape lines.

"Yes, Sir." I adjust to stand on the hash marks, with my feet about shoulder width apart. Brian circles me, observing like I'm a puzzle for him to solve. I tense, waiting for the first jolt. Brian smirks at me. He holds the wand up as he roughly strokes his free hand over my pectoral, squeezing, shoving against my shoulder. He pushes almost hard enough to knock me off balance. I press back into him to avoid moving my feet.

The buzz of his wand charging fills my ears. I get an acrid whiff of ozone, my only warning before the first jolt of electricity bites into my other pec. I yelp, arching into the tingling sparks. Brian steadies me with the hand on my shoulder. Jax is behind him; my eyes track to him, seeking confirmation that this is how it's supposed to feel.

Jax catches my eye, must read the uncertainty in my face, because he nods encouragingly. That first touch startled me more than it hurt. Still, the strange electric sensation is more intense than I expected. The reassurance that Jax is there in case I need him lets me relax and focus on Brian.

"Good boy." Brian's shoving turns into a caress. His fingers dance over my nipple. He strokes, then pinches, then twists, until I hiss at the pain and that's when I get another jolt of current. To the other side again, arcing through the barbell and jolting me with greater intensity than the first shock. Jax's shutter whirs, a reminder that I'm doing this for him.

"Ngh." I'm not sure if the sound I make is one of surprise, pleasure, or pain. Or all three. Brian steps closer and this time he runs the blunt head of the wand down my abs, sending a trickle of current tickling over my skin. The brush of that sweeping touch is nowhere near as intense as when he was applying it to my jewelry. But the prolonged sensation has me tensing my core muscles and shaking with effort by the time he steps back.

"Great, Brian, just keep my line of sight in mind when you're working in close like that." Jax interjects. I smile at the grounding reminder that he's here.

Brian shifts his stance, like he's making room to invite Jax into our scene. I like the thought of that. I'm performing for Jax as much as for Brian. That nuance, that I'm standing here and taking whatever Brian chooses to give me *for Jax,* helps me to relax into the posture Brian wants from me. The next time he shocks me, I lean into it, moaning at the cascade of tingles. I want nothing more than to show them both that I can be a very good boy for them. For Jax, really.

"That's it. Do you like it, boy?" Brian asks as he continues to touch me with the wand, over and over again. Jax moves around us, snapping photos. Does he like what he sees? Am I giving him the reactions he wants to capture?

"Boy?" Brian demands when I don't answer him. He tangles a hand in my hair and forces me to look at him.

"Yes, Sir." I agree, panting from the effort of holding my position through that last series of shocks. The sharp tug on my scalp helps me focus.

"Can you take a higher intensity?"

"Yes, Sir."

He releases me with a brisk nod, stepping back to swap out the broad electrode for one with much less surface area. This time, he starts with my lats. I arch away from the zap. Brian shifts his attention to my other side. Then my abs, making me tense and writhe and it's hard to keep my balance as each new jolt shocks me from a different angle.

When he aims the tip at my nipple, I arch away from the single point of biting pain. The electrode slips into contact with my piercing and the current arcs through my barbell, zinging into my nerves. The sensation burrows deep inside of me this time. I stagger, stepping off my mark. Brian removes the wand, curls his fingers into my harness and hauls me roughly back into position.

"Did you have permission to move?" he growls at me.

"No, Sir. Sorry, Sir."

"Did it hurt, boy?"

"Yes, Sir. It startled me."

Brian nods. "Perhaps it will be easier for you to hold your position with some help?"

I agreed to light bondage when we were talking earlier. He showed me the restraints he intends to use and I don't have a problem with them. So I nod.

Brian arches a brow, giving me a chance to correct my oversight before I earn more punishment.

"Yes, Sir. That would help. Thank you, Sir."

Brian sets aside the wand, switching it off, and gets the cuffs and spreader bar. He crouches at my feet to attach the ankle cuffs, forcing my feet to stay the proscribed distance apart. Then he binds my wrists behind my back with wide leather cuffs. There's enough slack to let me shift my balance, but I have to keep my shoulders back and it exposes my chest to him more. From his smirk when I tug against the bindings, that's entirely the point.

Brian emphasizes my newfound helplessness by stroking my chest again. He trails his fingers over my pecs, flicks, tugs, twists my piercings. I didn't give him permission to put his mouth on me while we were negotiating, but the look in his eyes says that he wants to. I shiver at the intensity of his gaze and the flash of sense memory. Cold ice cream and hot breath. Melted chocolate and a cool gust of air as Jax blows on me. Sweet cake and the burning heat of ginger. Warm eyes gazing at me. Jax and his camera move in the corner of my eye. I can hold still and be a good boy for Mx.

"Ready for more?" Brian asks, reminding me he's the one I'm doing this with tonight.

I nod. He doesn't wait for me to correct myself before pinching and twisting.

"Agh. Sorry. Yes, Sir." I try to crane away from him and almost topple over for my efforts. I forgot about the spreader bar already. Oops. Brian steadies me with a hand curled under my bicep.

"Steady, boy. My rules haven't changed; you still need permission to move your feet."

"Yes, Sir." I agree, leaning into his hold. Brian waits until I get my feet under me before releasing his grip on me and letting me stand.

Brian goes back to his toys and switches the attachments again. This time he doesn't plug in an electrode. The new part he pulls out is a cable that he tucks into the waistband of his jeans before he approaches me. I'm not sure what that bit does. Brian offered to explain it all, but I was too eager to get started to listen well.

I trust Jax wouldn't have introduced us if Brian didn't know what he's doing. And I trust Jax to step in if Brian steps outside the terms we agreed to. And I relish the thrill of the unknown. Brian reaches into his case and pulls wicked looking metal claws over the tips of each of the fingers on his right hand.

This time, when Brian reaches for me, sparks jump from each of his metal claws, all around my pec. He sweeps his hand down, bringing the tingling sparks across the sensitive flesh. The charge jumps through my piercing again. A sharp crackling energy that makes me arch into his touch and sort of regret taking sex off the table. That tickle of electricity has my dick aching in my jock.

Brian traces barely there touches on my skin, fingers dancing across my chest to the other nipple. The fingertip claws aren't sharp enough to cut, but electrified as they are, they give a similar sensation, just muted. Sparks trail in his wake, gone before they can truly register, building up to something just out of reach. I moan as the charges coil my nerves tighter and tighter, pleasure coalescing into—nothing. Brian pulls his hands away, smirking at me as I deflate, shoulders hunching protectively forward, as much as my bindings allow. I slouch limply, panting, and desperate for more.

"Sir?"

"You like that, huh, boy?" Brian taunts.

"Yes, Sir. May I have more, Sir?"

"Such a polite boy when you want something, huh?" He wraps his other hand around my harness again, hauling me into a better posture. The arc of electricity zings into the decorative metal grommets as he touches me. I pull my shoulders back, presenting him with my chest again.

"That's better." When he flicks my barbell this time, I jump and yelp. The double zing of pain and electricity magnifies the intensity. He repeats the action until my nipples ache and burn and the sensation goes right to my groin.

Brian pinches the sensitive nub between his electrified fingers and rubs, just this side of too hard. It's intense. So intense I wish my hands were free so I could touch myself. The tips of the claws feel like they're threatening to give me a new piercing. I get a rush of adrenaline from the fear that he'll take this too far. Unbidden, my eyes seek Jax for his silent reassurance behind the camera.

He gives Brian a quiet instruction about positioning us for the next shot. Something about going in slow. Brian adjusts us both before pinching me again, his metal claws pincering closed in slow motion. I arch away from the zing.

"Ugh, please, Sir." Only it's not really Sir I'm doing this for. It's Jax. I want to please Mx, give him the perfect shot for his gallery. And that juxtaposition, that I'm doing this scene with a stranger in front of the person I really want is the mindfuck that sends me floating toward subspace.

In that moment, Brian feels like an extension of Mx. Brian might be in control of what happens with the wand, but Mx is the one orchestrating the entire scene. In my head, Mx giving a command has me viewing Sir as an extension of Mx's dominance tonight. That makes it safe to let go and fully submit to whatever comes next. Submit to Mx and this person he trusts to give me something I've wanted to try for ages.

"Please, what?" Sir demands. He doesn't let up, touching me repeatedly, tapping the claw against my nipple and sending spark after spark straight through my piercing and right to my core, like magic.

"I can't." My knees are weak. I'm going to fall over if he keeps up the constant onslaught and I don't even care. I'm dimly aware of Mx snapping more pictures. Is he zooming in on my face? Waiting to catch that moment where I let go, and lose myself in the ebb and flow of electricity from Sir into my body? We're a circuit, the three of us, and my entire body is a live wire, feeding from his every calculated touch until I explode for Mx.

"Too much?" Sir checks.

I shake my head, then nod. "Don't know if I can stay standing. Sir."

"On your knees then, boy." Sir holds me firmly, helping me drop awkwardly to my knees despite my restraints. He steadies me until I find my balance. It's awkward to kneel with my ankles still forced apart and my hands behind my back. Mx hovers nearby, focused in on me as though he's bracing to catch me if I fall. His clear concern makes me determined to manage the change in position with as much grace as possible.

By contrast, my struggles seem to make Sir happy. His eyes track to my muscles straining from the effort. He tugs me around by the harness, making me arch and strain, all the while his touch crackles with electricity. The fizzing sparks bite into me harder around the grommets every time he adjusts his grip and comes into new contact with me.

Mx, moving to get a better angle with his camera, catches my eye again. The reminder that he's here makes me fight harder to obey. "Perfect, extend as far as you can for me." Mx murmurs as the shutter whirrs again.

I hold my position, straining into Sir's hold as he arches my body, bowing me backward as far as I can bend without needing him to support my weight. Leaning hard into the pose for Mx. Sir traces more fizzing energy along my jaw. The skin there is more sensitive and I whimper at the effort of holding still under his touch. Those claws prickle against my skin, convincing my hindbrain I'm in mortal peril. As if they could tear through my exposed throat with ease.

"Beautiful, boy." Mx praises me.

"How are you doing, boy?" Sir holds his hand up, shaking out the fingers of the hand without the claws. "With an indirect current like this, it zaps us both. Do you like it?"

"Yes, Sir. I'm good, Sir."

"Good. Jax, was there another pose you wanted before we wrap this up?" Brian turns toward Jax.

"If you're both up for it, I'd like to try to get a kissing shot with sparks." Jax gestures between us.

"How about it, boy? Would you like to feel it here?" Brian presses the tip of his finger to my lips and I flinch back at the sharp zap and crackle of it. The question jolts me out of the scene a little. Do I want to kiss Brian? Not particularly. Do I want to experience an electric kiss? Oh, hell yes, it sounds intense. Like a mouthful of supercharged pop rocks, if I can extrapolate from his fingers on me.

"Yes, please, Sir."

"Jax, want to zoom in closer for this? Just be sure to keep far enough back that we don't brick the electronics."

"On it." Jax moves in closer. He sets up his tripod near us, just outside another tape line on the floor. So that it's not too close to the wand. Brian waits while Jax gets in position and fiddles with the settings. I straighten up. My pose is hard to hold for long. Brian smirks at me, not missing my shifting, but not correcting me either. I'll take it.

"Ready when you are," Jax says.

"Good, we'll take it slow, right, boy?"

"Yes, Sir."

"Open."

Sir grips my hair and hauls me into position again, exaggerating the subservience of my pose. He leans over me from behind, forcing me to bend back and up to meet him, almost past the point where I'll topple back onto the mat. His knuckles sting like buzzing bees against my scalp when he adjusts my angle. I whimper at my helplessness. Mx is right there, in my peripheral sight, and his presence settles me as he makes his final camera adjustments. As long as he's here with me, this is a safe space.

I open my mouth to Sir, close my eyes so I can imagine it's Jax's lips hovering inches from mine. This kiss is for him. I surrender to the charge, arch back into him, trust him to give me this new experience.

The first brush of his tongue on mine is like the force of a slap, concentrated down to a pinpoint and delivered to my mouth.

"Perfect. Hold that right there for a second," Jax instructs. We stay there, tongues brushing for a long moment. "Great, you can move now," Jax says.

Brian's mouth moves against mine. I open reflexively to him and his lips seal against mine. The charge flows through my lips. It's like a mouthful of pure carbonation. The clean ozone scent of the wand fills my nose and sparks fill my mouth, millions of angry bubbles bursting at once. Firm unyielding lips against mine. Heat and lightning and I want, oh how I *want*. More of this. More of Jax.

The kiss ends, the sparkling sensation fades to a vague sting. I open my eyes to see Brian smiling down at me as he eases me upright again. The sight is jarring. His isn't the face I want hovering inches from mine. It's not his lips I want to taste.

"Got that?" Brian asks Jax once I'm able to kneel without his support.

Jax checks his camera. "Damn, yeah. These are going to be great when I get them cleaned up. Gorgeous, Con."

"Did you like that, boy? Want to give him another chance at the shot, just in case?" Brian winks at me.

"I don't know if I can take another kiss like that, Sir." I admit. My mouth still zings with the memory of his kiss. And I don't really want to kiss him again. Other than the electrical current, there was no passion in it.

"Fair enough. I think that's enough for tonight, boy. You look wrung out."

"Yes, Sir," I agree. He's not wrong. Brian sets aside his wand, then he moves behind me to unfasten my restraints, starting with the cuffs on my wrists. As soon as he releases me, I roll my shoulders to work out the tension there. Brian chuckles.

"Stiff?" Brian asks as he unfastens my ankles.

"A bit." I bring my arms forward to rub at my wrists. There are faint marks where I pulled against the cuffs. Nothing that won't fade by morning, though.

"How was it?" Brian asks me, and it's a relief that he isn't pushing me to keep calling him Sir now that our scene is over. He stands with his restraints and I flop down to lounge on the mat since I don't have to hold a pose anymore and I'm drained from the session.

"Good. It can seem so different, depending on how you use it. It got really intense on my piercings."

"So, you liked my toys, Connor?" Brian asks, and is that a flirty lilt when he says my name or am I imagining things?

"Yeah. I liked them a lot. I liked how you kept me guessing

about what you'd do next and made me work for it some. It was good. Thank you. I hope I did alright?"

"You did beautifully, boy. I'll give you my number if you want to play again sometime? No strings or expectations. Though, I'd be delighted to let you experience the wand on your other piercings next time, if you're comfortable getting naked with me." Brian winks. Okay. That's definitely flirting. And my stomach rolls at the thought of telling him I'm trans and having him revoke the offer. Just, no. I don't want to ruin the post-scene endorphin high I'm floating on with cold, hard reality. I let myself imagine it, if I could just say yes and take him up on some fun without that giant question mark hanging over his reaction.

"Bet it would be awesome down there. Like spilling champagne on my junk." I laugh at the thought. "Only less messy."

Jax laughs at that. The sound reminds me of warm honey, sweet and soothing. "You like messy, as I recall." He puts his camera on his workstation and retrieves my clothing from the shelf. I glance over at him and smile. His presence makes me feel safer. Like I can tell Brian and find out if another session is actually an option.

"You can get me messy anytime, my friend." I favor him with a saucy wink. Oh, shit, that came out way flirtier than I'd intended it. Oops. I shoot a guilty look at the guy who just took me to endorphin town.

"Ah." Brian looks between Jax and me, like he's adding up our friendly banter and reading some sort of relationship into it. "I didn't realize you two were—"

"Just friends," I assure him quickly. That way, I don't have to hear Jax deny any deeper connection.

"Right. Like I said when I called to arrange this, Connor is a friend who agreed to model for some promo shoots I've been hoping to capture for my website." Jax fills in the details.

"Mhm." Brian's tone makes it clear we haven't convinced him. "It's none of my business. What *is* my business is making sure you're good before we part ways, yeah? Need anything from me, boy?" The label is clearly him reverting to our roles to wrap up our evening together. That's fine with me.

"No, Sir." I shake my head. I don't really need much for aftercare right now. Just talking to the two of them and feeling like I'm safe. Which I do, because Jax has that big growly protector energy I've always liked about him when I've seen him in action at the club. He brings my clothing to me, placing the folded garments on the mat near my head. I stretch out on the padded vinyl.

"You'll call me if that changes, yeah? Or someone you trust?" Brian asks as he wipes everything he used down with disinfectant before storing it back in the carrying case.

"Yeah." I yawn. I lazily watch the meticulous care he takes with his toys. The mat is comfy. I could probably sink right into it, with how heavy my limbs are just lying here. "I have people I can talk to if my mood crashes later, but thanks for offering to check in. Do you need a check-in later? Or anything? I'll text, so you have my number."

Brian smiles at me, a big genuine smile. "That's kind of you to offer, boy, but I've got support people, too. You're a sweetheart."

"I try." I grin at Brian, then shiver because the room is a bit too cold now that I'm not doing anything stimulating. My head is a jumble over what just happened. I went in deeper than I usually would with a new person. And that is completely because of my trust in Jax, but the pile of clothing beside me makes me feel more naked. Exposed in the aftermath. Raw and I want—no I need to retreat into a safer headspace. I curl onto my side and wish I had a cuddle buddy.

"Want to get dressed, Con?" Jax nudges my clothing closer. And that...that's something I associate with a Daddy. Getting me dressed, helping me into my shirt and pants when I'm sleepy and lazy and I don't really want to get up at all. I'm already not quite in my usual adult headspace from the scene. Vulnerable.

I haven't really allowed myself to be little with Jax since we started fucking, not other than during the cake smash, but that's where my head goes tonight. To the safe small headspace where I can let someone else take care of me. Jax said he doesn't mind me being little sometimes when I told him intense scenes send me there. A distant part of me hopes that actually seeing it doesn't change things between us for the worse.

"Nope. You do it." I grab my clothing and ball it up to offer it to him. When he just looks at me, I wave the clothing at him. "Please?" I draw out the last word. I need him to take care of me and I don't have the words to articulate that any other way right now.

"You want me to help you get dressed?" Jax repeats my request to me and I roll my eyes.

"Yes. Don't wanna get up." I pout at him.

Jax reaches for the clothes and crouches down next to me. I offer him one of my legs. "Pants first."

"Is that so?" Jax unbundles the fabric, sets aside my shirt and positions my pants so that he can thread my foot through one leg, just up past my knee. Then he taps my other ankle, and I lift it for him. I sigh contentedly as he eases my foot through the leg hole. Then he pulls my pants up, leaning over me a bit to get them up to my bum. Mm, I like how he's gazing down at me. We should do this whole schtick in reverse sometime.

"Lift your butt." He taps my hip gently, so I press my feet into the mat and lift. Jax slides the waistband into position, his hands carefully not straying to my bits. Boo for that. I kind of want him to accidentally on purpose touch my ass. Or my junk. But he just dresses me like I'm a child in need of help.

Once my pants are on, he gently lifts each of my feet to slide my socks onto me, careful to adjust the toe-seam so it lies properly. I wiggle my toes, appreciating the tenderness of his care for me. Is this what it's like to have a Daddy to take care of me? I ache with want for that.

Except Jax isn't my Daddy, and he isn't the one I just had a scene with. That would be Brian, who is still packing up his things to leave. He doesn't look upset that I'm being a demanding brat with someone else right now, so I roll with it.

"Shirt?" I give Jax a plaintive look.

Jax stifles a smile, takes my hand, and pulls. "You have to sit up for that."

I let him haul me upright like I'm a rag doll. That thought reminds me of Jax's endearment for me and I smile giddily up at him.

"Arms up." Jax models the pose. I oblige. He pulls my tee over my head, tugging it into place over my chest. The fabric is a bit irritating on my abused nipples after all the attention Brian gave them. I'll have to moisturize later so they don't stay sore. Mm, or maybe Jax would do it for me?

"There, all dressed, doll. Want to rest in my office while I help Brian get his things out to his car?" Jax offers.

"Is that okay?" I look between Brian and Jax, not sure who I want permission from.

"I wouldn't have offered if it wasn't," Jax says dryly.

"It's fine, boy. Whatever you need after a scene is fine." Brian gives me the answer I need, absolving me of any lingering guilt over wanting Jax instead of him after he gave me a novel experience.

"Okay, then." I reach for Jax's hand and he pulls me up to my feet, correctly interpreting the gesture as a request for help.

"The office is right through here. You can curl up on the dog bed, if that's not weird."

I snort. "You know I'm besties with Q. It won't be my first time napping in a dog bed. Is it for puppy play?" I ask.

"No." Jax runs a hand through his hair. "Gia comes into work with me when I've got long days in the studio or a late night editing photos. I don't like to leave her alone for too long. Here." Jax grabs a fuzzy blanket from the prop shelf as we walk past. He drapes it over my shoulders before easing me down onto an overstuffed dog bed which takes up most of the floor space in his cramped office. I like how he lights up when he talks about his pet. It's cute. And the giant dog bed is further proof he's a devoted pet parent, as though I needed it. Major turn on.

"Bet she loves meeting all your clients," I observe, hoping to prompt him to gush about his best buddy some more. I lower myself to sit on the cushy pet upholstery. Nice.

"I told you Gia flunked out of guide dog training, right? Washed out because the poor girl is too friendly. I swear she hasn't met a stranger in her life. Excuse all the fur. I vacuumed last week, but well, you've met her." Jax gives me a self-deprecating half-smile. "Here, snuggle in, Con. I'll be back to check on you soon, okay?" He hands me a bottle of water he pulls from under his desk and tucks the blanket more firmly around me. His use of my little name and the easy way he takes care of me have my tummy all fluttery. This is what I want from a relationship. I'd be lucky to find a boyfriend like Jax.

The water is cold, like it just came from a mini-fridge or something. While I wait for him to come back, I sip from the bottle. I shiver under the blanket, wrapping it tighter around me. I'm going to crash soon. That's inevitable at this point.

I can hear Jax and Brian's voices from the studio space, but not clear enough to make out what they're saying. The comforting sounds of their conversation drift over me as I relax in Gia's bed. I can't help imagining what it would be like to do a similar scene with Jax as a direct participant instead of an observer directing us from behind his camera lens. It's a nice thought. Even nicer, is the thought of him curling up next to me.

CHAPTER 11

Jax

I didn't plan to end the evening with a needy little dozing in my office, but I have no objections to watching over Con while he naps. Other than him letting some of his little side through for our first photo shoot, this is the first time since we started fucking that I've seen him act little. As if it's his safe space, and he needs it after the scene with Brian. I wonder what that says about our scenes. Maybe just that he's comfortable with me in a way he isn't with Brian.

Even viewed through my camera lens, their scene got me hot and bothered. That reaction only magnifies as I review the photos. I could tell Connor liked the way Brian kept him on his toes. The photos I'm currently scrolling through while their subject snores on Gia's bed surpass my every expectation from before the shoot.

Brian and I took some practice shots to get my camera settings adjusted to capture the sparks and glowing electrodes. The practice paid off. And not just because we marked out how close I could risk getting with my camera since the electromagnetic field can damage electronics. The vibrant arcs from the wand attachments to Connor's body are in crisp focus. With his bare chest on display and electricity dancing over his piercings, the images of him are stunning. I couldn't be more pleased with the raw emotion on Connor's face as Brian pushed him harder toward the end of the session.

I flag several of my favorites to feature on the kinky part of my website and several more to list as stock photos. The last one I open to touch up is probably the most visceral of them. Connor has his head tipped back, lips parted and ready to accept a kiss, just before Brian leaned into his space. His expression makes it clear he's floating in subspace with his eyes hooded. The photo has me adjusting myself as I work on it. Connor's submission in that image is perfection. Everything about him is begging to be kissed. His neck arched gracefully back to open himself up to his top. He is gorgeous on his knees. It's easy to believe I've captured a piece of his soul in this photo.

Connor snuffles in his sleep, and I tear my eyes from my editing program. I blink in surprise at the clock at the bottom of my screen. Time got away from me.

"Pst, Con?" I nudge the boy with my toe when he doesn't wake up at my hissed call of his name.

"No school today," he mumbles, rolling onto his belly and burying his face in the dog bed. A moment later, he makes a choked sound and coughs as he sits up. "Why's my bed smell like dog?" He pulls an overly dramatic grossed out face.

"Probably because you're in Gia's bed. And she's a dog." I say dryly.

Con gags again, then claws at his tongue. "Ugh. Dog hair." He once again tries to cough it up.

"She's a shedder," I remind him apologetically.

Connor picks a strand of fur from his tongue, or at least I assume that's what he's pinching between his fingers as he shakes them at me. "Got it! You weren't kidding about that shedding."

I snort at his antics. "Sorry to wake you, but I need to lock up and head home."

Connor buries his face in his hands. "Oh, shit. How late is it?" He pulls out his phone and clicks his tongue in consternation. "I'm sorry. I can get out of your hair."

"Or you can crash at my place, since it's going to be at least an hour before you can get a bus at this point." It's late and I know the bus schedule for my neighborhood leaves much to be desired after midnight.

Connor peeks at me from between his fingers, expression torn. "I should probably still head home since I've got work tomorrow."

"All the more reason you need sleep. Let me drive you, at least?"

"I don't want to be a bother. It's fine. I had a good nap." He stretches again, twisting his back. "Thanks for letting me crash in your office. And the other stuff. I needed that."

I get the impression he means the entire night I arranged for him with Brian, not just the aftercare I provided. "Not a problem. You were the one doing me a favor since Brian's wife wanted nothing to do with stock photography. She was excited for him to be showcased, though."

"Oh." Connor bites his lip.

I'm pretty sure I know what has him looking so concerned. "She knows he was here tonight. And even if I didn't know he has an agreement with her for playing with other people, his actions aren't your burden to shoulder."

"Okay."

"She's fine with what Brian did with you tonight. How are you feeling about it?"

"Good." He rubs over his chest, recalling the probes and their charges. "It was so tingly."

"I'm glad you enjoyed it." I save out of the proofs so I can select the best of the batch to retouch and send to him later for his approval.

"Yep, I did. E-stim is a big yes from me." Connor comes around my desk as I minimize my editing program. He props one hip against the desk and leans there, watching me.

"Good to know. I can ask around about borrowing a box from someone." I offer.

"You'd do that for me?"

"Sure, Connor, I enjoy playing with you. And even if more e-stim isn't in the cards, I've got plenty of plans for you." When I rise from my chair, I loop my arm around his waist to pull him in for a hug. "I know we didn't play directly tonight, but thanks for coming."

"I'm always happy to *come* for you, Jax." He says with a wicked smirk.

"Good." I kiss his cheek, then hit the keyboard shortcut to hibernate my computer for the night. "Let's go; I'm driving you home now."

"You really don't have to. Gia…"

"Hush. I got Gia situated for the night before our photo shoot. If you're going to insist on sleeping in your own bed, I'm going to insist on making sure you get there safely. There's not much traffic at this hour anyway, so it's hardly a big deal." I drape my arm over his shoulders and steer him out through the studio's back entrance, since it's closer to where I parked my car.

"Yeah, okay. Thanks, Jax. We still on for this weekend?" Connor shivers in the cool night air as I lock up behind us.

"Yeah, but this might be my last free weekend for a while. Wedding season is upon us."

"The horror. I didn't realize you still shot those?"

"Eh?" I wobble my hand in a so-so gesture. "I don't advertise it, because of the potential for drama, but they pay well. So I don't turn them down either, at least not with my usual clients when they ask. I book at least a couple of ceremonies on most of the weekends during warm weather." We get into my car and he asks me more questions about my work. I answer, and it only occurs to me as I'm wishing him a goodnight outside his apartment that I have only the vaguest idea what he does. Other than saving the city by promoting social housing. We don't talk about our lives. Just sex and kink.

Except it felt so natural to share with him tonight. I could regale him with every wedding disaster story in the book, just to hear him laugh and catch a glimpse of his smile. And that is exactly the sort of thought that will lead to the downfall of our easy no strings sex.

I resist the urge to text Connor another goodnight when I get home. Gia is already curled up in my bed, keeping my spot warm, and I snuggle in next to her. It's just as well Connor opted for his own bed since Gia hogs all the covers. And if talking to him makes me question what I'm doing with him, then he's probably got the right idea, avoiding sleeping over.

CHAPTER 12

Connor

Marietta has a big soccer tournament with her development team a couple of weeks after Jax set up my session with Brian. The past few times we got together, it was even harder to make myself leave at the end of the night.

I've convinced myself I need space. So I took time off to visit the fam and cheer Marietta on in the stands. Bonus points for getting to see Eli and Noa's recitals while I'm in town, too. And hang out with Viv and her kids while she's still on leave with baby Edie.

Since I'm around while everyone else is working or in classes, my folks have me wrangle the twins home after school. They're doing their homework before I take them to Marietta's game to meet everyone else. Noa is helping Eli with a math problem when Q texts to tell me about a pipe bursting at Adventures.

I shuffle from the dining room, where they are studying, into the den so the twins won't see anything inappropriate my bestie sends before I open the attached image. That seems like a reasonable precaution. Their last text was a pic of their ridiculously oversized new sex toy and how they're dying to tell me about using it with Niko, after all. I take a minute to parse the new message, a GIF of a busted pipe.

Quent calls me as soon as I send back a message expressing

my concern. They babble out the whole sordid story, but it boils down to Martin has to close Adventures for a while. The news pretty much cancels most of my social life for the foreseeable future. That might be a tad overdramatic. But sometimes it feels like the club is the central hub for all my friends. Not that there's anything wrong with that. Except I know all the eligible Doms who frequent the place and none of them are a good match for me, so it makes dating frustrating.

It's hard enough to meet people who share my kinks *with* the club. Without it, I'm at a bit of a loss. Except, the more I think about it, I've barely been to the club outside littles' nights in months. Not since Jax and I started getting together on Sundays.

Now that his photography schedule is getting busier on the weekends, I was hoping to fill up the hole in my social calendar by getting to the club more often. Guess that's not the only hole that won't be getting any loving. I could use the free time to try dating again. That's on the back burner ever since Jax offered to be my fuck buddy.

Even though I love seeing my family, I miss my usual time together with Jax. It's only the third time in the past five months that we had to skip a week, but I regret the lost time. Jax more than made it up to me after the last time. I came so hard I thought I might actually burst the week after my last visit home.

Jax makes sex better than anyone I can recall being with. We might have agreed to nothing serious between us, but he's an attentive bedmate. He follows my cues about my body. Treats me with respect. I love the way he tugs on my sac while he sucks my dick. I should probably stop fantasizing about anyone touching my junk when I'm sitting in the den on the phone with my bestie. If for no other reason than that my baby siblings are doing their homework, not a stone's throw away. I glance out into the dining area to see Noa and Eli still bent over their math assignments.

"Hey, Earth to Connor...what were you thinking about just now? Something hot?" Quent teases me.

"The sun," I shoot back.

"Bullshit. I won't pry. For now. But if there's a hot daddy out there in the boonies, then I demand you spill all the details when you get home next week. Can you meet me for lunch on Monday?"

I grimace. "Probably not? I took off half of this week to drive out here, so I'll probably work through my lunch on Monday to catch up at work. Dinner instead?"

Q clicks their tongue. "Ugh. Fine. Make me wait. That's a deal if you bring me dinner."

"Sure. What do you want?"

"Indian has lots of veg options for you, right? Masala Palace?"

"That works," I agree. They make an awesome chickpea dish I like. And Q is a sucker for their appetizer combo. "I'll bring the food."

"Okay. And since you might as well have been a million miles away just now, TL;DR, I have a new favorite toy. Seriously, you've got to try it sometime, Con." Quent enthuses.

"A hot guy breeding you with your new knotting toy was all you dreamed it would be, huh?" I tease, because Q hadn't kept the original story brief. The summary helps, since I zoned out on some details while they chattered.

"Yes. We're *so* doing a repeat of that scene. Mommy already promised. Did you have fun with Jax?" Q asks with faux innocence.

They clearly think there's more there than friendship, but even if he did date, I'm not about to jump into anything with Jax. He's the first new friend I've really clicked with in a while.

With Adventures closing, time to see all of my other friends is bound to be scarcer than usual this summer. A light and breezy friendship with Jax is nothing to sneeze at. We've already got plans for me to model more of his kinky photo wishlist.

"Mhm." I agree, noncommittal, so as not to encourage prying questions.

"Fine, you don't have to share details if you aren't ready. I feel like we haven't dished in ages." They complain, and it's true that I haven't really seen them since my e-stim scene.

"Yeah, it's been a while. The session with Brian was a cool surprise. I guess Brian's wife backed out because she got cold feet about having her body immortalized on Jax's website or something? I had a blast, though. And no dick pics required."

"Ooh! So, do you want to see Brian again?" Q easily pivots to shipping me with someone other than Jax. Which is cool, except I can't picture dating Brian. The dynamic he wanted was fine for a scene. I have no problem verbalizing respect for a Dom while we're playing. But calling my partner Sir all the time just isn't the sort of relationship I want. Not to mention he's married. It's obviously an open thing, but that isn't for me either. I'm fine with sharing sex with multiple partners, but for romance, I want exclusivity.

"I mean, I've seen him around at play parties and stuff. He's more approachable one-on-one. Not too formal, but strict about using his title while we played. But, nah. No spark."

Q giggles. "Um, dude, wasn't the entire scene sparks?"

"Pshaw. You know what I mean, Q. Plenty of electricity, but no chemistry between us. I liked his toys well enough. I'd play casually with him again, but I don't think I'm into him. And there are other kinks I like more."

"That's too bad. There's always next time. What's next on your wishlist?"

"It's not like we wrote out a formal list," I hedge. But there are more things on my list that match up with Jax's photo wishlist. More things he's hinted he wants to do with me.

"Mhm." Q makes a noncommittal noise, holding out on a proper answer from me.

I sigh. "Fine, if you must know, Jax has been hinting that we might do a CNC scene with like tentacles and stuff."

"For real?" Q sounds skeptical. "Like *Alien*? I thought you weren't into impregnation and stuff? You want in on all this surrogacy fabulosity with me?"

"Ha! No. It's the body horror that does it for me." I shift on the couch, uncomfortably aware that I'm having this discussion in the home where I grew up. Right under the bedroom where I first discovered how much mental imagery that bothered me on a visceral level also turned me on.

"Figures. And you like the idea of being forced by an alien?" Quent teases.

"Yeah. Tentacles are hot. What's not to love about sentient bondage?" I reply flippantly.

"I mean, I'd call you a weirdo, but I get the whole breeding thing. Wanting to be held down and filled up and dripping. Some virile stud of a creature using—"

"Shh! Ok, yeah, enough, I'm supposed to be watching the twins..." I shush them, then add in a mumble. "I don't need you getting me all turned on, Q."

Quent chuckles. "Fine, fine. No platonic bestie phone sex in front of minors. Anyway, I'm happy that you're happy. I wouldn't be into having an alien fill me up with funky eggs. That sounds slimy, but you do you."

"I mean, I'm hoping someone else will do me, but yeah,

thanks."

"Is it your sexy photographer you want getting in your pants? Or just anyone? I saw the proofs he's put up on his website so far and the updated gallery makes it seem like Jax has a new favorite subject."

"I'm sure he's just got the pics of me up because the wand effects look really cool and that's his most recent stock photo shoot."

"Babe, I've snooped his site plenty. It's not just the wand session. He never puts up quite so many pics of one model like that. He *likes* you."

"What? No! He just likes photographing me." I protest. The little ember of a crush I'm nurturing needs no more fuel. I don't want to want impossible things. I've had enough of that for a lifetime. And I don't want to reach for more and risk missing out on the fun I've got planned with Jax and his photo sessions this summer. That's even more important now that my usual kinky outlet is closed.

"Sure, my bad, I won't push." Quent backs off. "So. Any new date prospects lined up?" Okay, so they aren't backing off so much as coming in from a different angle of attack.

I sigh dramatically. "Got a couple of feelers out on the usual apps." I lie. "Nothing that's caught my fancy." Truth, since I haven't actually checked those apps in months. Not since my fail date with Lorence. "And I found a singles forum that might be promising. More personal interaction and less all-knowing algorithms. They even have in person mixers that the mods arrange. I might check one out." I logged into the forum during a moment of weakness after leaving Jax's place last week, just to feel like I was being proactive about finding a long-term partner.

"Sounds fun. We should get the gang together and all go with you. For moral support."

"You aren't single." I point out dryly.

"Yeah, but that doesn't stop me from being ready to mingle." Q throws back at me. And if we were talking in person, they would for sure be giving me a big cheesy wink, or batting their eyes as they caress my arm.

"You're such a dork."

"And you love me for it."

"I do. So. Martin is really closing Adventures for the summer?"

"Yeah. Not like he had much choice. Tate says the damage was pretty bad, so it might last awhile. Sounds like he plans to reopen ASAP once he gets the work done, though."

"Good. It will be weird not having the club."

"Yeah. Mommy offered to invite all our friends over for some extra play parties to tide us over while it's closed."

"Fun."

"Mhm. Fun, but also kind of stressful." The phone crackles as they shift around again. "I miss your face." They whine.

"It's only been a couple of days since I saw you for lunch." I roll my eyes at them.

"Yeah, but now you're too far away to visit if we wanted. That makes it different."

"Not really. But I miss you too."

"And we were in public last time we met up, so I couldn't tell you about my session with Niko. I've seriously been dying to give you all the juicy deets." Quent continues to press their argument.

"Well, you've told me now. And I can see why you loved it. The kids are putting away their math, so I've got to go. I'll see you Monday for dinner. Thanks for letting me know about the club. And the progress on getting you knocked up by Logan's seed."

"Ew. I am gagging at that. Seed? Are you a secret regency romance fan? I don't want to think about Logan's biological contribution to this endeavor outside the abstract. Why is spunk so much sexier during sex than at literally any other time? Like, unless it's currently going inside or on me, I don't want to hear about it. At all. Ever."

"And yet, when those conditions *are* met…" I trail off, knowing they'll fill in the blanks.

"Yeah, yeah, I'm a filthy cum-slut during sex. And proud of it."

"As you should be, babe."

"Oh, speaking of coming…Mommy's got a movie night planned for us, got to go. Love you, Con. See you soon."

"Have a fun afternoon."

"You know it." Quent sing songs, I can picture them winking as they say it. We hang up and I mess around on my phone until the twins finish putting away their homework. They're bickering playfully, so I break up the argument and we head to meet the rest of the family. I love being surrounded by the entire boisterous crowd. This visit home is just what I needed to recharge my batteries and get my mind off Jax for a few days.

***

Marietta's team wins the tournament. I stay through the weekend to make the most of my visit. Shabbat dinner at my parents' home is always worth the trip out here. Last night, the entire family even made it to our parents' place, along with their dogs. Paul and Matt have Harvey, an old lab. Viv and Gretchen bring their pug. Plus, my folks have two terriers. Prior to getting to hang out with Jax and Gia, this time at home was where I had to get my fix of playing with canines. I still spent a lot of the evening down on the ground, playing with the dogs and my niblings.

My apartment in the city can't come close to comparing. When I'm there, I usually eat alone at the rickety table while my housemates go about their usual weekend plans. More than once, I've considered rearranging my work schedule to four ten-hour days so I can visit my family more often. Without the club to give me a social outlet, that scenario is even more tempting. But now that would mean no more Sundays with Jax, since I'm usually exhausted after a visit home. Still, I should talk to my boss, Nadine, about making that an option at my upcoming annual review.

Spending time with family for Shabbat is comforting and familiar. I've missed this. The closest I've done to carving out a special set apart time to just be is my Sundays with Jax. Not that there's any real comparison there. I could go to a synagogue in the city. There are plenty to choose from, unlike here, including ones that promise to embrace queer folks. But it's just another place where I never quite fit. My step-dad's religion isn't mine. There are small ways I honor that part of my family. I stick to the broad strokes of Pop's dietary restrictions, mostly out of habit these days, and celebrate the holy days with them, to the extent possible.

Regardless, it's good to see all my siblings and niblings, not to mention our parents. The familiar blessings are music in my ears. The soft glow of candlelight suffuses our meal in the hazy warmth of nostalgia for my childhood. I savor the yeasty sweetness of the fresh challah Viv brought to dinner and the astringent sweetness of the wine on my tongue. It's all the same as when I was a child. The tradition of it makes me homesick, even though I'm right here, sitting in the same chair I sat in as a teenager. These visits are always so ambivalent lately.

I love spending time with my family. The constant noise and motion used to be my baseline ambiance level. I still need the noise of a television or something going on to help me focus when I'm alone. Not that I don't have plenty of noise with my housemates around, but it's not the same as being with family.

Even so, there's still a sense that I don't fit here. Over the past few years, since I left to pursue my engineering degree, I've gotten used to the solitude of living apart from them. I get my people fixes where I can. Like at Adventures and with Quent and our friends. Much as I love every chaotic second of my visits home, I also miss my chosen family after my latest chat with Q.

My downtime earlier while everyone was at work and school let me catch up with Quent and text Jax for more floof pictures of Gia. It was a nice breather from all the smothering love of my family. They've not been subtle with asking if I'm dating anyone lately. I get it; I'm the last of the adult kids to settle down. Even Marietta has a girlfriend she's been dating for going on two years. Don't even get me started on that double standard.

All of us older kids teased the rents relentlessly about how they let the little kids date way sooner than the rest of us. Not that I actually dated much in grade school. Well, high school, we weren't allowed to have one-on-one dates until high school. Not that those rules stopped Matt and Prescott. The rest of us waited, though. Unlike the little kids, who have probably already had more relationships than I have. I'm not at all bitter about that either. Nope. Not at all.

At first, I was busy navigating my transition stuff. Then, when I dipped my toes into dating, it was a disaster. I thought Albert liked me. Turned out, he was settling for the only other out gay boy in our class. I thought we were in a genuine relationship right up until our prom night. That's when he made it crystal clear that I was perfectly fine friends with benefits material, but I was far too lacking in the penis department for him to consider me boyfriend material.

Albert liked my mouth on his dick well enough, though. It probably should have tipped me off when he always had an excuse not to return the favor, but I was young, naïve, and horny.

Getting off with his hand pressed against my bulge while he had his dick shoved down my throat was better than anyone else was offering me. I think he figured out how much I got off on having him order me to my knees before I did. He liked it, too, even if he called me a perv for it after the fact.

Albert isn't why I have trouble dating. It's the fact that he's not the only one who feels that way about my body. I've heard that same shit from too many cis guys to count and it's fucking depressing. It's not even that I don't get where they're coming from. I like dicks, too. A lot. You're attracted to what you're attracted to. Fine. And double fine if we're just talking about a quick fuck. But like, if I met a guy who didn't have a fully functional bio dick for whatever reason—cis or trans—finding out his junk isn't exactly what I expected isn't a deal-breaker for me. Not if he ticks all my other boxes.

There's just so much more to loving a person than their genitals. I wish there were more people who felt the same. Or an easy way to sort those who agree with me from the Alberts of the world. It would make dating so much easier.

I've gone on a ton of first dates since Albert. Even dated a few guys here and there and developed regular play partners at the club who have similar kinks. Nothing long-term or serious. No one I really connected with beyond sizzling sex and pleasant conversation. No contenders for the brand of forever love my parents and older siblings have found.

When I visit home, it's a sharp reminder of what I'm lacking. I want to have a loving family like the one I grew up with. Someone other than my housemates to come home to. Someone to hold me when I have a bad day. That one person who knows my kinks and wants to indulge in them with me. Q and my other friends tick a lot of those boxes most of the time. And now I've got Jax to share orgasms with. Not to mention the kinky games we get up to. But it's not the same as having a romantic relationship with someone I can rely on to always be there for me. A relationship similar to what Q and Miss Kylee have.

My morose mood lasts through a lazy Saturday spent playing board games. We end the day with a relaxing picnic at the park. Even though the weather isn't really warm enough for it yet. I mostly push my melancholy aside to be in the moment, but by Sunday lunch, I'm tired and withdrawn. And even though I'm the quiet one at home, my little siblings notice.

We meet up with the entire family at a restaurant so I can see everyone before I head back to the city this evening. Cameron has my car, since he took it for a tuneup earlier in the week, after Marietta's tournament. He's a mechanic, and it was due for maintenance, so he insisted I leave it in his shop for him to look at it. He promised to bring it to the restaurant where we're all meeting up for lunch.

I crawl into the back of my parents' van with the little kids. During the drive to the restaurant, Marietta and Eli squabble over the radio station until Pop flips the channel to Radio One, where they're airing a comedic monolog. Then all three of my siblings ignore the radio to talk over each other for the rest of the drive. I sit in the back of the van, soaking it all in. I thought my moodiness slipped under the radar until the three little kids all maneuver me into sitting across from Modaddy at dinner. They're the parent with the almost preternatural knack for ferreting out trouble with all us kids.

Marietta gives me a *look*. Eli nudges my arm with his shoulder. Noa flashes me an encouraging smile. And yeah, despite all their chatter about school and their plans for the summer, and catching me up on the local gossip, they noticed my heart wasn't in it. When the heck did they grow up so much?

After we all have our drinks and place our meal orders, Eli knocks shoulders with me and gives me a pointed glance. Once again nudging me to talk with Modaddy, who already has their concerned parent face trained on me.

"What's wrong, Connor?" Modaddy asks in an undercurrent. Eli and Noa both turn toward Marietta, offering me no escape. They've boxed Modaddy and I in at the end of the table with the little kids and Pop now acting as a buffer between us and the rest of the family.

"Nothing." I fuss with settling my napkin over my lap to avoid eye contact.

"Are you sure? You've been quiet this weekend."

"I'm fine, just basking in all the family time." I assure them.

Modaddy frowns. "If you're sure, dear." They pat my hand and I know they aren't buying what I'm selling. They respect my silence, though. Conversation rolls over me. The twins are kvetching to Marietta about their teacher, who apparently had a vendetta against Marietta when she had him two years ago. I didn't have the teacher in question, so I can't comment. Viv did, though. We weren't in the same class that year. Cameron and Prescott had that teacher as well.

"Yeah, that's my bad, y'all. I may or may not have convinced my entire class to prank him because I bombed a quiz and he might or might not have held a grudge about it." Cameron jokingly takes credit for their suffering.

Eli chucks a piece of his roll at him. "Why is it that out of all the siblings they had in class before us, it's always you who all our teachers remember?"

"I'm just that memorable." Cameron sticks his tongue out at Eli and shrugs it off.

"Yeah, you're hot shit, baby." Gail, Cameron's wife, shoves him playfully. "Giving the family a bad name. Don't forget our kid is going to have to deal with your legacy, too."

"Babe!" He protests. The force of his wide-eyed non-verbal exchange with Gail seems out of place, until he gives up just why he's on edge by unsubtly gritting out, "ixnay on the idkay," through the side of his mouth. The pointed look between his wife's belly and our parents erases all doubt.

"No!" Pop sets down his fork. "For real?" Pop beams at my brother and Gail. "Are you making us grands again?"

Gail smiles and nods, a hand going to her belly. "We were going to wait to tell everyone until a little further along, but, well, surprise!"

Pop stands and goes in for a bear hug. Modaddy is up to offer a congratulatory hug next, and pretty soon we're all talking over each other to congratulate Cameron and Gail on their first kid. Prescott, Viv, and their respective partners chime in with parenting advice and pregnancy talk and I'm thrilled for them. Excited about having another new nibling to spoil. One who will probably be the same age as Q's eventual nibling. I'm bursting with happiness for my family.

The news shouldn't make me sad. I feel like the worst brother ever for the pang of loneliness stabbing me in the gut. Once again, I'm being left out of the club my siblings so effortlessly join. It's the same social catch up I've never stood a chance at. It seems like I will forever be hitting all my social milestones miles behind my peers from the time I was old enough to realize I wasn't like the other kids.

Viv and Prescott get it, to some extent, except in some ways they really don't. Prescott married the boy he's been best friends with since kindergarten. Viv and Gretchen had a rockier start, bitter rivals for cheer squad captain, but they've been together since high school, too. Other than wanting a wife instead of a husband, she fits here. Same with Prescott. I don't.

I paste on a smile, say all the right things. Listen to them compare notes, advice, and stories. I focus on my meal with single-minded devotion when it arrives. And when we're all leaving and dividing up into cars to head to our various homes,

Modaddy opts to ride with me. All three of the little kids go home with Pop.

It's still weird to realize my three youngest siblings aren't so little anymore. I remember changing their diapers. The collective nickname is probably going to stick with Marietta, Noa, and Eli for life, regardless of age. They'll be in their seventies and the rest of us will still be calling them the little kids.

Modaddy tucks my arm under their elbow as we walk to where Cameron parked my car. They pat my hand and guide me, like I'm a little kid again. I kind of like being tucked up close to them and given one-on-one time. We get in, but I don't start the engine right away.

"You don't have to talk about it. Tell me about life in the city," Modaddy says, adjusting their seat.

I sigh, knowing they mean it. They won't pry. It's equally true that we both know I'm going to spill my guts to Modaddy before we get back to their house. "I'm happy for Cameron and Gail." I grip the steering wheel with both hands, squeeze, release. Then I fidget with the mirrors, adjusting them because Cameron is a little taller than me.

"I know you are, dear. And they know it, too. You're a wonderful uncle and brother." Modaddy observes.

"I'm fine. Things are good. Work is good. My friends are good. Our club is closing because of a busted pipe, so I probably won't be making any special friends there anytime soon. Quent is trying to get knocked up."

"Oh. That's new. Are you worried they'll have less time for you when they've got a newborn to look after?" Modaddy asks.

"Huh? Oh. No!" I pull a face. "That's not an issue. It's a surrobaby. For their brother. I mean, I'm sure they'll want to spend time with their nibling, but I don't think it will change our friendship much."

"I see."

With a sigh, I twist the key in the ignition. "There's really nothing going on with me. I'm just tired."

"Makes sense; you work hard."

"Yeah." I put the car in gear and back out of the parking lot. We drive through town in silence.

When we get to the empty stretch of rural highway that my folks live on, I rest one arm on the console and try to relax. Modaddy pats my hand. "I'm glad you made the time to visit us."

"Yeah. Me too. It's good to see everyone."

"You know, you could see more of us if you moved closer. Princeton needs engineers, too." They mention the nearest town of any appreciable size.

With a rueful smile, I shake my head. "I like my life in the city, Modaddy. I've got my dream job, and amazing friends."

Modaddy nods, like they expected that answer. "Well, if you ever change your mind, there's a place for you here."

I swallow the lump in my throat. My family has always made it clear they accept and love me just the way I am. I will always be welcome with them. But Modaddy is wrong. There isn't a place for a queer kinky sort of Jewish trans municipal engineer here. Not if I want to find someone to share my life and my home with, not if I want to be true to every part of myself. Not if I want my career to continue on its current trajectory. "I guess."

"There is, Connor. I know you didn't always have the easiest time growing up here, but times are changing. I hardly ever get misgendered to my face anymore."

My stomach churns. Right. Anymore. Because they used to get misgendered and have slurs thrown at them when they first came out. And I'm not naïve enough to believe some of it wasn't about me and how they raised me. How they let me transition socially as a kid and start on puberty blockers when I needed them. Not just let me; they fought for me to get the care I needed.

Those meds spared me from having top surgery. They meant I only had to endure the wonders of puberty once, and when I did, it was the correct version for me. Sure, I was a late bloomer since my doctors didn't let me start hormones until I turned sixteen. But at least I didn't have to dread my body morphing into something that felt completely alien and wrong while I waited.

"That's just it. I'm so sick of everything being harder because of how I was born. It's not fucking fair that we had to spend years fighting with my doctors and my body to achieve the effects of puberty when it just *happened* for everyone else. It's not fair that dating is a fucking minefield because I have to disclose what's in my pants and it's a deal-breaker to a lot of people. And of the people who stick around past that point, half of them just see me as an easy way to cut out the middleman for having a kid with another dude. I feel like, if life is a race, everyone else started several laps ahead of me. It's like I'm always going to be playing catch up and I'm never going to make any headway."

"Good thing life isn't a race then, honey."

"Really?" I growl my frustration and Modaddy relents with a click of their tongue.

"I know. I know things were harder for you. It killed me when I couldn't fix that for you. I told you that your courage to be yourself helped me find the strength to come out, all those years ago, when I thought it was already too late for me, right?"

"Yeah."

"Well, that's still true. You still inspire me, every day. All you kids do. You are an amazing son, Connor. I'm so proud of the man you've become and the life you're making for yourself in the city."

"You don't wish I'd stayed here like all the rest of us?"

"No, baby. I'd be lying if I said I didn't wish you felt like you could live a full life here. But I understand why you had to go. And I'm grateful you come back as often as you do to visit, even though it's hard for you."

"It's not—" I protest, but Modaddy flashes me a 'cut the bullshit' look and I change course. "This is the only place in the world where I feel like I'm just 'that weird trans guy with way too many siblings.' I hate everyone knowing our business. I don't know how you stand it."

"This is home." Modaddy shrugs, like it's that simple. "But it doesn't have to be your home. Are you happier in the city than you've been since you got home?"

"Yeah. Mostly. I think it's just been getting to me that I'm still single and dating is hard and seeing all the others happily coupled up chafes. I know that's a shitty way to feel, but..." I shrug.

Modaddy squeezes my hand. "There's no such thing as a wrong feeling, my boy. Your hurts are valid, and I hope you find what you're looking for. Just you remember you can always talk to me and your pop. I'm only ever a phone call away, yeah?"

"Yeah. Thanks. I love you."

"Right back at you, kiddo. Now, stop crawling under the speed limit and let's get home so you can pack up to get on the road. I don't want you driving too late."

By the time I head home later that evening, I'm ready to get back to the city and my usual routines. I miss Quent and our other friends. Jax. The familiar ache in my chest at feeling alone when I see all my coupled off siblings hurts more after I see them with their own happy families.

I could call Jax to see if he's free, since this is our usual time to get together. I won't though. A quick fuck is only going to remind me of what I can't have with him when I'm in this mood. I don't want that. My friendship with Jax isn't romantic, and that's what I'm missing right now. Romance with a partner. An orgasm, no matter how good, is only going to make me resent all the things Jax already told me he can't offer me. Anyway, I'll probably see him at Q's play party next week.

At least I don't arrive home to an empty apartment. My housemates are watching the end of a hockey game in the living room, so I join them. I'm not much interested in the game, but I am craving the comfort of being around people. We talk little, other than to kvetch about the game and terrible calls from the refs and coaching staff.

The three of them remind me of home, and rehashing Marietta's soccer games over dinner. That familiarity eases the ache of longing for what I don't have. I feel at home and adrift in equal parts. Lonely, despite the company.

Times like this, I wish I had someone to hold me. Q would, if I really needed it, but I try not to abuse their open invite to crash in their guest room when I need closeness. Eventually, I retreat to my not-quite-to-code bedroom, which is more of a partitioned off nook in the corner of the living room. The television droning and my housemates' continued conversation lull me to sleep.

CHAPTER 13

Jax

Q and Connor are thick as thieves, so it's no surprise when he tells me he'll meet me at the play party Kylee and Q are hosting. I'm just glad I get to see him after he gets back from his visit home. He canceled our standing Sunday arrangement, and I missed having him over. Restless energy drove me to spend the evening catching up on admin in my office with Gia by my feet. In her bed, where Connor napped the last time he came to the studio.

Connor promised to help Q set up tonight, since his friend has been feeling under the weather this past weekend while he was out of town. As soon as I get down to the basement play area, my first sight is Con throwing a soft cloth toy for Q and another pup.

There's no doubt he's in his little space. Con is adorable, with his face caught in a carefree grin as he throws the toy. Hard muscle hidden under soft fleece PJs. Head thrown back in laughter over Q's antics, chasing the other pup with the toy.

I want to capture the pure, mischievous joy on his face when he tricks both pups by pretending to throw the rope. They chase after it, only to turn back with reproachful, pleading eyes. He wiggles the toy in front of himself with crooned praise for the pups. Both pups jump on him, licking his face and showering him in affection until he throws the toy, laughing all the while.

Part of me wants to approach and see if he wants to play

with me later. We danced around the fact that we'd both be here tonight, but neither of us suggested any solid plans. If he's little, he might want to look for a caregiver to play with. Someone who can give him the relationship he craves. I don't want to intrude on that, no matter how much I enjoy our current friends with benefits arrangement.

Considering that basic incompatibility, I don't interrupt his game. Someone I know catches my eye, and before I know it, I'm drawn into a quick conversation with a friend of a friend who wants to book a photo session. I'm not here to network, but it's silly to pass up good word-of-mouth leads, so I always bring along some cards at events like this. I pass them to the interested parties.

When the conversation ends, I notice Tate has joined Con in his game of fetch. And there is someone I don't recognize watching the boys with an avidity I'm not sure I like. At the back of my mind, I'm pretty sure it's jealousy and not legitimate internal alarm bells about the stranger. Well, he can't be a complete stranger if Q and Kylee invited him into their home. Still, I'm familiar with most of the people our hosts know in the local kink scene. I make my way over to the couch where the stranger is sitting and strike up a conversation.

"Hey, I haven't seen you around before. I'm Jackson." I introduce myself with a handshake that he returns politely.

"Rory. I'm new to the city."

"Welcome. How do you know Q and Kylee?" I try to play it cool.

"Tate invited me for a playdate, since I already know Kylee and Q from the little/pup munch they organize," Rory says. There's a twinkle in his eye that tells me I'm not being subtle with my over-protectiveness of the boys and pups playing a few yards away. Still, a tension within me relaxes upon hearing that Tate is the one who captured the man's interest. I shouldn't be jealous.

It's not like I have any claim to Con's attention. He's a friend, and I was just thinking of how I should back off tonight to let him explore his options.

Except he's a friend I've fantasized about ever since I got my first taste of him under this very roof. And I have some pretty kinky friends, but Con's the only one I want to strip naked and lick every inch of. He's a friend I love getting off with.

So I might have blurred the lines on what we're doing. He might be more of a crush than a fuck buddy. That isn't his problem, and if he was interested in Rory, I'd have no right to be jealous. Still. My gut reaction should tell me something about what I really want with the sweet boy standing so close I could almost touch him. Taste his sweet lips. I shake off that fruitless line of thought.

I chat with Rory for a while longer. At first, I stay because there isn't really a polite way to disengage now that I struck up a conversation. Not without letting Rory know, with no pretense, that I was concerned about his interest in the boy whom he can't tear his eyes off of. We chat idly about the local scene. I tell him about my photography.

The fact Rory's eyes remain locked on Tate frees me up to ogle Con for a while, at least. Tate crawls over and Rory seamlessly picks him up and plops the boy on his lap, as though Tate isn't larger than his potential daddy by a fair margin. Tate gets all cozy and the contentment in his gaze seals it for me.

Rory seems like a decent guy, someone who's into the daddy thing to be a nurturer. I notice the pronoun pin on his shirt, and it further eases my mind that he'll mesh with Tate and Con's crowd. From what I know of him after our chat and observing the pair, Tate and Rory could be a good fit. I can see why Q extended the invite to this man, new to the city or not.

That pup thinks they're subtle about their introductions, but I know better. I realized they wanted me to talk with Con the night we shared Q's ice cream. I also know that the introduction is all the pushing they'll do, no matter how good a match they think I'd be for Connor. Which is good, because I know what's between us is temporary. Just scratching an itch while Con looks for his forever. I'm about to excuse myself to give Tate and Rory some time together, when they beat me to the punch, going off to find some toys.

That leaves me free to seek a distraction. Anything to keep me from monopolizing Con's time when he's clearly looking for a caregiver tonight. Clark interrupts my thoughts to suggest some locations for a photo shoot to celebrate his wedding anniversary with his pup. Niko is a handful when he's in his pup space, but the couple are among my oldest customers. So I'm willing to go to some extra trouble for the duo.

Nicholas's boyfriend apparently has a family cottage outside the city with enough privacy to do an outdoor shoot in his pup gear. We arrange for them to email me pictures of the location and I agree to see if we can make something work soon. By the time I'm done talking with the pair, Con has gotten absorbed in a game with his friends. I resent seeing him gazing at Rory for direction. I want to be the one he looks at that way, hanging on a dominant's every word.

Kylee sidles up beside me and pulls me into a quick side hug. "I know that look." She greets me with a chin tilt toward Con.

"We aren't looking for the same things." I don't bother denying that I have feelings for Con.

Kylee snorts. "Q and I also want vastly different things from each other, and look how well we work."

"You know what I mean." I give her shoulder a shove and track her gaze to where Q is on all fours next to Niko. The pair of them go down on Clark with enthusiastic zeal and much tail-wagging.

I glance over at Kylee. Even though I know the two of them

are open with their sex life, it's still jarring to see her contented smile as she watches the love of her life with someone else. I don't think I'd be that chill if it was my partner.

The tender look on Kylee's face leaves me with no doubt she is truly happy that her pup is enjoying the evening. "Even if it's not about wanting the exact same things, but I'm not sure we can meet each other's needs."

Kylee turns to face me. "Oh? What are you looking for? Because that boy wants a Dom to take him in hand and give him the moon."

"He's a sweetheart who wants a Daddy-Dom. That isn't me."

"Hm. Is that what he told you? Because I'm no expert, but I think relationships work better when both parties talk about their wants and needs instead of assuming you know it all. Even if you are the D type in a D/s dynamic." She thumps me on the back.

"You're more of an expert than me." I glance at Q, focusing on the collar around their neck that marks them as Kylee's to everybody here. She's probably right that I should at least talk to Connor. The worst that can happen is he turns me down. But I don't want to lose what we have already.

The game he's playing appears to be ending. Monty leaves the group of littles gathered around Rory. The others continue to play. I don't want to ruin Con's fun. I mingle until he and his friends tidy away their toys. Now's my chance to make a move. Bonus good deed in that Connor won't be a third wheel for his friend if he plays with me.

I'm not sure what I'll offer him until I approach the gathering and catch the boy eyeing the books half-buried under a mishmash of toys.

"Hey, Conman. Would you like me to read you a story?" I offer.

Con turns big brown eyes on me, and grins like I offered him a free puppy.

"Yes, please!" He plunges a hand into the toy box and comes up with a stack of picture books. He hands them to me one at a time, like he expects me to tell him he's reached his book limit. I suppress a laugh at his calculating expression when I take them all. He goes back for another couple.

"As many as you want." I encourage him. He snags two more, adds them to the stack and calls a distracted goodbye to his friends. Then Con drags me away by the hand. I follow him to a cozy reading nook in the corner and he waits until I sit.

"Can I sit in your lap?"

"Of course, doll."

Con frowns, catching his lip between his teeth. He shakes his head. "You're not a Daddy, right?"

"Right."

"What can I call you, then?"

I've given that an undue amount of thought since we started down this path. Can I give Con the little time he needs? Is that a benefit I'm able to add to the list? Playing with littles isn't really my kink, but I don't dislike it, either. "You can still call me Jax when you're little, or Mx Jax if you want to be formal. But if you want to know what I am to you for this sort of scene, how about your babysitter?"

Con's face falls at that. I made a mis-step. "So, like a temporary placeholder until I find my Daddy?"

Ah. No wonder his mood changed and his smile looks so fake now. Did he think I was offering more than our existing arrangement? Did he want me to be something more to him? When he's little isn't the time to discuss that kind of nuance.

"No. More like someone you can trust to take care of you when you need it." I pat my lap. He clambers up to sit on my knee. "That made you sad; can you tell me why?"

"Babysitters don't love their littles." Con admits, picking at the seam of my jeans.

"And you want me to love you?" I ask, barely daring to hope he wants more with me than something casual. We still need to discuss it more when he's big. And I need to figure out if I'm willing to make an exception to my no relationships rule for him.

"No." Con hunches his shoulders. "That isn't what I meant. I don't expect any big to love me the first time we play together. I just want that to be part of the scene. That type of caring."

"Okay. What would make you feel cared for? If I'm not comfortable being your Daddy and you aren't comfortable being yourself with a babysitter?"

Con shrugs.

"Take your time to think about it, okay?"

He nods. "Okay."

"Want me to read these stories to you while you think?"

"Yes, please." He squirms in my lap, interest piqued by the story I pick from the top of the stack.

I read the book to him, holding it so he can see the pictures is easy with him sitting on me. He gets excited about the puppies going on missions to save people. And when we get to the caterpillar book, he pretends to eat all the food pictures.

"Can I be a beautiful butterfly, too?" he asks, pointing at the picture.

"The beautifulest," I agree, quashing the urge to kiss his face.

He's adorable like this. Free and unencumbered with his adult worries.

Con nods. "You should take my picture with fairy wings."

"Oh, so you're a fairy now instead of a butterfly?"

"Yep. And you can be my fairy godparent."

My heart squeezes at his thoughtfulness. He took into account both our needs to come up with that. And the title fits what I want to be to him, if I let myself consider doing age play with him. Someone he can trust and come to for anything without the gendered role or familial undertones that don't work for me in bed. A trusted friend, that's not much different from our current deal.

"Is that okay?" Con cranes around to look at my face and gauge my reaction. "Did I say something wrong?"

"No, my little fairy, you said something very right. I can be your fairy godparent if that's what you want. It's a bit of a mouthful, though, huh?"

"You're right." His brow crinkles in thought. "Hmm. How about initials? FGP?"

"Fugup?" I tease, pronouncing the three letters.

Con giggles. "That sounds like a naughty word. Would you spank me if I called you that?"

"A fuckup?"

Con presses his hands to my mouth. "You said a naughty word!" He sounds delightedly scandalized by that fact.

"Hm, I guess we need to work on a different nickname then." My lips press against his fingers when I talk, and it makes him giggle. I take his hands and move them away from my mouth. He turns it into holding hands. "I can't make my sweet little fairy get in trouble when you're just trying to call for me, huh?"

"Uh huh." Con nods solemnly. "That would make you a bad Guppy."

"Guppy?"

"Yep. Like, GP for godparent."

I chuckle. "Sounds like you figured out what to call me, huh?"

"Uh, huh. Can we read another story, Guppy?"

"We can. Which one do you want next?"

Con sorts through the stack and picks another puppy book. This one has the unfortunate line calling on the puppies to 'come back' and Con giggles at the command every time I say 'come'. A disproportionate number of Q's books feature dogs. We read them all. Then Con tells me all about his dress up toys and how he wants me to see his fairy costume because it's fantastic. I agree to take his picture in it if he brings it to my studio sometime.

"I have a bunch of costumes. Do you like to play dress up? When I was a kid, we had a humongous trunk of old costumes to play with. Modaddy would hit the post-Halloween clearance sales." He gestures with his hands to show me how big the box of costumes was, nearly smacking our stack of books onto the ground.

I rescue the books and relocate them on the side table next to our chair. "Was that your favorite holiday?"

"Nuh-uh." Con shakes his head, his whole body getting in on the gesture. "Second favorite. Purim's better. We get to dress up in costumes, and make noise. It's more special because not everyone celebrates it. And there are cookies and stories and noisemakers. And a girl hero beating a bad guy."

"Sounds fun. When is that?"

"Adar, so the Gregorian calendar date changes. I got to take

144

a long weekend to visit home for it this year, back in February. We celebrated with a few other local families. My folks' town isn't big enough for a proper shul, so that's what we do for most holidays." Con kicks his feet, squirming in my lap like he isn't sure how I'll respond. "You know I'm Jewish, right? I mean, my family is, anyway."

"Sounds fun. And yeah; I knew that."

"Cool." He beams at me.

"You are very cool, little fairy." I boop him on the nose, which earns me another giggle and more squirming in my lap. That's going to have me hard if he keeps it up. That's probably his intent, knowing the little imp as I do.

"I'm gonna call you about taking fairy pictures for me. I have the best costume and makeup, and it's going to be awesome."

"Sounds fun." I'd happily take the boy's picture in whatever he wants to wear, or nothing at all. But I can picture him playing with a cheap pair of dress up fairy wings and it's a cute image. I know a couple of bigs with nursery setups for their littles that would make a great backdrop for that kind of shoot. I could totally pull in some favors to use their spaces or borrow props. There's a giant teddy bear that would be perfect for something I have in mind with him.

"Guppy?" Con pats my cheek, like he's trying to get my attention back from artistic planning mode.

"Hm?" I ask.

"I asked if you want to see pictures from Comic-Con. I just dressed up as a generic fairy. But I loved how the makeup came out and I got some pics with a group dressed up like the cast from *Day Dreamer*. You know that video game?"

"I'm familiar with it, yeah."

"Leya has a fairy wing skin, so I got pics with someone who

was cosplaying her."

"Nice." His description has me second-guessing how involved his costume might be and whether a more fantasy backdrop would be more fitting than a nursery. I can totally make that work. Add in some special effects in editing. I don't get to do much of that sort of design work, so it could be fun. Or turn out terrible, but it's always an interesting challenge to try something new. "Send me the pictures when you get home, okay?"

"Okay, Guppy." Con nods excitedly. His butt shimmying in my lap has me more than half-hard. "I will. You really want to see?"

"I really do. Can't wait. You're getting awful wiggly right now, though, Conman." I grip his hips to still his movements. And he leans back to gaze up at me.

"Hafta pee. But I don't want to stop playing with you."

"Up, boy, if you have to potty, you need to go right away. We can play more when you're done."

"You sure?" He bites his lip and glances toward the washroom on the other side of the basement play area.

"Yeah, little fairy, I'll still be here when you get back." I ease him forward off my lap.

"Come with me?" Con turns and reaches for my hand. I let him pull me up and twine our fingers together. He practically skips along at my side on the way to the washroom. I expect him to let go when we get to the door. I can wait outside, but he pulls me inside.

"Help with the zip?" He demands. After a moment's pause, he seems to realize how forward he's being. "Sorry. Would you want to help me potty, Guppy?"

"Sure, doll. What do you need help with?"

"Mostly for taking off the onesie. Don't want to drip on it since

I'm still getting used to a new stand-to-pee packer. Can you hold my PJs out of the way?"

I help him unzip, pull his arms out of the sleeves, and take the one-piece pajama off enough for him to free his packer and point it at the toilet. It's not the same one he wears when he visits me for sex. This one is hollow and more detailed.

"Do you like having a big help you potty, Con?" I ask as he pees. The sounds of it are too intimate, and I need to offer us both some sort of coverup from the raw vulnerability of the moment.

"Yeah."

"What does your dream Daddy do to help you?"

Con glances up at me. "He'd stand behind me, real close. And then he'd hold my penis for me, to show me how to aim. And then shake it all clean and tuck me back into my undies."

"You want that from me?" I offer, even though he's pretty much already done.

Con nods once, looking away from me. I step in close, and wrap my hand around his shaft. Our fingers brush and a bit off moan escapes from Con as my stiffy brushes against his ass. "D-Guppy?" He glances over his shoulder at me.

"Sorry, little fairy. You're sexy; it'll go away if we ignore it." I give his STP a little shake to clear out the droplets clinging to the tip.

Con gives the balls a squeeze to remove any lingering moisture, so I give another gentle shake. Then I carefully tuck him into his underpants, patting his bulge gently once it's clothed. I lean forward to flush, pressing more firmly along Con's back. He makes another soft involuntary pleasure sound.

Part of me would happily stand there pressed against him for as long as he'll let me, but I'm conscious of the roomful of party guests just outside the door. Also, bathroom sex is against the house rules since there's a limited number of toilets here.

"We should go." I say, at the same time Con clears his throat and speaks.

"I, uh, need to rinse it out first." He fishes the packer out of his pants, swabs himself with some toilet paper, and takes the STP device to the sink. I watch as he handles the packer with care, shakes it dry, and tucks it back into place, adjusting his bulge before he turns to face me.

"Wash hands now?" Con asks, giving me a plaintive look. I take the excuse to step up behind him, pressing in close again, and we share the sink to wash our hands. Con hums a song under his breath as he scrubs. It's definitely a caregiver thing, and I'd do this for him as often as he wants me to.

"All done?" I ask when he turns off the water and reaches for the hand towel.

"All done." He flashes me a sweet smile.

I reach for his hand, and we step out of the washroom. The crowd still playing has thinned substantially since earlier in the evening.

"How did that compare to the fantasy, little fairy?"

"I liked it. Made it feel like a real part of me." Con doesn't meet my gaze. "Like I'm no different from any other boy who needs his Daddy's help. Or a big's help."

"You're all-boy, Con. Screw anyone who makes you feel any different. Next time, Guppy can hold it for you the whole time."

"You want to play with me like this again?" he asks, a world of disbelief in that simple phrase. Past rejections color what he expects from anyone who plays with him. It's almost enough to make me wish I could be the Daddy he craves, even if he seems willing to settle for less. But that isn't who I am. I'm not a Daddy. Still, after tonight, I'm determined to be the best damn Guppy he's ever dared to dream of having until he finds what he truly wants. If I fill the role well enough, it might keep him from settling for someone else until he meets the Daddy he deserves.

"Yep. You're not getting rid of me." I confirm.

Con flings his arms around my neck and kisses my cheek. "Thank you. I'm having the best time tonight."

"Me too. It's a shame things seem to be winding down." I gesture at the distinct lack of a crowd as more people wander up the stairs and out of the room. Hope and Clark are both helping Kylee tidy up and encouraging guests to wrap up what they're doing.

"Oh, crap, what time is it?" Con asks me.

I turn to locate a clock. Con, more familiar with the room, has already seen the time, though. He groans. "Crap. It's after one. I'm going to be waiting an hour for the next bus and I have to work in the morning. Guess I should have driven."

"I could give you a ride home." I don't ask why he took the bus. The first Sunday he canceled our get together, he mentioned that the only reason he has a car is that he uses it to visit home. I didn't pry into why then, and I won't now.

"Are you sure?" He bites his lip and dances from foot to foot. "I know Q would let me crash here, but I don't have work clothes. I'm going to be dragging ass tomorrow, even if I don't have to get up early enough to go home to change before my shift."

"It's fine, Conman. I'd be happy to help a friend."

"Okay. If you're sure." He nods. "Um, mind if I find Q to say goodbye first?"

"Of course not."

He flashes me a smile. "Cool. Q is a worrier and I'll get my phone blown up with messages if I don't let them know I'm going."

"It's fine. You don't have to explain yourself to me, little one."

Con grins, kisses my cheek once more, and darts into the thinning crowd to find his friends. I scan the room to see who's left. No one else I need to talk to from a business perspective. And no friends I'm close enough with to require checking in before we leave. That's a downer. I know everyone here, but it's all superficial. Well, I'm sure Kylee would appreciate it if I said goodbye before leaving. She's a friend, but she's also busy playing hostess.

Before I can feel too sorry for myself, Randy approaches me with a backslapping hello. He's one of the pup handlers I know decently well from seeing him around the scene.

"I hear you do boudoir shoots now?"

"I do."

"Excellent. Clark tells me you shoot all kinds of kink, is that right?"

"It is."

We hash out the details for a photo shoot. Once Randy walks away with a satisfied smile, I search the crowd for Con, hoping to leave before anyone else corners me for more work talk. That's the biggest problem with mixing my business interests with my leisure activities. The two always seem to clash when I'm trying to relax and let off steam. It's why I rarely get to play at parties like this. It makes my friendship with Connor that much more special.

Kylee catches my eye and winks. I'm not sure why, until she darts her gaze to Con, who is heading back toward me with a purposeful stride. She mouths something to me, but I don't catch it, and then Con takes my hand and tugs me toward the stairs.

"Ready to leave, Guppy?"

"I am. Are you?"

"Yep. Let's go!" He leads the way upstairs and waits patiently while I collect my light spring jacket. We talk more on the way home. About his friends, and his favorite cosplays, and what he likes to do when he's little.

When we get to his place, I catch him staring at my mouth. It doesn't take much imagination to guess that he wants a goodnight kiss. He licks his lips. I shouldn't cross that line. A goodnight kiss would make this seem like a date. It's not, though, just friends hanging out at a party.

A play party. Where we played together and made up sweet coupley nicknames and he let me hold his dick in my hand. I lean across the console, into his space.

"Kiss me goodnight, little fairy?" I murmur.

He squeaks, a surprised little noise, then presses his mouth to mine, giving me a chaste peck that's more teeth than tongue. I reach up to caress his cheek, hoping to relax him. It works and his mouth softens, opening to me. My tongue dances with his for a moment before he pulls back with a sigh.

"I should *really* get to bed now. If we do more of that, I'm going to invite you inside with me and that's a bad idea when I have to be at work in, like, five hours." He fumbles out of his seatbelt and opens the car door.

"Another time then?" I ask, reaching for his hand to slow him down before he dashes away from me.

Connor grins and nods. "Definitely."

"Don't forget you promised me some wing pics."

"I won't." He winks at me. "As soon as I get inside."

"I'll look forward to hearing from you, my little fairy."

"Night, Jax."

"Good night, Connor." I wait until he waves from inside his building to pull away from the curb. Never hurts to make sure the boy gets home safe.

By the time I open the door to my apartment, I've already got a new message from Connor. Gia wakes up and greets me with a sleepy tail wag, but she doesn't rise from her bed in the living room. I stop to give her some scritches and she huffs a sleepy little bark before nosing her face under her favorite stuffed squirrel and falling back asleep. I wait until I'm in bed to open the attachment from Connor. And I'm glad to be cozy in bed when I see my sweet boy in full fairy makeup. His costume includes a gorgeous set of ethereal gauzy fairy wings, and not much else.

Connor: This is the sexy version for home viewing ;P I wore some strategically placed cool plant-based armor pieces to cover the naughty bits at the actual convention.

I send him back a line of fire emojis, already palming myself through my pants. The semi he's had me sporting for half the night is raging to life at the image of Connor with a full face of teal and purple fairy makeup. It makes him look otherworldly. I joked about making a mess of him, but damn, I can just picture him painted in wax to match the eyeshadow in this picture. Or wearing a pearly necklace of my cum. Or on his knees for me, wings trailing behind him. Not that I have a wing kink. More, I've recently discovered a very strong Connor kink.

Connor: Sorry, too much?

Jax: Nope. I'm going to jerk off to this. You're a sexy little fairy.

Connor: Send me the cum shot?

I laugh at his request.

Jax: I'm not that kind of photographer, boy.

Connor: I'll show you mine ;)

Jax: I thought you had work early in the morning.

Connor: *pout* you aren't my Daddy :P

Jax: I'm your fairy godparent, and if you're a very good boy, I'll make all your dreams come true.

Connor: You said I'm already a good boy.

Jax: You are. But if you want to have dreams, you have to go to sleep.

Connor: I'd fall asleep faster if you send me a dick pic to jerk off to, Guppy.

Jax: You want to think about me while you touch yourself, boy?

Connor: Mhm. I want to think about your mouth on me again, hot and wet and needy.

I work my hand into my pants to stroke myself, reaching for the lube on my bedside table with the other hand.

Jax: I'd suck and tease and pinch your tight little nipples until they're as hard as your little cock.

Connor: Would that make you hard?

Jax: Yeah, Connor, I'm hard and leaking for you, wet enough to jerk us both off with no lube.

It's the truth, but I still add a glob of lube to my hand as I work my fist along my shaft in a leisurely glide.

Connor: Mhm. I want to taste you.

Connor sends me a GIF of a blowjob. The boy in the porn clip bears a vague resemblance to him. He gazes up at the guy whose cock he has in his mouth, submission clear in his posture. The clip is short, but it's plain to see that the boy giving the blow job has lost himself in worshiping the cock in his mouth. I can imagine Con looking at me like that. His tongue swirling around the head of my dick like he's thoroughly enjoying an ice cream cone, desperate to savor every drop. I have to give my balls a gentle squeeze to hold back my orgasm at the mental image of Connor on his knees for me. Adoring me.

Jax: Nope, not today. I want your mouth free to moan and beg me for more. You'll pull me down on top of you.

Connor: Uh, huh. I'll wrap my legs around you while you rub your fat juicy cock against my little dick and torture my nipples.

The next image is his chest. Perky little nipples pinched hard as he twists his piercing. Fuck, I can remember how jewelry feels in my mouth, surrounded by the soft wet cotton of his shirt and flavored with ice cream. Or smeared with birthday cake. Or swollen and sensitized after I pull off a nipple clamp following hours of touching and teasing him. The way his skin flushed with blood when I released him. I've fantasized about every one of our weekends together countless times.

Jax: I'd lick them first. Get them nice and wet. Blow on them, so the cold makes your skin pebble and you're desperate for heat. Twist and tug on your piercings until you're a needy little mess for me.

Connor: Fuck. Yeah. I'd arch into you, beg you to take me into your mouth.

Jax: Play with your nips, boy, make yourself ache for me.

Connor: Already there, Guppy.

The title he came up with, just for me, makes my dick pulse, close to the edge. I stroke more slowly, drawing out my pleasure. Savoring the experience with him.

Jax: Good boy. When you're desperate for more, I'll suck your nips into my mouth. Hard, so hard it makes you gasp and moan. Does that make you horny?

Connor: You know it does. I want to rub off against you. Hump my little dick into you.

Jax: I know what my boy needs. I fuck my dick into yours, rubbing our lengths together. Then I demand that you reach between us, wrap your hand around both our junk and jerk us both.

Connor: Mm. Yeah, you fuck your dick against mine until we need to come so badly it hurts. And then you tug on the barbell through my nipple with your teeth until I can't stop myself from bucking up into you. I fuck my hand and your dick until I come.

Jax: I come too, spurt all over your belly, make a mess of you. And then I'll kneel between your legs and lick it all clean. Lick your spent little cock until you get hard for me again. Suck you until you come. Again and again until it hurts too much to keep going and you beg me to stop giving you orgasms.

Connor: Ngh. Yeah. Fuck. I'm coming.

His next message is a picture of his face, head tipped back, mouth open in pleasure, eyes squeezed shut. It's hot. I can't get enough of his O face. His familiar groan falling from his lips as I drive him wild with lust and need. I wish he was here so I could smother his sex sounds in kisses.

A few more hard strokes to my dick tip me over the edge, too. I snap a picture of my spent cock and the puddle of cum in my palm to reciprocate.

Jax: Me too. You're a bad influence. We both have work in the morning.

Connor: Mm. Worth it. No regrets. That was hot. And I like your big fat dick. Can't wait to see it in person again soon.

Connor: Though now I'm curious. How many O's do you think you can milk out of me?

Jax: Hm, good question. My record is four times in one night. But I was nineteen, high as a kite, and the last one hurt more than it felt good. What's your personal best?

Connor: Um. More than that. *shifty eyes* It hurts after the third or fourth go in a couple hours. But I kind of like that? I savor the ache for a while afterward.

Connor: Sorry. TMI?

I laugh at the absurdity of that.

Jax: We just got off together, pretty sure TMI is off the table at this point. ;P

Connor: *Snort-laugh* True. It was good, too ;)

Jax: Better than good. I'd be down for a repeat. Several times, if that's what does it for you.

Connor: Mm. In person next time. Anyway. I'm yawning and I should probably actually take advantage of the post-O drowsiness to get to sleep. Talk to you later?

Jax: For sure. Good night, little fairy.

Connor: Night, Guppy. And thanks. I had fun tonight.

Jax: Me too. Sweet dreams.

I wait a minute to see if he sends another message, but he doesn't. Setting aside my phone, I go to clean up before bed. I'm not entirely sure what I'm doing with Connor now. Tonight blurred the lines for me. We're something other than friends, and still less than lovers. But I like him, and he likes me, and maybe that's all either of us needs to know to enjoy whatever this is while it lasts.

CHAPTER 14

Connor

Adventures' temporarily closing blasts my social calendar wide open. I've been missing having the club as a venue to blow off steam more than I thought I would. I still see my friends, but it's more of an effort without the club as a central hub that we all gravitate toward. They seem to be busy all the time lately.

Tate is all tangled up with Rory, his new-in-town daddy. Monty thinks he's being super discreet about screwing around with Luke, but I recognize rope burns when I see them at our usual D&D sessions. And I've seen the way they look at each other when Tate isn't around. Why Monty thinks Tate would be upset about his bestie dating his brother, I have no clue, but Monty is prone to overthinking things. So Monty has vague excuses about what he's doing instead of hanging out with us. And Tate brings his new beau to any kinky events with him. And I feel left out.

Unfortunately for me, Q is sick as a dog for a while and can't hang out as much either. It's easy to piece together that they won't be needing another insemination scene. Not that I say anything about their happy nibling news until they bring it up over lunch. That only happens once they finally feel well enough to meet up with me on a rare mutual day off.

They've been spending a lot of time at home with Kylee this summer and seem reluctant to go out with me, which is fine. I get they need time with their partner, and I know that surrogacy would be a nightmare for me, so it's probably no walk in the park for them either. It just makes the ache of missing my family harder to bear.

Not that they're available much lately, either. My older sibs are busy with kids on summer break from their usual schedule, and work, and vacations to visit with their in-laws. The little kids have back-to-back summer camps and I'm just as stuck in a rut as I've been for ages.

None of that would be too big a deal, except that of course it all aligns with the wedding season for Jax's photography business. More often than not, the receptions go late enough into the evenings to make meeting up afterward impractical. Especially since he's been on his feet for hours and seems exhausted by the end of the day.

Despite that, we text daily. I squeeze in quick visits to his place during the week, since he prefers not to leave Gia home alone more than he has to. Not to mention my bedroom hardly affords me any privacy. Neither of us broaches the idea that I could spend the night. That's a partner thing, not a friends with benefits thing.

I don't know why it's a limit for me with Jax when I'm perfectly content to sleep with Quent, and it doesn't mean anything romantic. Probably because Quent is so tactile and so very committed to Kylee that the possibility of it meaning anything more than that Q likes to cuddle is laughable. Sleeping in Jax's bed would cross a line for me. One I'd hate to walk back.

Jax asks me to model for him a few more times after our shoot with Brian, so that's one way we carve out more kinky time together. It's not always easy to fit the modeling sessions into my work schedule, but I do it anyway. Just to see him.

It's for his stock photos, so we avoid anything too intense. Generic bondage photos, mostly. An edging session with nipple clamps and weights attached to my piercings that make my sac ache in the most delicious way. Those photos are for the private gallery on his website, not the stock site. I got to snuggle with Gia in her dog bed while I was coming down from that scene. Jax insisted on pampering me and driving me home since I was super tender after the endorphins wore off.

Last week, he even asked me to bring my cosplay stuff, so we did that fairy photoshoot he promised me. It made me slip into my little headspace, and I swear he loved it when I called him Guppy. Unless I was reading what I wanted to see into his sappy smile and his tender touches. He seemed so into me when he was positioning me to pose with the giant fake flower props that looked like something out of a CG fairy movie.

Afterward, I let him play with my cheaper costume makeup. The kind that really smears well when you get your throat fucked so hard your eyes water and then smears more when your partner shoots all over your face. Let's just say I left his studio with us both covered in makeup smears and blissfully fucked out. Best night I've had in ages. He was so sweet to me that night.

We've been texting nonstop since Q's party. And sexting when getting together in person isn't workable, but it's not the same as going to his place and actually fucking. Except after the fairy pictures, when I let myself be little with him, he's seemed more distant when we talk. And he always has excuses when I ask to get together.

I miss him. I don't say as much, just tease him about missing our usual Sunday fuck-fests and how I'd gotten accustomed to seeing him regularly. He must think I've gotten too clingy, so I try to back off.

Of course, the work week is busier for me in the summer, too. That's when I've got more frequent site visits to oversee. Plus a passel of student interns and volunteers to train and mentor.

And that's on top of all my usual duties. Besides which, summer is a better time to drum up publicity for the fundraising that sustains our organization year-round. So in a nutshell, I'm busy as heck during the week and Jax has all his weekends booked off for work until well into autumn.

We aren't dating, but not seeing him as much feels like a breakup. It gets to where I leave more time between my responses to him, too. Just to dull the ache of disappointment. My sex toy drawer has certainly gotten a workout this week, now that my source of regular orgasms has dried up. It's not nearly as satisfying to play solo. Even with the explicit pics that Jax and I have been sending to each other to use as fap fodder. At least he still sends me those when I ask for them.

I go to save the latest photo of Jax to my collection. In it, he's gazing down at the camera with his phone at some effortlessly artistic angle that shows off his chest and makes me want to lick my way up to his mouth. When I hit save, I get a warning that I'm running low on storage.

My phone suggests freeing up space by deleting unused apps, and it's a surprise to realize I haven't opened my dating apps in months. Barely at all since Jax and I started our no strings sexcapades. With the less than memorable exception of a crappy coffee date here and there in the early days. And all of those were meetings I'd arranged before Jax offered to be my fuck buddy.

Has it really been that long since I made any effort to find a boyfriend? Yeah, I guess it has. Not like I was holding out much hope that Mr. Right was waiting for me on some vanilla app. But I've been placing an unhealthy importance on my friendship with Jax. I've let the buzz of something new develop into feelings he won't reciprocate.

Heck, when we were at Kylee and Quent's latest party, I was ridiculously jealous of the other people I saw him talking with. And he has to realize that giving him a special name for when he's big, telling him I want to be loved, means more to me than meaningless sex.

I hover my finger over the button to delete the apps. Do I still want a relationship? Yeah, I want it so badly it hurts sometimes. I want what I've got with Jax, only with someone who wants to share a life with me. Someone who wants to take care of my little side and do all the filthy, sloppy, kinky things with me in bed. And hold me while I fall asleep afterward.

Do I still need the apps to find that? I'm not sure. Either way, it's not fair to Jax or myself to use our friendship as some sort of stand in for a romantic relationship just because he's convenient. I shouldn't be putting that pressure on him when he made it clear he isn't into dating. I should pull back. Or at least discuss things with him.

Instead of deleting the dating apps, I go through all my in-app notifications to see what's new. I've missed a few potential matches. Some got passive aggressive when I didn't reply to their messages right away, even though the messages are clearly marked as unread.

Not missing anything there. Hello red flags. If they think I should make my life revolve around them before we've so much as exchanged a hello, that's a big yikes. I delete those along with the obligatory unasked for dick pics or giant boob shots from people who didn't bother to read my profile.

The kinky singles group I joined a while back has a notification that they're organizing a mixer. That might be a low pressure way to meet someone. I might not have Jax to rely on for kinky fun and orgasms for much longer, and even if we aren't over, we aren't exclusive. Might as well dive back into the dating scene. I should do this. I worry my lip and hit the button to tell the organizers I might be attending.

Then I text Jax that I have a date along with the day and time, so I won't back out at the last minute. Jax leaves that message on read all weekend. I try not to obsess over it, since I know he's busy with weddings, but he usually makes time to text me. Even if it's just silly selfies in his downtime.

Monday, he texts that he hopes I have fun and he's got a work engagement that night, anyway. When I message back to see if he wants to fool around on video chat, he says Gia got into something rotten at an outdoor photo shoot. She needs a bath. 'Sorry, but I have to wash my dog's hair' sounds like a fabricated excuse. But Jax sends me pics of her in his spacious shower, so it's probably the truth.

Connor: Aw, she looks so sad and pathetic with her fur unfluffed.

Jax: But she smells at least 1000% better now.

The quick reply eases the ache of missing him. This feels right, talking to Jax like everything is normal and we're friends. And I'm on solid ground teasing him about his doggo.

Connor: LOL. But just look at those big puppy eyes begging you to let her keep her foul stench.

Jax: Not happening. You'd thank me if you were here ;)

Connor: You're a big meanie, scrubbing away all her hard work getting messy ;)

Jax: Uh huh, I should have known it was only a matter of time before my messy little monsters banded together to try a bath boycott.

I grin at the implications. He has to mean me. That I'm his messy little monster, too. Gah. Reading too much into his teasing is begging to get my heart broken, but I can't seem to help myself.

Connor: Solidarity, Gia!

Jax sends me another picture, this time with Gia rubbing up

against a brush.

Connor: Does she at least enjoy getting brushed after?

Jax: Yeah, except when I get to the tangles. Her majestic butt-floof is all bedraggled and studded with burdocks. Don't ask me how she finds them the second they're in bloom, but the girl is a burr magnet.

Connor: It's because her floof is a perfect transportation vector for them to spread. Give her extra pats for me.

Jax: Will do. She got all excited when I said your name.

Connor: Aw, your doggo misses me?

I'm tempted to ask which of them misses me more, since it's been ages since our last hurried in person quickie when I stopped by after work on an impulse. But no, I've got to cut back on the blatant flirting.

Jax: I think she knows that when I say your name she gets a tasty Kong to keep her occupied so the humans can have private alone times.

Connor: Well, I'd hate to disappoint her royal floofiness.

The dots bounce for a long time. Jax leaves me on read for the rest of the night but I wake up to a message from him.

Jax: We should talk in person, Connor. Is next week still busy for you?

Connor: I can always make time for a friend. Lunch? Tell me which day works best.

My gut clenches at the obvious implications of that phrase. 'We need to talk' never means good things. Does he want me to back off? Or perhaps he wants to 'just be friends' without the benefits? Am I pushing too hard and all the scheduling issues we've had lately are just his way of letting me down easy? It would hardly be the first time I was too dense to realize I was way more into a guy than he was into me.

The fact Jax leaves me on read all afternoon only makes me more certain I know where this is going. I know we both have busy schedules this week, but it still stings. We arrange a lunch meetup downtown, close to my work, for next week. I go back to the singles mixer page and change my answer to definitely going. It will be easier to handle Jax pulling away from me if I have something to look forward to. A solid plan to get back out there and throw myself into the dating pool.

I message Quent about the mixer, but I don't mention Jax probably breaking up with me. Or breaking off our benefits. Same difference. It's silly to be upset; I knew it was too good to last. I shouldn't be a soppy mess about Jax, when we were never even really dating.

That doesn't stop me from digging out the oversized puppy stuffie from its spot at the back of my closet. It's too big to be practical, but Q got it for me to snuggle with when we were shopping for my niblings' holiday gifts last fall. I'm glad to have the oversized stuffie as I hug it close and cry into the toy's silky fur. When they explained the logic behind the gift, I laughed at Quent. I'd joked about wanting a date for the holidays. So they said a stuffie was the next best thing, that way I'll always be able to snuggle with them, even when they aren't around. It's comforting to have something to hold now.

I'm tempted to call Quent, but I'm not ready to talk about this yet. Not when I know Quent will remind me not to jump to conclusions and persuade me to lay my cards on the table with Jax. But the fact remains that he doesn't date and I want a partner who is proud to claim me as his. That's a pretty basic incompatibility, no matter how amazing the sex is between us. Even if he's not breaking up with me next week, I should probably let this go before I break my own heart.

I cry myself out, falling asleep with my stuffie. And then I let work consume my energy for the rest of the week. At least Saturday is our regular gaming session, so I have a distraction from missing Jax. When we discuss the mixer, all my friends decide to tag along for moral support. Which is ridiculous of them, since Harry is the only other one of them who is actually single, but I appreciate the support more than I can say.

It's a pleasant reminder that even when they're busy with their own lives, they're still there to support me when I need them. And I need the moral support to make sure I attend the event. Let alone do more than hide in a corner sipping a drink and trying to work up enough courage to talk to anyone.

If nothing else, Monty and Quent will see to it I meet people. And Tate is good at getting them to rein in their enthusiasm, if there aren't any bigs around to take the lead. My heart aches at the thought of meeting someone else. I don't want to get to know a new partner. I want Jax, but it's childish to cling to the familiar when it isn't working, so I smile and try to be enthusiastic about my prospects at the mixer.

It's a relief when Harry starts the game and I can just enjoy the in-game revelry. Today's feast is our reward for rescuing a goblin village from the big bad meanie our heroes have been fighting against.

Goblins are apparently good at gobbling up tasty treats. Harry's descriptions of the feast shouldn't make me think of Jax. Of how he indulges my messier interests. I try not to think about him licking frosting off my skin. Or how much fun we could have with the giant toad caviar. Apparently the bowl overflowing with globs of squishy eggs served in their own goo are a goblin delicacy. All I can think about as Harry describes them is how similar it sounds to the gelatin eggs that go along with the funky ovipositor toy Jax sent me a link to a while ago.

"Can I try those?" I ask when Harry takes pains to describe them, mostly because he's been known to throw in fun food related props. If he's got a bowl full of edible slime balls, I am here for it.

I try not to dwell on the pang of loss at realizing Jax and I will probably never get to play with his new toy. Not if he's planning on breaking things off with me. Maybe he'll agree to one last hurrah. Or I can get myself a similar toy to try out solo. It's not the same as doing it with him, but it could be my promise to myself that I'll hold out for a partner like him. One who shares my relationship desires *and* my kinks. Ugh. I always do this to myself, getting over invested with guys who don't want the same things I do.

Quent nudges my dice toward me, and I realize Harry said something to me. "What?"

"I said you need to roll a D8 since you ate the eggs." Harry repeats with an ominous smile.

"Am I going to regret that?" I roll the eight-sided die and wince at the result out of habit, even though a low roll on something like this doesn't necessarily mean bad things are a guarantee. "One?"

"Oh man, be right back." Harry chuckles and rubs his hands together with glee—like an evil sadist—and excuses himself to the kitchen. Sure enough, he returns with a serving bowl full of what appears to be egg-shaped Jello shots. He nudges the bowl toward me and they all jiggle. "Go on, take a red one, Connor."

I pluck it from the bowl with some effort, since the thing wants to slip from my grip, and wiggle it toward Quent. "Want to try delicious giant eggs with me?"

They gag and shuffle back with a vigorous head shake. "That is all you, babe."

I shrug, tip back my head, and swallow the morsel. It's just normal Jello. That Harry apparently doctored with some unholy combination of cinnamon and hot sauce. Fiery cinnamon completely obliterates the initial sweet cherry flavor as it slides down my throat and I fan my face comically. "Ew, that burns all the way down." I reach for Quent's water and they press the bottle into my hand.

"Anyone else want a shot?" Harry wiggles the bowl at us.

I glance at Quent who shrugs back at me. "Are they boozy? I'm driving after our game."

"Nope, just used some additives to mimic the flavors." Harry proffers the bowl.

"Oh, fun. What was yours, Connor?" Quent pokes at one of the green globs.

"Fire." I take another swig of water.

Harry gives me a faux-sympathetic smile. "If it's any consolation, you feel energized."

"Oh, goodie, are we about to be ambushed while we're all enjoying the drunken revels?" I whine.

"Hey, that would be meta-gaming. Do you want another fireball shot?"

"No. Can I pick a different color?"

"Go for it. I made them for you all to eat." Harry urges.

"What's in the green ones?" Quent holds one up to the light to examine it.

"Guess."

Quent eats it, and smiles as they declare, "Oh, mojito, nice. Mint and lime. Don't suppose you added peanut butter to the grape ones?"

"Sorry, no. But it does make you feel refreshed," Harry says.

"Too bad. Are these magical? Magic buff eggs? Can we bring them with us for our next adventure?" Monty chimes in.

"You can." Harry nods.

"I stuff a bunch of the eggs and their goo into my spare flask for later." Quent grins.

"Me, too." Monty reaches for the 'eggs' as well.

"The nearby goblins give you disapproving glances, but no one tries to stop you," Harry says.

We spend a while comparing giant frog people egg colors and what they taste like versus the buffs they might give us. Harry did a good job mimicking various drink combos without booze, and the Jello is fun. I like the way it jiggles around, so it keeps me occupied while Tate hashes out some armor upgrades for his character. We all seem a bit distracted today. I hope the others have more positive reasons for their inattention.

When our game ends, Tate hustles Monty out the door like he has somewhere he wants to be ASAP. Quent offers me a ride home, so we get to chat. I've missed seeing them as much as usual over the past couple of months.

"How's the nausea and fatigue treating you lately?" I ask once we're alone in their car.

"Better. Almost a third of the way through. I need to let the others know soon. How about you? You seemed down today. We don't have to go to that mixer if you're not into it."

"No, I want to."

"Ah. So, you and Jax aren't a thing?"

"It's not the thing I want it to be, anyway." I shrug and fuss with my seatbelt strap.

"I'm sorry, Connor."

"It's fine. Can't make other people want a relationship." I fidget, uncomfortable with their sympathy.

"Still, this calls for a movie night. Come stay the night at my place? Mommy won't mind."

"Shouldn't you clear that with her first?"

"Nah, you're always welcome and I haven't had you over for cuddles in decades. Please? You can pick where we order dinner from."

I snort at that. "As long as it's one of the three places that don't make you want to hurl?" We might not have gotten together in person as much as usual, but we still talk and text all the time.

"Well, yeah. Sorry."

"Don't be. Dinner and a sleepover at your place sounds perfect."

CHAPTER 15

Jax

I've been itching to show Connor the glossy portraits sitting on the edge of my desk from the minute I uploaded the files from my camera. Okay, no, from the moment he sent me the grainy selfie from a comic convention. The same night where I let myself be his caregiver for an evening. That night changed something for me. Made me seriously consider if I can give him what he needs.

I've wanted to do him justice in the fairy costume ever since. The finished photos will make his jaw drop. It took hours of editing and learning new techniques from tutorials to get just the right magic effects to accentuate his ethereal beauty. I love the results, though.

I low-key want to hang the image of Connor, looking stunning in a fantasy setting, on my wall. If that wouldn't be weird. It's weird as fuck to put a picture of your fuck buddy on your wall, though, right? Right.

But that's not really what I want, anyway. I *want* to hang up a picture of my boyfriend. I want Connor to agree to seeing me. Not just for sexy times and kinky fun. I want him to want me the way I've started to want him. And the only way to get from the awkward avoidance of the past few weeks to where I want us to be is to sit down and have a frank talk. I need to tell him how things have changed for me since we started this all those months ago.

I'm meeting him downtown for lunch today, and my eyes keep drifting back to the clock. It seems like time has been dragging all morning, but if I leave now, I won't be too early to grab a table for us. It's not like I'm getting much accomplished when all I can think about is Connor and how he'll react. To both the photos and me asking if he'll date me. We're so compatible when we're together, it's easy to assume he'll agree. But I know he has a little side, and he knows I'm not comfortable being his Daddy.

I grab my stuff, tuck the envelope with the pictures under my arm and whistle for Gia. I lock up the studio before I take her for a quick walk around our neighborhood. Then I leave her to chill at home with music streaming on low to keep her company. I snap a photo of her to send to Connor once I grab a seat on the bus, just to break the text silence. This way I won't have to worry about parking and I can message him along the way.

Jax: Gia wants you to know her big meanie said she can't come to the restaurant with us.

There aren't a ton of people riding into the downtown area at this hour, so I get comfy and wait for Connor to reply. The fur baby picture gets an immediate response, as I'd hoped, so that might mean Connor is already on his way to meet me. Then again, sending him Gia pics is a sure way to get a quick response if I go too long between hearing from him. I should feel bad about shamelessly using my girl as an unwitting wingman, but Gia likes Connor. And the way he loves on my dog when he visits is one thing I love about Connor.

Connor: Poor baby. Tell her I'll make her some doggie cookies to make up for it next time Quent and I have a baking day. If that's still okay?

Jax: You can spoil my dog anytime, Connor. Are those for human pups or bio dogs, though?

Connor: Q has a recipe that's good for both. And we use the xylitol free peanut butter, so no worries. You haven't mentioned if she has any dietary restrictions?

Jax: No allergies, or anything. Sounds awesome. We should try that recipe at my place sometime?

I get extended bouncing dots. They stop. Then reappear. I stare at my screen and consider clarifying or walking back the invite. Does he not want to hang out with me outside our current parameters? Is he looking for the words to let me down easy? I thought he was interested in more, but maybe I was just seeing what I wanted.

His extended silence makes me doubt that our lunch date is going to end the way I want it to. I put my phone away a few stops early and walk the rest of the way to meet Connor, too anxious to sit. He's already standing in front of the restaurant we chose and when he catches sight of me, he forces a weak grin.

"Hi, Jax." Connor lifts a hand to wave.

"Good to see you, Connor." I'm sorely tempted to pull him into a hug, or kiss his cheek. His closed posture and hunched shoulders warn me to keep my distance. I know he's shy with strangers, so it could just be a desire to avoid drawing attention in public. I deliberately chose a lunch spot in a part of town where same sex PDA is fairly commonplace, so I don't think it's that.

"Yeah." He scuffs a toe against the sidewalk, expression glum as he won't quite meet my gaze.

"Well, I, uh, brought you something." Instead of pushing his boundaries, I hand him the envelope.

The gift perks him up as he takes it from me, and slits open the envelope before pausing. "Oh, is this safe for public consumption? What is it? Can I open it here?"

"Go ahead." I gesture for him to pull out the photos.

When he does, he lets out an excited little squee and covers his mouth with his hand. His eyes are shiny with tears as he darts his gaze between me and the portrait. "Jax? I don't understand." He shakes his head.

"What's not to understand, little fairy?"

"Why are you making me artwork and inviting me over to bake cookies if you want to break this off?" He gestures sharply between us.

"Huh?" I gape at him. Did he really think that's what I wanted to discuss? No wonder he looked so miserable.

"Isn't that what you asked me out for today?"

"Not at all. I asked you out because I wanted to have a sit down conversation with no distractions so we could talk about where we both want our relationship to go. I told you why I don't date, right?"

"Because you don't want a jealous boyfriend making you choose between him and your work." Connor nods.

"And when have you once shown me anything but support for my work?"

"Uh, never? It's your passion as well as your job. You know I would never ask you to give that up..."

"I do. Which is why I want to make an exception for you. I was wondering if you'd be able to make an exception for me?"

"What do you mean?" His brow scrunches, making him look adorably puzzled.

"I mean, you wanted a Daddy, right?"

Connor shoves my shoulder and rolls his eyes. "No. I want a boyfriend who can be my caregiver when I'm little or who wouldn't begrudge me spending time with other caregivers to get that need met. A Guppy is just as good as a Daddy in my book, as long as he or they love and care for me."

"Are you sure you wouldn't want all the little stuff? I can give you some of it, but it's not an all the time thing for me."

Connor laughs. "It's not for me either. Mostly, I enjoy being little with my friends or for a scene, and occasionally as part of my aftercare, I like to feel small and cared for. You've already seen how I get. Like with the smash cake and after my scene with Brian."

"Yeah, you were adorable as fuck." I nod.

"So, is that something you can live with in a boyfriend?" Connor offers me his hand, the gesture still tentative.

"Yeah." I twine our fingers and bring his hand up to my lips to kiss the back of it. "For you, I'd be willing to try a lot more than helping you get messy, or get dressed, or holding your cock for you while you piss."

Connor's gaze darts around us to see if we're being overheard. I pull him in against my chest and murmur into his ear. "Big or little, I want to give you all your dreams, Con. I want to make a filthy mess of you."

"Yes, please." Connor squirms in my arms. I suspect he's as hard as I am under his packer. "Could we skip lunch and find a place to, uh, celebrate?"

I kiss his cheek, then bring my lips to the shell of his ear to murmur my next words where no one can overhear them. "No, you've been working yourself ragged. Let's have lunch and we can celebrate tonight. Bring clothes for tomorrow so you can spend the night. I want to take my time with you the first time I make love to you as my boyfriend, Connor."

Connor jerks his head around to look at me, eyes wide and

hopeful. "Are you sure?" He bites his lip. His tentative smile makes me ache to reassure him I'm as sure about being with him as I've been about anything in my life.

"Yes, about all of it. Unless you don't want to?"

"No, I want to. I just...I was sure you wanted to meet up to—well, not break up, since we weren't really together—but break things off. I need a minute to process. You're sure you want me as a partner. Like, neither of us sees anyone else romantically?"

"Yeah, Connor. I told you from the start that I like you. And we're compatible in bed and out. Why wouldn't I want a gorgeous boy who makes me come buckets and lets me dirty him up?"

Connor shrugs, still glancing around self-consciously. "I dunno. Lots of reasons. I guess you were right that we have plenty to talk about, but want to go inside first?"

"Of course. Or we can get the food to go so we can find a place to talk more privately?" I offer, since it hasn't escaped me that he isn't entirely comfortable discussing our sex life in public.

Connor smiles sweetly at me. "Oh, I know a spot on the waterfront that's usually not too crowded, and there's a burrito place along the way. They make the best fish burritos, if you like those? Gah, I barely even know what foods you like."

I chuckle at his flustered hand-waving and sling an arm around his shoulders. "Taco Fino?" I wait until Connor nods. "Yeah, I like their burritos. And a stroll along the waterfront to enjoy the sunny weather sounds perfect."

Connor glances at his phone and nods. "Okay, I should have enough time for that. No more meetings today and I can always stay a little later to finish paperwork. Heck, I might actually get some of it completed without interruptions to answer everyone else's questions if I'm there after hours." He winks, like it's a joke, and I realize I know little about his work beyond the broad strokes.

"Right, so you don't know about my food preferences, and I am woefully unaware of what you actually do with all those long hours and frustrating meetings."

"I guess you were right that we needed to talk, but for future reference, can we find a better way to word that?"

"Yeah. Sorry I made you sad." I squeeze him closer.

Connor shrugs off my arm and twines our fingers. "It's fine. And it'll be easier to walk like this." He swings our arms. "I'm glad the conclusions I jumped to were wrong. Next time I will clarify before I go all doom and gloom. So. If we're doing this dating thing, everything is on the table, yeah? I can tell you about my family drama and whine about how busy Quent is lately. And complain that Harry fed me a virgin fireball Jello shot. It was awful, but also made me think it would be fun to try those ovipositor gelatin eggs with, like, ginger extract...do you think that would be safe?"

"Ah. I'd wondered if you were intentionally vague about your life with me. You know I enjoy hearing about you, right?"

"Well, I get that *now*. I just figured we were both using the sex to scratch an itch and you wouldn't care about my sister's high school sports prospects. Or my baby niece scooting around and painting her entire body, let alone her nursery, in butt paste."

"Oh my. The little troublemaker sounds like her uncle." I tease him.

"Hey!" Connor squawks.

"What? Do you deny that you both enjoy being messy little goblins? Want me to smear you in vaseline?"

"Only if you want to try pinning me down and fucking me when I'm slippery as a greased pig. Those suckers are hard to catch."

"You know this from experience?" I arch a brow at him.

"Well, yeah, country boy, remember? We didn't keep pigs." Connor bumps shoulders with me. "But, yeah, our neighbors raised them. My oldest brother, Prescott, was besties with their eldest son, Matt. They thought it would be hilarious to grease up all us younger kids' hands to chase a bunch of piglets around the yard to keep us occupied when they were babysitting us. Pretty sure they wanted us worn out early so they could make out before our folks all got home. Anyway, he's my brother-in-law now, and they have two kids."

I chuckle at the animated way he tells the story, gesturing and grinning at me, warm as sunshine. It's good to hear him talk about himself. To have him share his memories and the things that matter to him. It's obvious he's close with his big family and equally obvious that keeping them out of our chats has meant keeping a huge part of himself hidden away from me. No more of that. I want all of him.

I pull Connor in close to kiss his temple and he gives me a bemused grin, like he has no idea how endearing he is. How much I want to put my hands on him and kiss him all over. "I will never say no to covering you in whatever mess your heart desires, Connor. You know I splurged on the high end rubber sheets, so it would be a shame not to grease up and try our hands at naked wrestling."

He giggles. "Yeah? Maybe you can fill me up with that alien goo you mentioned, too?"

I laugh. "Just you wait, boy. The sky's the limit."

"Nope, I think tentacle aliens and their eggs technically come from beyond the sky, so that isn't a limit at all."

"Look at you, being all full of sass."

"So, if we're officially dating now, does that mean you want to be exclusive? Like, would you be okay with me messing around with my friends during scenes at the club?"

"I think I'd want to be there if you're having sex with other people. But I won't say you can't do whatever scenes you want, as long as we talk about it first. And I know you and Quent are close, so if you need to go spend the night with them sometimes, I trust that will not change things between us. You love them, right? Just not romantically?"

"Pretty much." Connor agrees with a relieved huff of breath. "Are you sure I'm not dreaming this?"

In answer, I pinch his cheek. "You seem awake to me."

Connor laughs, swatting my hand away. "Hey, no fair! I never said I wanted to wake up, yet, if I was."

"My bad. I did promise to help you live your dreams wide awake, though, remember?"

"I remember." Connor kisses my cheek, then tugs me toward the line of people waiting to place orders. We're at the little hole in the wall for the burritos, so we pause our conversation there to get our food at the order counter. As we make our way to the waterfront, Connor tells me more stories. I enjoy learning about his family. And hearing his anecdotes about growing up as an openly queer Jewish kid with queer parents and siblings in a small town helps me to understand my shy boy. When he gets to his ex, it's easy for me to understand why he assumed the worst from me last week.

His high school boyfriend sounds like an immature asshat, but Connor already knows that. So I just squeeze his hand and tell him I see him as so much more than the sum of his parts. And it's the best date I can recall having. It's hard to tear myself away from him so we can both get back to work. We'll definitely have to schedule our next date on a day off. Still, I can't wipe the grin off my face at knowing there will be a next date. Hopefully, a lifetime of them. I'm already looking forward to seeing him again tonight as we part ways for now.

CHAPTER 16

Connor

J ax wants me. He wants to be with me. Not just fuck me or get kinky together. He wants all of me. His words from our lunch date run through my mind on a giddy loop all afternoon. I want to blow up my family chat thread with excited babble about my boyfriend. Jax.

Jax is my boyfriend now. Or is he my partner? My date? I'll have to ask him what title he prefers, but regardless, I want to shout it from the rooftops. I guess it's true what they say about cliches being that way for a reason. Normally, calling attention to myself is my worst nightmare, but I'd make an exception for letting the world know Jax is mine.

I've pulled up Quent's contacts half a dozen times, to tell them I might have found my forever, except they're busy today and I want to celebrate together. In person. So I just text to arrange dinner together later this week when they ask how my meeting with Jax went. I told them we were grabbing lunch, but not that I suspected Jax wanted to end things.

In hindsight, I'm glad I didn't make any rash decisions before I heard him out. Well, other than signing up for that kinky singles mixer. Now that we've agreed to be romantically exclusive, I log into the site to rescind my RSVP. Next, I text my friends to let them know I can't do the mixer after all. I leave a voice recording for Tate, like he prefers. I doubt any of them will mind the change in plans. Tate and Monty might not have officially announced anything about their Daddies, yet, but I know they're each seeing someone.

As I get off the bus in Jax's neighborhood, it strikes me how quickly his home and studio have become a familiar part of my life. Ever since that first session where he photographed me obliterating a cake, I've associated being here with a buzz of excitement. It's a joy to know I'm going to end the evening totally satisfied in a way I rarely achieve outside the safety of Adventures.

I love the way Jax takes me apart and lets me experience new things within the haven of his home. And I love the explorations he's facilitated for me at his studio when he can't provide what I want. Like the session he set up for me with Brian. Even better, he gave me the courage to try new kinks under his watchful gaze. His steady presence made me brave enough to trust the tops he brought in to play with me and let go.

It's been exactly what I said I wanted the first time we had an actual conversation, and he let me vent about my failed love life. Jax has given me just over six of the most sexually satisfied months I can recall. He helped me check off kinks I've wanted to try with no strings, from my e-stim session with Brian, to an artistic needle play shoot with Doc.

Jax being there for me to arrange logistics and talk out what I enjoy and what I'd rather not try again. With the club closed and my friends wrapped up in their own romantic dramas, it's been easy to lean on Jax to fill the gaps in my social life. Even with our schedules making our time together more rare lately.

I couldn't help getting to know him, seeing the person past the friendly but distant facade he presents at most of the social functions where we've interacted in the past. I treasure my glimpses of the real him. When the clients are gone and the lens cap goes back on the camera at the end of the night. The person who dotes on his dog and tucks me into a warm blanket cocoon in his office.

I haven't missed the way my presence distracts Jax from his work when I need time to gather myself after a scene. It's part of the reason I've been so careful to leave his bed as soon as possible after every play session at his house. Jax is easy to love.

Over the summer, I've started looking forward to the aftercare he gives me as much as the scenes he arranges for me. Well, for us. I know part of the reason he set up playdates with other tops for me is for upgrading his website's private page, not for me, per se. In hindsight, it seems obvious that it was no coincidence his photo gallery shoots helped me fulfill almost every one of the kinky desires I divulged to him in a low-risk setting. Jax is amazing at taking care of me. I just hope he gets as much out of our relationship as he gives.

I've been hoarding the quiet moments we spend together in his office after the dominant party du jour leaves. That quiet time when it's just Jax and me, and I never want it to end. There's nothing quite like the sleepy lassitude of coming down from a scene in his space. I love resting at his feet while he edits photos and does his computery work things.

The absent way he touches me when a file or program takes a while to load or when he takes a break between tasks fills me with contentment. Those casual little touches are everything. They're like the way Kylee touches Q when I hang out with them. An outward display of the affection between a couple who are in sync with each other.

When it's just Jax and me, I can imagine what it would be like to be with him like that, just Jax and me. And when I walk up to his door, still walking on air after he asked me to be his boyfriend earlier, that's exactly what I find awaiting me. Just Jax.

"Hi," I wave at him, bouncing on my toes to keep from glomming on and hugging the stuffing out of him right here in the entryway.

"Hey, you're right on time." Jax beams, stepping aside and gesturing for me to enter. I follow him, removing my shoes by the door. Gia galumphs over to greet me, her tail wagging her entire body in excitement.

"Hey, Gia, sit." I greet the dog calmly so I don't rile her up more. She drops her butt to the floor, tail sweeping the ground behind her as she nudges her snout against my hand for pats. "Are you excited to see me?" I croon as I stroke her head. That works her up more. She scoots closer, pressing against my leg while I scratch her ears. "Yes, you are, aren't you, sweet girl?"

"She's almost as excited to see you as I am," Jax observes wryly as he steps closer, arms open for a hug. I lean in to give him a side hug so as not to disturb his dog.

"Aw, I missed you both, too." I give into my impulse to kiss his cheek. Jax grins at me. He cups my jaw in his hand and takes another kiss. This one is on the lips and brimming with raw passion that has me turning to face him more fully and forgetting to pet the pup at my feet. Gia whines at the loss of contact, nudging her nose into my hand to demand affection. Jax chuckles and the heat of the moment passes. I still enjoy the way his soft lips move, smiling against mine.

"Guess she isn't ready to share you." Jax drops his hand to ruffle Gia's fur, and our fingers brush as we both pet her.

"We could take her for her evening walk first?" I suggest.

"Sounds perfect. Especially if you want to grab sandwiches along the way. Nothing too heavy, but I don't want you fainting on me." Jax winks at me. "I'll even let you walk her. If you want to do the honors?"

"Sounds good. I need my fur-puppy fix. There's a kosher deli nearby that I've been meaning to try. What do you say?"

Jax agrees and hands me Gia's leash so we can walk the dog

together. For all that she flunked out of her guide dog training, Gia is easy to walk, staying close to my side. Jax takes my free hand, tangling our fingers together and letting them swing. It's so totally domestic and I love every moment of the walk with him. This is the mundane sort of belonging with someone that I've been looking for with every failed first date.

Jax tells me about the session he shot this afternoon and asks about my day. Then he checks in about my family, cinching that swoony feeling I got when he kissed me. I get joyful flutters in my belly every time he jostles our joined hands, reminding me he's holding my hand in public. He wants to be seen with me. Nothing is different, except that we've taken down the artificial boundaries between no strings sex and being involved in each other's lives. Everything has changed with that one choice.

"How did Gail's appointment go? You said she had one today?" Jax asks. The reminder that I can share these things with him now, and that he cares enough to ask for updates, warms me to my toes.

"Good. Nibling number five is apparently measuring in the 90th percentile and breech, so Gail is looking at a possible scheduled C-section. Cameron tried to flex about his baby being above average until Viv told him it was probably just that the baby has their dad's fat head."

Jax chuckles. "They sound like a hoot."

"Yeah. Cameron likes to stir up trouble, and Viv keeps him in line. Oh, and you know how I mentioned Eli was on a waitlist for a summer dance camp in Victoria? He got a call that they had a last-minute cancelation, so he's over the moon excited about going. Noa is grumpy that he isn't going on the camping trip they planned together when he thought it wasn't happening. But she's trying really hard to be supportive and not act grumpy, so that's been drama all afternoon."

"Oh no, will that mean Noa's trip gets canceled?"

184

"We're figuring out logistics to avoid that. Pop was going to take them both, but now he's got to go to Victoria for the camp with Eli. Modaddy can't get the time off at this point. Gail and Cameron are visiting her family in Washington for a baby shower that week. Prescott and Matt are trying to get time off, but it's short notice. Viv and Gretchen said maybe, but I don't think they're thrilled about camping with two toddlers and a tween. If they can't supervise, I might try to shuffle around some work stuff so I can go with Noa for some quality sibling bonding. Heck, I might go, even if Prescott and his husband can get the time off to help them wrangle their two kids and Noa out in the wilderness." I shrug, self-conscious of all my rambling. Not everyone wants to hear all the latest family drama, so I stop there, waiting to see if Jax wants me to continue.

"Aw," Jax wraps an arm around my shoulders and pulls me close to kiss my temple, then releases me without breaking stride. "You're the best big brother."

"I try to stay involved." I smile over at him. "It's hard living further away, but I can't imagine living so far from the city and my family here. Oh! That reminds me, Q is inviting everyone over for a pregame party at their place the Friday after the Summer Fling."

"Yeah?" Jax asks, smiling wide, like my excitement makes him happy. Gia perks up at my change in tone too, nosing at my hand. I give her a reassuring pat and modulate my voice, which has her settling into a more relaxed gait at my side again.

"Yeah. So, would you want to come with me? Like, as my boyfriend?" I ask, biting my lip because maybe it's too soon for that? Even though he already knows all my friends, so meeting my family doesn't need to be a big deal. "Are you cool with that? Or my date? I forgot to ask what term you prefer earlier."

"I like the sound of date. Let's go with that."

I grin at him and tug on our joined hands. "Cool. That's settled then. You're my date."

"Yep." Jax grins back at me and squeezes my hand. "And If you're ready to introduce me as your date, then I want to be there."

"Good. I know we haven't technically been dating for long, but they're important to me. I want you to know them. And I want you there too, if I'm taking time off work."

"Then I'll see what I can do about rescheduling my shoots for the week of the trip. Gia and I would love to go camping with you."

"Thanks, this will be fun." I stop, overwhelmed at what it's like to have a partner who will go out of his way for me. I know that about Jax, that he's kind and giving, but it's still a lot. Gia tugs at the leash, then turns to sit by my feet.

Jax gives me a questioning look, but the little frown forming on his lips turns into a smile when I pull him in for an impulsive kiss. I don't draw it out, but I do have a growing sense of urgency about getting Jax back to his place. Where we can have the sort of slow and sensual sex I haven't allowed myself to dream of with him. Sex that has nothing to do with kink or getting off and everything to do with showing him how much I care. Tender lovemaking that will leave me breathless and boneless in his bed. Sex that comes with 'I can fall asleep until tomorrow and wake you up with a full on morning breath kiss' levels of intimacy.

I haven't ever really had that before, and I want it with Jax more than anything.

CHAPTER 17

Jax

When we get home, Gia goes straight to the kitchen. She gazes longingly between me and where she knows I've stashed her treats in the freezer.

Connor snorts. "Does she get freezer yums every evening or just when her human is getting laid and wants privacy?"

"Let's just say there are multiple reasons she likes you." I wink at him as I get Gia's toy for her from its spot in the freezer. "I'm glad you came over. Dinner now, or after sex?" I hold up the deli bag with our sandwiches inside. Gia waits until I give her the release command to gather up her treat to eat it on the living room rug.

"Definitely after you make love to me, date." Connor points to the fridge and flounces toward my room. It no longer takes me off guard when he loses his shyness around me to demand what he wants. It's something I enjoy about playing with him. That I get to see the bold boy who knows what he wants instead of the shy, reserved sub who lets himself fade into the background at the club and play parties with our mutual friends.

I can't help smiling as I shove our dinner into the fridge for later and follow my boyfriend to my room. Even in my head, the title fills me with a warmth it hasn't in the past. Connor wants the total package with me. We're fire in the sack, he's a sweet and willing submissive when we get kinky.

I love the innocence of his little side when Con comes out to play and the tender streak he inspires in me. He encourages my photography, and he loves my dog. I'm not far behind him, but when I walk inside, Connor has already stripped down to his underwear, his packer bulging in the front. He turns to face me when the door opens, shoulders hunched, one arm angled across his chest to rub at the opposite elbow.

"So…" he draws out the single syllable, fidgeting with his waistband and looking everywhere but at my face. He hasn't been body shy during our kinky scenes. Not since the first time he showed himself to me naked. "How do you want to do this?"

"Vanilla sex?" I ask.

"Yeah." His throat bobs as he swallows hard. "Like, it's different without our dynamic and a clearly defined role."

I take a cautious step toward him. Connor doesn't step back, but he tenses up more. "Even in our dynamic, I'd let you fuck me if that's something you want, Connor."

"I kind of figured that?" His eyes dart to mine and away again. His answer only leaves me more puzzled.

"Okay, so what's your question?" I sidle closer. Connor mirrors the movement until we're face to face, and he's close enough for me to reach out and tip his chin up so he'll look at me. He bites his lip and shakes his head before answering.

"I prefer being told what to do in bed. Even if we aren't doing anything kinky. Will you still do that?"

"I can. Do you want me to be completely in charge? Like telling you when to come or to only touch me if you've gotten permission? What would it look like?"

"You would tell me what to do, where to touch you, get rough if I'm not quick enough to obey. But if I like, want to kiss you, you wouldn't make me stop just because you didn't say I could.

Something like that?"

My dick is fully on board with that idea. "I like rough sex, too. What if what I want is to make love to you soft and tender? Make you ache for every caress, every thrust, every kiss until you're quivering and desperate for me to take you over the edge?"

Connor licks his lips, his breath catching as I describe how I want to fuck him slow until I drive him wild. "That would also be good."

"Good. Since you want me to get rough, or 'make' you do things, do you want me to stop if you say no, or use stoplights?" I put air quotes around making him do anything. Connor might like to submit, but I have no illusions that he couldn't overpower me if he wanted to. He's more buff than me, even if I have a few inches of height on him.

"Stoplights. If that's okay?" He finally looks at me with a tentative smile. It strikes me that stripping away the kink tonight also took some of the vibrant confidence he's exuded every other time we've played. Maybe that's it, that this isn't play, and the stakes are so much higher.

"Sure. So, I know you're a filthy little slut after a scene." I try to lighten the mood by teasing him with something playful that I know he likes to be called during scenes. "And you mentioned that you prefer to bottom, but would you want to top me sometimes?"

Connor's smile brightens, so I must have hit the right note. "Yeah. I, uh, cleaned out and put on my play packer when I stopped home for my overnight things. In case you wanted to mix things up?"

"Do you want to fuck me?"

"Thought we could maybe flip fuck?" He licks his lips.

I grin at him. "That's my greedy boy. You want it all, huh?"

189

"With you? Absolutely." He flashes me a lopsided little grin. "Can't get enough of you, Jax."

"Well, you're in luck, because I want to give you everything. So, you prepped for me?" I step closer and push my hand down the back of his pants to finger him and check for myself. I meet the soft rubber of a plug when I delve into his crack.

"Duh. The real question is, did you prep for me?" Connor grinds against me. And that's my brazen boy back. His shyness overcome now that we've discussed where tonight is going. Good. I want him to always be confident in telling me what he needs and wants.

"Yep. I had hopes about how tonight would go." I tap the base of his plug, eliciting a moan. Connor loops his arms around my neck and pulls me into a kiss. I grip his hips and open to him as his tongue explores my mouth. We kiss and grind together until we're both breathless and Connor hooks his leg around my thigh. He's trying to bring our groins into alignment to get more friction on his dick, instead he nearly sends us both sprawling onto the ground.

We break apart, laughing at the near mishap as we catch our balance. "Maybe we should get into bed?" I suggest, my heart bursting with love for him and the fun he brings into my life.

"Naked first." Connor shoves off his pants, leaving nothing but the packing strap that holds one of the more lifelike packers I've ever seen in place.

I scramble to get naked, too, grabbing condoms and lube and holding them out to him. "Want to top me first? And do you want this?"

"Yep, thanks, the condoms help protect the custom paint job, among other things." Connor tears open the foil packet and rolls it onto his dick. "How do you want it?"

I jerk myself slowly as I watch him. "Take me on my back. So we can kiss. I want to see you entering me. Watch your face light up as you give me every inch of that gorgeous cock."

"Mhm." Connor palms himself and groans. "Get over here."

"I thought you wanted me to call the shots..." I tease him, even as I climb onto the bed and position myself before reaching for him to join me. Connor kneels between my legs. He parts my cheeks and drizzles more lube along my balls and crack, tracing along the path the lube trickles, fingering me open with two digits. I lift my hips toward him as he scissors his fingers against my rim, then slips in deeper to find my prostate. The jolt of pleasure has me fisting the sheets. "Right there, Connor. Need you right there."

Connor strokes me again. "Yeah? You want my cock to milk your spot, Mx?"

I laugh. "Here, I thought you liked to be the one begging."

"I can share. Do you like to beg?" He arches a brow at me.

"Not nearly as much as I love hearing you beg, doll. I want you to stop teasing your loving date and get inside me."

"Hm." Connor gives me another stroke. "I like that. You being my date. Mine to love."

"All yours. Now, fuck me already." I reach for him, and Connor leans in to let me cup a hand around the back of his neck and pull him in for a passionate kiss. He moans, his fingers slipping out of my body, his dick rutting into mine, the slick lube making us slide together without resistance. I need him. "Connor," I moan his name.

"How do you want it?" He pulls back, arranges my legs to give himself access, and lines up his dick with my hole. I bear down as he presses his girthy member against my rim, not quite teasing, but not quite giving it to me either. Like he's waiting for me to guide him. That's hot.

"Press in slow," I instruct. Connor does, and I bear down to get the head past my rim. "Mm, just like that, now gentle thrusts, in and out, take me a little deeper each time."

Connor pulls back out, fucks into me again. He goes a little deeper with each thrust, opens me up, over and over. His obedience is almost as intoxicating as the visual of him thrusting into me. His cock disappearing inside me as he gazes down at where our bodies join with a reverent sort of awe. Like he can't believe he's really inside me. I love putting that joy on his face. Love the way he stretches me and makes love to me. Love knowing that this is the first of many times we can connect like this.

"Yes, baby, thrust it all the way in." I moan as he does, still going slow, sliding in until he bottoms out inside me. We're joined as close as can be. His body presses flush against my ass. "Fuck me harder; make us both come, doll." I encourage him.

Connor pulls back until just the tip is inside me, then slams home. He fucks me hard, grinding against me at the end of each stroke. He grunts with the effort, moans as the packer presses into his t-dick when he bottoms out and drives the perfect curve of the shaft right over my spot. His every move makes pleasure sing through both of us.

It's so good I have to hold myself back from coming, I need him to fuck himself to completion first. He might like penetration after he comes, but I need more time to recover between rounds. So I bite the inside of my cheek to hold my orgasm at bay. I try not to let the gorgeous boy thrusting inside of me push me over the precipice. My universe narrows to the sexy little sounds he makes. The precise snap of his hips now that he's found a rhythm that works for us both.

"So, good." He moans, fingers squeezing my shoulders, lips seeking mine, grazing over my mouth as he gasps in pleasure and grinds against me more forcefully. "Need to come, please, Jax. Let me come inside you."

"Do it, Connor. Fuck me. Come for me. Let go."

"Oh, fuck, ngh." Connor's breath comes out on a keening pleasure sound as he drives in deep and comes in a series of sharp, hard thrusts that lose all rhythm. I cling to him as his body rocks against me. The orgasm makes his thrusts fall apart until he stills, following a full body shudder and kisses my neck sweetly. Like he wants to hide his face against me.

"Was that good?" I ask, more to ease him into talking than because I have any doubt he enjoyed fucking me.

"Mhm. So good." His voice is muzzy and soft after his release.

"Still want to switch?" I check.

"Yeah." Connor nods against my neck, then kisses me there again, sucking on the skin until I'm certain he'll leave a mark. Good. I want him to mark me. I stroke his hair, subtly holding him in place. He licks over the spot where he left a hickey. "Mine." He rubs his thumb over the spot, pressing just enough to make it ache. Sometimes I think he's a bit more of a switch than he'd likely acknowledge. "You know I like it when you fuck me after I come."

"Good, because I want to watch you ride my dick. And this time, I don't want you to hide your pleasure from me, Connor." I grip his chin and make him look at me. He gazes at my face with hooded eyes, clearly liking the commands I'm giving him. So I give him more. "I want to see your face when you come while I pulse inside you. Think you can do that for me? Time it, so you come when I shoot my load?"

"Y-yeah. I can do that." His voice wavers, but Connor doesn't seem at all uncertain as he nods eager agreement. He eases his dick out of my ass and lifts enough to work the plug out of his hole. "Fill me up, Jax."

I reach down to finger him, wanting to feel his muscles squeezing me at the loss of the thick plug. Connor doesn't disappoint, clenching around my finger in a way that has me entirely eager to have those same tight muscles working my cock. "Who did you want in charge here, again?" I tease him.

"You, Mx. I want you in charge." Connor moans as I play with his hole.

"Good boy. Grab the wand from my top drawer." I gesture to the bedside table, and Connor scrambles to obey. He holds up the fully charged massage wand I stashed there, special for tonight.

"This?" Connor holds the glittery pearlescent handle out toward me.

"That's the one. And grab a condom for me. No extra lube, you prepped, so you'll have to live with the job you did. Seems fair, no?"

"Yes." Connor agrees with a sibilant sigh. "So fair, Mx." He tosses the condom to me. I suit up.

"Ready?" I stroke my achingly hard cock. The interruption might have staved off my orgasm, but I'm still hard and horny as fuck.

"Yes, Mx." Connor knee-walks back to me with the vibrating wand in hand.

"Then mount up." I grip the base of my dick and aim it up toward where I want him. Connor straddles me, kneeling over my groin. "Lower yourself onto my dick, Connor." I urge him. He does, the tip slipping against his rim at first. He reaches down to help guide me inside, his fingers gentle and his rim soft when he bears down and swallows my cock whole. I gasp at the rush of heat and pressure when he lowers himself all the way to the root.

"How's that?" Connor teases.

"Amazing. Like my boy was made to take my cock. You fit me like a glove."

"Mhm. We belong together. So good together. Need to feel you moving inside me, please?" He rocks up and down, front to back. It's good, but it's nowhere near enough friction for me.

"Lift, I want you to fuck yourself on the entire length. Work every centimeter of my shaft with that hot little hole of yours."

Connor nods. "Yes, Mx. Want to ride you." His abs tighten as he does exactly what I asked of him. His eyes flutter shut as he rises, and he moans as he lowers himself back down, muscles squeezing and working me with his every motion.

Connor is everything I've ever wanted and more. He's incredible, sex with him is incredible. My hips roll up to meet his every thrust, almost without my volition. I want to share this sort of pleasure with him for the rest of my life. As often as we can. He's everything.

I fuck up to meet him harder, bucking wildly. Our bodies find a perfect harmony. Connor is clearly enjoying the ride, even if he needs more stimulation to come. I'm barely holding onto rational thought as I command him. "I'm close. So close. Use the wand to get yourself off, Connor. Press it against your sensitive little dick and make yourself come for me. I want to feel your ass clench around me while you come again. Don't take the wand off your dick until you've milked every drop out of my balls, boy."

"Yes, Jax." The low buzz of the vibrator starts up. Connor presses the blunt head of the toy between us. I notice the gentle thrum of it before he runs it up over his sac and works it under the base of the prosthetic he's still got strapped into place. The maneuver makes his thrusts falter and I compensate by lifting my hips off the bed to keep on fucking him. "Oh, fuck, there. Right there, Jax! Fuck me."

I do, grabbing his hips and slamming him down to meet me

thrust for thrust as the vibrator gives him the added push he needs to come. I want to fuck him forever, revel in the sweet way his body takes me in and makes me fly. Never stop being connected to him. The first wave of his orgasm squeezes me tight, and I tip over the edge. I press in as deep as I can get, wishing I could crawl inside him and never leave. Holding him tight with my cock buried balls deep inside him as I come has to be good enough.

I pull Connor down into a kiss, devouring his mouth as his moans mingle with mine. The two of us tangle together in every way possible. I never want it to end, pleasure pulses over us in a rush. The vibrator seems to draw more shuddering waves over us both, drowning us in an undertow I can't hope to fight. I lose myself in him, and he grinds against me, our bodies rocking together past the point where it's too intense to bear another moment of ecstasy.

"Jax," Connor sobs out a plea, "too much. I can't…" I know what he means. I can't take another second either.

"Turn it off." I agree. He does. I can still feel the residual tingle. His body still presses tight against and around mine, as if we've merged into one flesh. He clings to me as our breathing evens out from the ragged panting of a few moments ago. I don't want to pull apart, but we eventually have to. Connor grimaces when I slide my limp dick free from his body.

"I love having you inside me." He mumbles as he shuffles toward the edge of the bed. I grab for his wrist to keep him from going. Never again do I want to lie here while he walks out my door before the cum even cools. I want him to stay.

"Me too. And vice versa." I pull him back down into my arms. "No running off tonight."

"We'll make a mess." Connor protests.

"I don't care, and you like messes. It's only a bit of lube." I gently take the wand out of his hand and set it onto the bedside table. I remove and tie off my condom before tossing it toward the trash.

"True." He snuggles into my arms, relaxing into my hold. I press my luck, wrapping my leg around him, snugging him more firmly against my body so I can breathe him in and just savor having him here. It's anchoring, a confirmation that this is real. More than an emotionless booty call.

Connor is here because he wants me. Not a warm body to fuck or any kinky top who will have him. Me. And I want him in a way I haven't allowed myself to want anyone in a long time. I adore this boy in my arms, and he reciprocates.

CHAPTER 18

Connor

As a country boy, I'm used to waking up with the sun. All the years and distance now between me and my youth spent doing morning chores with my siblings have made it easier for me to sleep in. But the first morning I wake up in Jax's bed is jarring.

I don't remember the last time I spent the night with someone. The unfamiliarity has me disoriented until Jax's arms tighten around me and he pulls me back against his big, warm body. The heady citrus and spice of his body wash reminds me of where I am, and I relax into his touch.

"It's too early to be up," Jax grumbles into my neck without actually rousing enough to check the time. I glance over at the clock. He's right. We set an alarm last night after getting cleaned up and it hasn't gone off yet. The door is closed so Gia won't join us in bed. I wouldn't mind that, per se, but I don't really want to fool around with a canine audience. Waking up with my date's morning wood jutting against my ass has me all kinds of fired up for sex, though.

I don't even feel bad about shutting her out in the living room, since Gia seemed content to sleep on her dog bed out there. Last night, she dozed at our feet while we ate our dinner on the couch with a cheesy superhero show streaming in the background. She didn't stir when Jax took my hand and led me back to his bed.

That might have been the best part. The domestic moments together after we came down from the rush of shared orgasms. Soaping each other's backs in the shower before sharing a meal. How we exchanged tidbits about our days between bites of food. Simple contact with him while we watched our show. And best of all, laying down next to him outside the immediate aftermath of sex and with no expectation that it would lead to more. Just being together. Although, the sex is damn good too.

I wriggle back against Jax's hardness, hoping he'll take the hint. He chuckles. "Horny, are you?"

"Mhm." I agree. "Do you have time for a quickie?"

Jax cranes his neck over my shoulder and grunts. "Not really. I have to drive out to Port Moody to take some engagement photos. How about I get you off, though?"

"You sure?" I squirm against his dick again. Jax shoves his hand down the front of my pants and takes my dick between his fingers to stroke along the length. I buck into his touch.

"Yes, I'm sure. Get my fingers nice and wet." Jax holds his other hand up to my mouth, probing past my lips.

I try to get him slippery, mouthing at his fingers. When he's satisfied with my efforts, Jax switches which hand is stroking me, my spit slicking the way and making the sensation unbearably good. He uses his other hand to play with my sac, tugging on the piercings and overwhelming me with sensations.

I can't hold back when he places open-mouthed kisses along my throat. Heat and suction combine with his slick fingers on my most sensitive bits and the deep ache of him playing with my Guiche ladder, just this side of rough.

He doesn't stop stroking me until I'm utterly spent. I flop onto my back to see him better. "Mm, that was nice. I could go back to bed now."

Jax snorts as the alarm goes off, as if to punctuate my words. "You're welcome to sleep in after I leave, but you have to work too, right?" Jax swings his legs out of bed.

I heave a put-upon sigh and stretch out over the blankets, starfished across the warm spot he just vacated when he stood up. "Boo to work. I want to stay home and celebrate us getting together for real."

I cross my arms over my chest and pout at him. My little headspace feels right, like I'm safe to show Jax all of me. Here in this early morning space that I only rarely get to share with anyone. Not counting Quent. That might explain why I slip into this headspace. I'm used to being little when I'm sharing a bed.

"Yeah?" Jax asks, gazing down at me with a soft smile. "What would that entail, Con?"

I hunch up my shoulders in an exaggerated shrug, pleased that he correctly guessed that I'm having a little moment and switched to my little nickname. "I dunno. How about an all day fuck-fest? And you could make us pudding. We could fingerpaint each other with it. And lick each other all over. Or wrestle. You said we could have slippery wrestling!"

"I promised my little fairy that, huh?" Jax's eyes are dancing with mirth as he leans over me to give me a gentle kiss. He trails his sticky fingers over my face and I squawk an indignant protest, batting his hands away. His fingers smell like me. And sex. "Now you need to get up to clean your sex juices off your face before work." He settles back on the edge of the mattress and pats my thigh to encourage me to get up.

"What if I just go to work like this, Guppy?" I stick my tongue out at him.

"Nope, my messy boy is just for me. We can still play with other people. As we agreed, I wouldn't ask you to give up your playtime with your friends. And they can see the photos we take together, but when I get you filthy for me, I want that to be mine. Is that alright?"

I nod, squirming closer to him so I can lay my head in his lap. "Yeah. I'm your filthy boy. Just yours. Will you make me messy this weekend? After the Fling? Can we go together? Or, I guess you have a wedding, huh? Meet me there?" I demand. Jax cards his fingers through my hair, smiling down at me indulgently. I reach up and poke the hickey I left on his neck last night, delighted that it's right there for the world to see my mark on him.

The swell of pride I feel at leaving an impression on Jax's skin reminds me of how Monty shows off his bruises and welts after an impact scene. I might have to let Monty know I get it now. That sense of pride over something so primal as knowing he'll carry the shape of my mouth on him all day. Jax takes my hand, squeezing before I can prod the bruise again.

"Yes, you left your claim, little one, but that hurts when you jab it. I have a wedding on Saturday afternoon. But Martin asked me to take photos of the Fling, too. So I'll be there as soon as possible and we can come back to my place afterward for a scene, if you aren't too tired. Now, why don't you let Guppy help you pee and get ready for work?"

"Oh, yes!" I roll onto my feet. I tug Jax toward the washroom, almost forgetting to grab my packer that doubles as a stand-to-pee device from my bag along the way. Jax follows me. He waits while I drop trou and fit the packer in place.

"Ready?" Jax asks, as he steps in close behind me. His bulge presses against my ass, and I wriggle closer.

"Ready." I nod. Jax reaches around me and holds my dick for me as I pee. It's exactly what I asked him for months ago. A big who helps me with something so intrinsically personal. I lean back into him as my stream tinkles into the bowl. Guppy presses his other hand flat on my belly, keeping me in place. Almost like he's gently pushing on my bladder to be sure I empty it.

"That's it. Such a big boy, using the potty." Jax praises me in much the same way I've heard him talk up Gia when she does her business on our walks. Much like the dog, his praise makes me want to wiggle around and kiss him, but he holds me firmly in place until I'm all done peeing.

I give the balls of the packer a squeeze to work all the liquid out. Guppy shakes the last few drops from the tip of my dick before releasing his hold. I tuck away my packer, then turn to kiss him. "Thank you for taking care of me, Guppy."

He drops a chaste kiss on my nose. "Anytime, little fairy. Want to get in the shower and clean up with me?"

"Yes, please. Let me grab my clothes first." I duck out into his room to get my overnight bag while he adjusts the water temperature for the shower.

We don't have time to get handsy or anything, but it's still nice to be close to him. Share in each other's personal routines. And I'm still feeling little when Jax steps out of the shower and wraps me in an oversized towel. He dries me off, tousling my hair and pressing a chaste kiss to the crown of my head, then helps me into my clothes. I can't help falling for him a little more with every caring gesture.

When I remind him I'm big enough to be responsible for pets, he lets me feed Gia her breakfast while he fixes us breakfast. The coffee he serves to both of us alongside warm slices of sweet cinnamon toast he makes in the toaster oven pulls me back toward my adult headspace. It's just not something I associate with being little. Coffee is for grownups, and I want my warm, steamy mug. Jax hands it over.

"Not sure how you take it; I've got all the typical fixings. You can help yourself." He tops his unadulterated coffee with cinnamon.

I help myself to a generous glug of cream, a spoonful of the sugar he nudges toward me and the cinnamon shaker, since it's on offer. "Do you need to get on the road? I could walk Gia for you, if you need me to."

"That's sweet of you, but I'm bringing her with me. These are clients I know well, and they have a fenced yard where she can run around while we do their photos."

"That's cool." I take a sip of the brew and sigh happily. Jax makes tasty coffee. Definite tick in the date benefits column.

"It is. Do you need anything from me to ease out of little-space before work? I could give you a ride into downtown?"

"I'm good. Thanks, anyway, but that's totally out of your way and the bus would probably be just as fast, if not faster during the morning rush. And uh, thanks for rolling with my little time this morning. I know age play isn't really your thing." I rub at my neck, hoping my little mode won't give him second thoughts about dating me.

"Nah, no need to thank me. It's my pleasure to take care of you when you need it, Connor. I told you I'm comfortable playing that way sometimes. You stuck by the parameters we discussed. I'll never be your Daddy, but if you're happy with a fairy godparent who takes care of you when you're little, then that works for me. And you told me you're more likely to need little time during or after emotional scenes and situations. I'd say last night was emotional for both of us, no?"

"It was. In all the best ways. And I don't need a Daddy, just a big who lo—" I bite back the word. We've been dating for a hot second; it's way too soon to fish for declarations of love. Jax is smiling at me like he knows exactly what I almost said. "—*likes* me. I really like you. A lot." I press my hands to his countertop to keep from fidgeting.

"I really like you, too." Jax pats the back of my hand, turning it to twine our fingers together. "I love spending time with you and that you're comfortable being little with me."

"Cool. Me too. Guess I already said that, huh?" I gulp hot coffee and try not to overthink things. Jax squeezes my hand, still firmly gripped in his, reassuringly.

"You did." Jax sips his coffee, too. We lapse into a comfortable silence punctuated with small talk and sweet glances, eating our breakfast together at his table. I smile at Jax, and think of all the times I've visited my family or stayed the night with Q and ached for someone to wake up to like this. Someone to share a quiet moment before a busy day at work. Gia finishes her breakfast and noses at my leg, looking for pats. I oblige.

"We should probably get to work before we're late. I'll see you this weekend?" Jax says as he stands with his dishes.

"Definitely." I nod, dusting my toast crumbs onto my plate and trailing Jax to the sink with my plate and cup.

Jax takes them from me to load into his dishwasher. "Prep before the Fling because I have plans for when we get back here."

"Oh? Do I get a hint? Boyfriends get more hints, right?" I press myself against his side and try my best rendition of puppy dog eyes on him.

Jax gives my ass a gentle squeeze. "Nope, boyfriends get more surprises."

"Do I at least get to know what it is before you shove it up my ass?" I pout.

"Do you want to know? Or would you rather guess?"

I sigh dramatically. "Fine, I guess I'll just have to guess what you made the cream filling out of."

"It really is fine, if you'd prefer to know. But if not, I promise it falls under the category of things we've discussed and I think you'll enjoy the scene I have planned."

"Are you going to make me take whatever this surprise is?"

"Yes."

I lick my lips, mild arousal pooling low in my belly. I don't want to act on it just now, but it's nice. Nice to be with someone who doesn't view me as some sort of compromise. Someone who likes all of me. "Can we use those restraints you've got on the rubber sheets?"

"It's an under the mattress system, so we can use it with or without the sheets, but yeah, I can arrange that."

"Good. Then I look forward to my surprise."

"And I look forward to having my boyfriend at my mercy." Jax plays up an evil laugh. I shove at his shoulder and he wrestles me into a bear hug. I kiss his lips, giving up all pretense of resistance. Gia whining and pawing at my pants breaks up the love fest. I glance at the clock on his stove and curse.

"Shit, now I *really* have to go. See you soon?" I grab my overnight bag from the floor where I left it earlier. Jax assures me he will see me soon, and follows me to the door to give me one more kiss for the road. He fondles my ass and I leave with a smile on my face and a spring in my step.

CHAPTER 19

Jax

The Summer Fling at Adventures is an all evening affair. The party is in full swing by the time I get there from the wedding luncheon I spent the afternoon shooting. I figured it would be busy. I didn't count on it feeling like coming home after a long absence.

Of course, I noticed the gap in my usual social circles over the long months while the club was closed for renovations. But it didn't strike me just how deep the sense of community Martin has built over the years runs. Seeing the smiling faces of friends and acquaintances I've barely seen all summer puts that in perspective. The club truly is a home away from home for so many of us. A safe place to be ourselves and explore experiences that aren't always welcome outside this haven.

I'm not the only one to get emotional about it, either. I snap candid photos of dozens of heartfelt reunions. Play partners excitedly planning scenes with the updated space. Lovers snuggled together on the new lounge furniture. Friends negotiating over the catered spread of snacks. Everyone seems eager to get back into everything the club offers, whether in the newly updated public spaces or the private rooms.

I check in with the folks I photograph to see if they're okay with the images. Many request personal copies once I send them to Martin for his promotional materials. Most of them agree, a few with stipulations about cropping out faces or identifying marks. I delete anything that I don't get permission for, filing away electronically signed releases on my phone. I'll double check everything gets documented when I edit the photos. Most of the pictures I take are candids of the regulars I know Martin is friends with. It's more about documenting a big night in his professional life than promoting the club.

Connor gloms onto me with a big hug when he sees me in the crowd. But he seems to understand that I'm on the clock and goes off with some of his friends to check out the upgrades while I work. Whenever we run into each other amongst the crowd, he beams at me, lighting up like the sun. He brings me a drink when he overhears me casually joking with an acquaintance that I haven't been off my feet all day. Later in the evening, he seeks me out again, checking in to see if I'm close to done.

"Hey, just wanted to let you know I might head out soon. Q and Kylee offered me a ride, and it's, uh, getting late, so I'm probably going to go with them. You can call me if you still want company when you're done here?"

I appreciate Connor not pushing me, or trying to guilt me about our plans. He respects my job, even when it intersects with our social life. Truthfully, I have enough photographs of the event to work with. "Oh. Did you want to ride home with them? Or would you rather come with me?"

"Do you still want to do our scene?" Connor rocks back on his heels.

"I do. Unless you're too tired, we can reschedule if you'd prefer. Time got away from me tonight, sorry." I click the lens cap onto the camera and get it ready to put away. I really am done working for tonight, regardless of Connor's answer.

"It's fine." Connor waves off my apology.

"I didn't realize how much I missed being here." I gesture toward the common room. The crowd is thinning more and more. The empty food platters got carted away by catering company staff hours ago. Martin and his new boy are gathering up trash and tidying the common room, along with a few other regulars.

Connor favors me with a hint of his playful grin. "Right? It's like the first time I went to an inclusive queer club and felt that sense of belonging."

"Yeah. A place where we fit. Sometimes I forget how much I need that. Shall we help pick up before we head out?"

Connor glances around at the folks helping Martin clean and nods. "Good idea. You take care of your camera and I'll go check in to see what Martin needs us to do."

He turns to go, but I grab his hand to stop him. "Wait."

"What?" Connor shoots me a questioning glance.

"I can't wait to get you naked in my bed, boy." With that, I raise his hand to my lips and press a chaste kiss to his knuckles. He beams at me before going off to talk to Martin. I stow my camera in its protective case, then secure it in the locker room. This place might feel like a second home, but my camera equipment is my livelihood, so there is no sense in taking careless risks with its safety.

Once I leave the locker room, Connor waves me over to where he's got a ladder. I help him with tearing down the rest of the Summer Fling decorations and tidying the common room. The entire process is boisterous and fun. Most of the remaining guests are regulars who I consider friends, so it's nice to chat and joke together while we work.

Once Martin calls it quits, Connor and I head back to my place. He chatters about the Fling and all the people who were there on the drive. I can tell he's buzzing with energy again. Good, I was worried he might not be up to playing tonight, and I really want to do this scene with him. We discuss all the freshest club gossip until I pull into my parking spot behind my apartment.

"Scene time?" Connor asks, wriggling excitedly in his seat.

"Scene time. You still ready to play?" I check.

He nods vigorously. "I'm dying to know what you've got planned, Mx."

"Soon, boy. So. When we get inside, you are to give Gia her Kong if she wakes up. Then you go right into my bedroom and prepare your tight little virgin ass to be stuffed to bursting. Do you understand?"

Connor licks his lips and nods. "Roleplay?"

"Yes."

"Mhm. Yay. So, did the little virgin bite off more than he can chew? Should he beg you to let him go?"

"You can play it however you want. We've discussed CNC being a big fat yes, so if you really want anything to stop, I expect you to use your safewords. What are they again?"

"Traffic lights. And if I can't talk, I should tap out."

"And if you can't talk or tap out?"

"Shake my head three times?"

"Good boy." I reach over to ruffle his hair and hand him the keys to my place. "Now, go inside. I'll join you soon."

I give him time to follow my instructions and settle into my room before heading into the house to get what I need. Gia wags her tail at seeing me, but Connor already gave her the Kong stuffed with goodies, so she doesn't abandon it for my sake. "Nice to see you too, girl. I see you have a new favorite human." I joke. She wags her tail harder and huffs out a subvocal little bark. As if to agree that Connor is her favorite lately. "Yeah, can't blame you there; he's my favorite, too."

I can hear the muffled sound of the shower running in my en suite, so I take my time gathering what I need. Connor is going to love this.

CHAPTER 20

Connor

I run the washcloth between my legs, getting myself squeaky clean after the very thorough fingering I just gave myself. I cleaned out earlier, but I want to be ready for this. Not that I think a little mess will scare Jax away. I just want tonight to be perfect. It's our first scene together together. With him as my date. The label makes champagne bubbles of happiness fizz low in my belly.

I'm not sure what to expect when he comes into the bathroom, but it's not for the door to burst open. A Jax-sized person wearing a fuzzy bathrobe and a facemask of what I can only describe as inspired by some sort of eldritch horror enters the room. He's got face tentacles. I glance toward his hands and see that the sleeves of his robe are also be-tentacled.

Part of me wants to laugh at the absurdity of the moment. But then he makes some sort of over the top alien glorping noises. They sound like commands, before he wraps me up into a headlock that presses his dick against my bare, still dripping wet ass. And I don't care if the scenario is ridiculous.

"Hey! What are you doing? Get your tentacles off me!" I struggle against his hold. Jax applies pressure to the back of my head and neck, bending me forward, which shoves my ass back into his crotch. I groan at the hardness of his bulge pressing against me.

"Silence, human."

"What are you? What are you going to do to me?" I struggle until he applies more pressure. He uses the leverage to throw off my balance. I don't want to break free for real, or make us fall on the slick tiles, so I give in to him.

"I said silence." Jax abandons the pretense of making weird alien sounds as he manhandles me toward the bed. Or is that monster-handles? Forces? He shoves me sprawling onto the mattress, then climbs on top of me and quickly fastens the soft restraints at the four corners of the mattress to my flailing limbs. I struggle, but the tethers hold me firm and he tightens them until I'm helplessly spread-eagle, face down on the familiar rubber sheets. Just walking past them to get to his shower had me sporting a semi earlier. Talk about Pavlovian conditioning. Jax's bed covered in these sheets means good things are about to happen.

"Let me go!" I thrash. Jax reaches under me and gives my sac a hard squeeze and a sharp tug. I hiss air through my teeth at the rough handling.

"I'm afraid I can't do that, boy. We have selected you as a carrier. Lay still and this won't have to hurt."

"But you can't, please! Just let me go." Tugging on the restraints adds to the sense of being overpowered. My Mx is going to use me for whatever depraved tentacle sex he has in mind, and I can't do a thing to stop him. My dick twitches against the sheets at the thought. I bite back my moan.

Mx slaps my ass. "I told you to hold still."

"Please, I've never..." I protest, squirming harder.

"You've never had anything in here?" He squeezes a big handful of my flesh, then parts my cheeks aggressively and spits at my hole.

"No." I whimper and buck.

"Good, then you'll be nice and tight when I fuck you." He slaps the other cheek before holding me open again. Something soft but unmistakably wedge-like presses against my hole, forcing the glob of spit or lube inside my body. The soft tip presses against me, unable to quite penetrate me.

Mx adds more lube and something else opens me up; a plug? A fat taper that fucks into me rough and dirty, before he quickly replaces it with the soft tips of his narrow appendage. Or is it a toy? Whatever it is slips past my rim. I think it's some sort of tentacle toy. The textured girth widens with every bit of length he forces inside my body.

Mx doesn't give me time to adjust. So it's intense as the squishy toy continues to stretch me wider and wider until my hole burns. I don't know if I can take the entire thing.

"Please." I gasp, tears pricking my eyes. In an effort to block out the burn of being stretched too far, too fast, I squeeze my hands into fists. Mx is walking the line of what I can take, but so far he's staying on the right side of my physical limits.

"Hush, now. That's it. You're taking my breeding arm. Going to milk all my eggs out, aren't you, boy? Need to fill up this sexy little hole." Mx pushes the last inch inside, leaving me open and aching. Something flat presses against my ass. The base of the toy. I groan, gasping for breath, adjusting to the toy. It doesn't narrow in before the wide base, so my rim still burns from the stretch.

"Too much. You're too big." I whimper. He adds more slick to the base of the toy where it enters me, but otherwise ignores my protest, fucking it gently in and out of my hole.

"You can take it. You're going to take even more." With those ominous words, he fucks me more vigorously with the toy, quick hard thrusts that he knows I like, until, without warning, the toy loses some rigidity. The snick of a lube bottle opening, and then something presses against the walls of the toy. Slick squelching fills my ears. The tentacle fills my ass. A series of fat bulges move down the apparently hollow interior, stretching me to the point of pain.

I sob a wordless protest. The expanding girth is too much; I can't possibly stretch another millimeter as the tentacle deposits what has to be the eggs he was talking about inside of me. And then I do, and it slides in deeper, past the resistance of my rim to stuff me to bursting. Oh fuck.

Jax really is filling me up with his eggs. On an intellectual level, the idea he might shove literally anything into my body isn't quite as alarming as when he figged me without warning. I know Jax well enough now to be certain he wouldn't do anything that might cause actual damage. He won't put anything inside me he can't get back out. Right? He wouldn't. Or would he?

The tentacle seems more massive the longer it stays seated inside me. My restraints combined with the fact I can't see Jax from this angle to gauge what's going on, leaves a small, deliciously scared part of me that doesn't quite trust my judgment. I've been wrong about partners before. And the part of me that likes the thrill of a good scare latches onto the tiniest scrap of doubt that maybe he would.

I embrace the flood of adrenaline that thought sends coursing through me. So good. This is why I love this type of scene. It's like getting fully immersed in a scary movie magnified a hundredfold. Adrenaline and fear pulsing through me like a second heartbeat.

"Please, I…don't fill me up. I don't want your eggs." I toss my head and tug against my restraints. That's true. I don't want it, but I absolutely want him to make me take it, anyway.

"Nonsense, of course you do; your greedy little hole is slurping them right up." Jax normally touches me a lot when we play, but he isn't now. He isn't soothing me or praising me. He gives me another hard slap when I try to wriggle away from the tentacle jammed firmly inside of my body. That lack of connection to ground me makes everything more real for me. As if he's really some random tentacle monster and I'm really at his mercy.

I struggle harder against my restraints, bear down on the toy until I think I might pass out from the effort of fighting him. The tears that threatened earlier spill down my cheeks. "Mx. Please. Jax. I can't. Ungh. Please." Fear makes my heart pound. What is he doing to me?

"Hush, almost done. You have to take the entire clutch now that you're stuffed full of my breeding arm." Mx rocks the tentacle against my ass.

It hurts, but in a good way. A way that helps me let go of everything and float on sensation and inhabit the scene he's creating for me. My alien captor is stuffing me full of some strange eggs. And some tiny part of me believes it could be anything bulging up into my ass, even Mx's actual eggs. A slick series of little pops creates the weirdest sensation, followed by an overwhelming fullness deep inside me.

Mx does something, and the tentacle is a soft, squishy, empty sleeve again. Much less rigid and easier to take before he repeats the process. Stretching me wide with another series of eggs bulging up into me. More dull pops as the eggs fill me to bursting.

"Breeding arm? W-what even is that?"

"Something cephalopods have. Now, hold still, you should feel honored to be chosen as a receptacle instead of blubbering over it." Mx works the tentacle more slowly inside of me. When he withdraws it, he leaves the tip pressed against my rim as though to trap the eggs inside if I try to expel them. I'm still full enough to explode as I lay on the bed, breathing into the lingering ache. "That's it, hold them inside. They need time to incubate."

"Yes, Mx." I whimper, fighting the urge to push out whatever he's left inside me.

He pokes my hole with his finger, and I clench tighter around him. "Such a greedy hole. Need me to fill you up with my spunk, too? You've still got room for more, huh?" He doesn't wait for a response before pressing the blunt head of his cock inside me.

His fingers dig into my hips hard as he thrusts. I'm still slick and stretched open so his cock doesn't hurt, but I am uncomfortably full. A part of me worries about him fucking whatever he used as eggs too far inside me. What if they get stuck?

"Oh, fuck, boy, you're such a tight little hole. Love feeling my eggs inside you, warm and wet and perfect. When I'm done inside you, you're going to lay me a clutch, aren't you, boy? A nice big healthy clutch, bathed in my seed. You think you can do it?"

"No." I plead with him. "No, no, no."

"Yes, you can do it. You took my eggs so well and now you're going to milk my dick, too. Take it all, every drop." Mx fucks me in slow thrusts, his cock bottoming out inside me with each thrust.

I get the idea that talking about depositing his eggs inside me does something for him. Something validating, and I love that I can be that for him. A partner who affirms him the same way he does for me. He moves over me, fucking me into the mattress. His fingers find their way to my t-dick and he rubs me just right, letting me ride waves of pleasure as he fucks me. He comes first, and when he pulls out, I don't want it to end.

Jax unfastens my restraints and flips me onto my back, refastening the straps around my ankles to hold my legs apart. He scoots me closer to the end of the bed, so I'm lying with my knees bent and feet forced wide.

"Sit up. I want you to watch as you lay the eggs, boy."

I swallow hard, letting him prop me upright. "What are they?"

"My eggs. It's time for you to deliver them. Are you ready?"

I shake my head once. Jax rubs my back. "Can you give me a color?"

"Green."

"Okay. Then I need you to lay my eggs for me. I want to see them squirt out of your body. I want to finger you with egg goo and feel them moving inside you."

"Yeah. Okay." I nod and bear down. Nothing happens at first. Jax forces two fingers inside my tender hole and probes around.

"There's one right here. Push."

I do. At first there's nothing again, and I'm starting to worry that whatever is inside me isn't going anywhere without a trip to the hospital. Did he really insert something inside of me? The niggle of fear claws at me, growing with every ineffectual grunt and push.

Mx rubs my back, encourages me to push, and then something sort of slips out of my body, and then another. Until half a dozen perfect gooey ovoids puddle on the sheets between my ass cheeks. I rest panting, partly relieved to have done it, and partly afraid I didn't get them all. I can't recall how many of those hard little bulges he inserted. Am I missing one? More than one?

Mx scoops one up and rubs it against my hole. "There, good boy. Think you've got anymore in there?"

I shake my head, hoping I'm right. He grabs my wrist and forces my fingers against my hole. "You better check. Feel how wet you are for me." I find my hole brimming with a viscous goo as I finger myself for him.

"Fuck." Mx strokes his hard dick as he stares at my fingers moving inside me. "Spread yourself open; I want to see what I did to that tight little virgin ass, boy."

I obey and Mx moves so he's at eye level with my hole. He adds his fingers to mine and shines a flashlight inside me. It's like he really wants to examine my insides. The whole thing is humiliatingly invasive and awful. "Are there any more inside me?" I ask, voice quavering.

"Hm." Mx makes a noncommittal sound. "Push for me." Mx shoves his fingers in deep.

I don't think there's anything left inside of me. And then he lifts his mask to go down on my ass. Licking my rim, fucking me with his fingers and tongue, using his slick digits to jerk my dick and his mouth to drive me wild. I hold his face against me, the eggs forgotten as I come hard while he plays my body like an instrument.

Afterward, Jax pushes me onto my back and ruts his cock along my junk, frotting against me until he comes on a low groan. The slick flavorless gelatin lingering on his lips from going down on me makes our kiss viscous and I kind of like it. More of the goo leaks out of me, feeling alien and strange.

Jax eventually rolls off of me to release the restraints on my legs. He drags his fingers through the sloppy mess leaking from my ass. He plops the wet eggs onto my belly, smearing thick lube over my skin.

"I laid an egg," I reach for one. The surface is slippery with whatever slick is coating it. The goo sticks to my fingers. A perfect replica of what I imagine as some gross alien's progeny.

"You did. Six of them." Jax smiles at me, the tentacle mask and robe long since discarded. It's just my date looming over me now, not a tentacle monster, here to do unspeakable things to me.

"Umhm. Can you hold me now, Guppy?" I'm all floaty after the rush of our scene, and I need him to ground me.

"Absolutely, babydoll. Are you all done playing for now?" Jax scoops the eggs up and deposits them in a plastic bag along with his used condom. Hm, maybe we can talk about testing and getting messy without condoms soon.

"Yeah." I nod, reaching to pull him close. "There's nothing still in me, is there?"

"You got all six of them out." Jax joins me in the bed, smoothing a hand along my spine in reassurance. "But just so you know, they're made of plain gelatin. Any you didn't expel would finish melting at body temperature. Leaving them in would only make you even more of a gooey mess for a little while. They're body safe, but there are similar recipes that are less safe and silicone ones that aren't meant for anal play, in case you want to have that element of fearing the unknown if we do this again. So what did you think?"

"I liked it. That insertion thing was intense."

"The ovipositor? Yeah. Well, I enjoyed using it with you."

"I could tell." I pull him in for a kiss. "It's fun that it sort of flips the biological script a bit."

"That occurred to me." Jax smiles against my lips. "Would you want to use it again sometime? They make bigger egg molds too, for added girth."

"Yes." I kiss him again, lazily, my legs twining with his. I want to soak up having him close. We stay like that for a while, the adrenaline crash making me sleepy and clingy.

"Jax?" Before I can drift off, I need to tell him something.

"Mhm?" he asks, rousing enough to prop his head on an elbow and look at me. Mirroring his posture, I sit up, too.

"I love you." I murmur with our faces inches apart, no filter left to keep it in after he stripped me raw for our scene. Post-orgasms might not be the best time for declaring my love, but I don't think I could find the courage to say it to him first and risk a rejection if I wasn't utterly fucked out and floating on an endorphin high.

Since I'm already an oozing, clingy, emotional mess and he's still holding me close, in that moment it feels like Jax will accept anything that comes out of me. It's easier to open up my heart and tell him what he means to me after I let him open my body to the point I thought he might crack me in half. And now, having said it for the first time, something in me settles. I love Jax and he knows it. No more room for misinterpretation or assumptions colored by my past to come between us.

Jax's eyes sparkle, and even exhausted and coming down from the high of our play, I know before he says it that he feels the same. He's so expressive. I love the way his eyes alone can sometimes tell me what he wants to do with me. And that he's aware enough of his tells to hide them from me when he wants to fuck with my head in bed.

"Me too, doll." Jax pulls me closer. He gazes at me with a world of tenderness in his eyes as he says, "I love you, too, Connor." And then our mouths are far too busy for any more words.

CHAPTER 21

Connor

I submitted my PTO request to take Noa camping late last week, so I'm hoping to have a response from Nadine, my boss, today. Prescott and Matt can't get the entire week off, but worst case, they can take her for a few days. That's not what she wants, though. So my littlest sister has been blowing up my phone, begging me to come along as her chaperone so she won't have to cut the trip short by several days.

Camping in the Okanagan is no real hardship. We went all the time, growing up, since camping made family vacations much more affordable with all us kids. The scenery and hiking trails out that way are picturesque.

I've fantasized about sharing the views with my special someone since I wasn't much older than Noa myself. So I'm actually as excited as she is to go on this trip. It will be my first vacation with a lover, and I'm glad that it's Jax I'll be sharing that with. Plus, it will be good to hang out with Noa and introduce my date to the entire family.

Jax seems excited, too. He's already re-booking the appointments he had for the week that we'll be out of town. It could just be a combination of new relationship energy and the bliss of declaring my love and having it reciprocated for the first time, but I want to spend every waking moment with my date. What better way to celebrate Jax's new role in my life than a vacation together, combined with a chance for him to meet the other people I love?

That means I need to confirm taking the time off. It should be a formality, since Nadine has been on me to use my PTO. We've lost too many talented co-workers to burnout for her not to be on top of doing what she can to encourage a healthy work-life balance.

Still, when Nadine calls me into her office around lunchtime on the Monday after I made the request, I suspect I won't like her answer. It's the one thing that could put a damper on the buzz of happiness that thrills through me every time I think of Jax. And how he loves me. I have a partner, and we're in love. The thought still makes me smile, even through my nerves about this meeting with Nadine.

"Hey, you, uh, wanted to see me?" I poke my head into her office, leary of how this might all go.

"I did. Come on in, take a seat." She gestures to the chairs in front of her desk.

"Uh, sure." I shuffle into her office, shutting the door softly behind me. "Is this about my PTO? I'm sorry I submitted it so late. There was a last-minute change of plans with my younger siblings and they needed an adult to help with some child-care logistics."

Nadine waves a dismissive hand. "It's fine, Connor. I already approved your request. You're the only full-time staff member who hasn't taken time off yet this summer."

"Oh. Well, I mean, I usually take long weekends to visit home. So…" I shrug, flustered at being the focus of the conversation and not knowing what it's about.

"You do." Nadine nods. "And I was auditing time-cards after your performance review last month, and I noticed you've been staying late most days. Is there a reason for that?"

"Yeah. I've been getting more done when I have the office to myself. Fewer interruptions, I guess." I shrug. "The interns are great, but some of them this year require a lot of hand-holding."

"That's fine, but we can't approve extra overtime hours. You know how tight the budget is."

"Yeah. I know. I wasn't—"

She holds up a hand to stop me from justifying myself. "I'm also not the sort of boss who asks people to work for free. So, how about this? The board approved your request to switch to a new schedule. They've been considering this sort of change for ages, anyway, so you can be a pilot case of how it works for us. We'll schedule you to come in four days a week. We'll still expect a forty-hour work week from you, but this way you'll have more flexibility."

"That would be amazing." I agree, not entirely sure I heard her right.

I mentioned doing something like this in passing last month, inspired by my newfound confidence in asking Jax for the scenes I've been wanting to try for ages. Something about getting an easy, judgment-free 'yes' makes it easier to ask for more. But then Nadine offered me a raise, so I figured I'd have to wait awhile before asking again. It's almost as if Nadine and the board really value my contributions to our efforts as an organization.

"Do I need to sign anything?" I had to sign for the raise last month, so it would stand to reason.

"I'll get a contract amendment written up and on your desk by the end of the day. You do good work for us, Connor. We want you to stay with us. If there's anything else we can do to ensure you continue to be happy working here, my door is always open to you, alright?"

"Yeah. Thanks, Nadine. I appreciate it." I smile at her.

It makes sense that they'd want to keep me. Or really, anyone competent, there's a high rate of turnover and burnout among our colleagues. Still, I'm pleased at the recognition, and even more pleased about what it might mean for me. More time with the people I love. And all I had to do was speak up and ask for what I wanted.

"You are very welcome. Have fun on your camping trip next week. Oh, and let me know when you finish the draft briefing on the Howard Street development?"

"Will do." I tip her a playful salute as I stand to leave her office. Nadine laughs and shoos me back to my desk.

I leave her office in a dazed state of disbelief. This is my dream job. We do tangible good in the community. And now Nadine is offering me the exact change I needed to make this job more sustainable for my future. Time to spend with the people I care about. A weekday off to spend with Jax when he's busy shooting back-to-back weddings all weekend long in the summer months. More time for Quent and my other friends. Travel time so I can see my family more regularly.

Nadine just offered me the flexibility I need in my life to find a balance that won't leave me burnt out by thirty on the harder parts of the job. The placements for vulnerable clients that fall through despite our best efforts to find them housing. Those contracts and grants we don't land. The developers who go back on their word, preferring to take a fine when the time comes to include promised social housing in their new builds. All the disappointments that build up and make it easy to become jaded.

One of the best lessons I've learned from Nadine is not focusing on the bad and celebrating even the small wins. This new schedule is a win. And I want to celebrate it with my date. Jax. On an impulse, I message him a selfie of me grinning at my desk.

Connor: Hey, our camping trip is on for next week. Can't wait to get you alone in the woods. ;)

Jax: Where no one will hear you scream. ;P Except for your baby sister.

Connor: Well, if you're coming, I hope we can bring Gia along too. So no one but Gia and Noa will hear me screaming. Should we pack a gag?

Jax: Ha, I see how it is, using me for my dog? Also, maybe no screaming?

Connor: Obviously. And your camera. Bet I'll look super rugged in my hiking gear posed in front of nature with Gia and all her majestic floof.

Jax: I'm not taking your next dating app profile picture. You're taken, and don't you forget it, boy.

I snort out a laugh, realizing as I read his message that he has a point.

Connor: Oh, wow, that *does* sound like a dating app picture, now that you mention it. *cringe* Does that make me a bad boyfriend for asking you to take it?

Jax: Just a bit. You'll have to make it up to me. ;)

Connor: If only there was some way I could…

Jax: Also, kidding aside, I don't think I'm comfortable having sex in a tent with your sister right there.

Connor: That's fine. I was mostly kidding anyway. If Matt and Prescott come along for the first few days, we can swap child-minding duties for alone time in the tent.

Jax: We'll see about that.

His response is a little disappointing, but I get where it might be awkward to fuck while my older brother and his husband know exactly what we're doing. It will also depend on how private our campsite ends up being. And wrangling Carl, Camile, Noa and Gia to give Prescott and Matt similar alone time might prove daunting if Jax isn't used to kids. He doesn't have any siblings, so that means no niblings either.

Jax: Are you sure you want me to meet your family already?

That question makes me regret discussing this via text. Without body language cues, I'm not sure if he's giving me a chance to back out, or getting cold feet, or what. It gives me a queasy flashback to Albert being condescending about doing anything with me in public. And just like that, my earlier confidence that asking can really get me what I want abandons me. Cue text babble.

Connor: Well, yeah. You don't have to, though.

Connor: Like, I get if I'm being too pushy. Or if it's too soon.

Connor: Sorry.

My phone rings. I bite my lip and glance toward the rest of the office. The interns are still on their lunch break, which I am technically currently working through, so I answer the call.

"Hey, doll." Jax's voice is warm, and I want to fall into his arms. "I would love to meet your family whenever you're ready to introduce us. In case that wasn't clear over text. I just don't want to muscle in on your sibling bonding time with Noa."

"It's fine. She'll want to meet you. They all will. But I don't want to pressure you into anything. My family can be a lot. Even Quent was a little overwhelmed the first time I brought them home."

"Right, well, as tempted as I am to make a joke about Quent's sociability being rivaled only by Gia's, this is important to you."

"It is." I stifle a smile at the apt comparison between Gia and Quent.

"Then I'll be there. You said the trip is next Monday to Thursday?"

"Yeah. So we won't miss Q's party or my game this weekend. Or the wedding you're shooting. And I was going to spend Shabbat with them after we get back. If you don't have a Saturday wedding?"

"I do not. The busy season is winding down."

"Awesome. And I didn't tell you the best part. Nadine offered to let me change my schedule to working four ten-hour days. So I can visit them more often, and our days off in the summer won't be completely at odds anymore." As I say it, I realize that I'm implying we'll still be together next summer. The thought doesn't seem scary or far-fetched. Jax and I fit. There's no reason to think we won't last that long.

"That's wonderful, Connor. Congratulations."

"Thanks." I grin at the genuine warmth in his tone, pleased he seems to think we're in it for the long-haul too.

"Come over to celebrate after work?"

"Sure. I should get back to it."

"In that case, I won't keep you. I love you." Jax blows a kiss into the phone and I want to do a happy dance in my seat at those three little words. I doubt hearing him say that will ever get old. Despite my best efforts to keep emotions out of our sex life, I've felt it for a long time now.

"I love you too, Jax. See you tonight?"

"Yep, I'll order dinner if you text me what you want. Include your celebratory beverage of choice."

"Will do," I agree, already envisioning the crisp bite of bubbly cider paired with the homey comfort of pasta and garlic bread. Hopefully Jax won't mind garlicky kisses. "See you soon."

We hang up just as the door to the office opens and our rowdy group of interns returns from their lunch break. Work is chaos for the next several hours, but I'm smiling through it all, knowing I get to go home to Jax and Gia when it's over.

CHAPTER 22

Jax

Connor, Gia, and I head to his parents' place Sunday after I finish shooting a morning wedding. The two and a half hour drive flies. He's driving since he's familiar with the route, but we took my car since it's already covered in Gia's fur. We put on a rock station and listening to him sing along, serenading me and my dog with lines from love songs melts my heart.

As we're getting close to our destination, the station we've been listening to turns to static and Connor turns it off. "No point searching for a new signal; we'll be there soon."

"Is it just going to be your folks and the younger kids?" I ask, mentally trying to run through all the siblings he's started talking about more lately.

I might have spent most of my spare time over the past few days studying his socials like there's going to be a test. Hopefully, I get all his siblings' names right. His oldest brother, Prescott, is married to Matt and they have two kids, Carl and Camile. Then comes Cameron and Viv, who are married to Gail and Gretchen, respectively. Gail is pregnant with her first child. Viv has two kids, Chuck and Edie. And Connor's three younger siblings are still in grade school. Marietta, Eli and Noa.

None of them seem to differentiate step versus half versus full sibling. Though from what Connor has said, Viv and Cameron are his Pop's kids from a previous marriage. And the three youngest were born after his parents got married, so I can extrapolate the details, if that matters. I've totally got this.

"Probably not." Connor chuckles. "If I know my siblings, they'll all be over there, just 'popping by for a quick visit.' I haven't really brought anyone home to meet them as a love interest since high school." Connor drums his fingers on the steering wheel, like the admission makes him anxious. "So, please don't let them scare you off."

"I'm not going anywhere." I squeeze his thigh. The glance he shoots me, like he wants to believe me but isn't sure he can, makes me want to wrap him in a big bear hug. I long to reassure him we'll all get along because we all love him, but I think he'll take that as a cheap platitude. "Have you told them much about me?"

"Just that we've been seeing each other casually for a while, but now we're getting more serious, so I wanted you all to meet. And I mentioned you're genderqueer and my date. So they know you get what it's like to be trans and so they won't misgender you, or call you my boyfriend. You said that was okay. It's okay, right?"

"Yeah, Connor. It's fine. This is all going to be fine."

Connor grips the steering wheel tighter and nods, focusing on the road as we come around a sharp bend and approach a freeway exit. We sit with our thoughts for several kilometers of rural driving until he signals to turn up to an old farmhouse.

From the road, I notice the flowerbeds are a cacophony of colors, spilling across the front of the house and along a paving stone walkway. As we pull up the long gravel drive, I notice that there are several cars parked on the grass beside the two-car garage. A cluster of adults wave from the front porch as Connor parks my car beside a teal minivan.

There's a swing set behind the garage. All of Connor's niblings appear to be playing on it, along with several of his siblings. It's a decent crowd of people. When they all turn to face us as he puts the car in park, I get what he meant by them being 'a lot.' Even with the doors closed and the windows up, I hear raucous laughter from the children as one of the little ones screeches joyfully on the swings. This many people can get loud. But it all sounds happy.

Gia whines in the backseat. She's used to her doggy car harness from coming along to location shoots with me. Still, it's been an hour since our midway rest-stop to stretch our legs and let her pee. She dances in place, eager to explore her new surroundings and greet all the new people. Her whining gets more urgent.

"Settle down, girl, I'll get you in a minute." I promise. She subsides, tail swishing on the seat in anticipation of getting out of the car. I glance at Connor. He takes a deep breath.

"This is it; last chance to change your mind. You want me to turn the car around?" Connor jokes. His attempt at an accompanying laugh is strained.

"Nope." I grab his hand on the gearshift and squeeze. "I'm all in." I reach for him, sliding my fingers into his hair and gently making him turn toward me for a semi-chaste kiss. Connor softens into the affection, giving me just a hint of tongue. I tighten my grip on the back of his head and have to remind myself we have an audience, so this isn't going any further right now. Connor rests his forehead against mine as we take a moment to carve out space for just the two of us. "Relax. I'm excited about meeting your family, Connor. I love you."

"Love you, too. That's why I'm nervous. You're sure about this?" He searches my face for any hint I'm blowing smoke. I meet his gaze until someone tapping on my window startles us apart. Connor's door opens and his Modaddy pulls him into an awkward hug while he's still wearing his seatbelt. Gia barks excitedly, once more shuffling her paws and whining to get free. I unbuckle and open my door.

"Hi! I'm Viv." Connor's sister opens her arms for a hug as soon as I step out of the vehicle. I give her a quick squeeze, then step back. Viv tucks some hair behind her ear. "Connor says you use he/him pronouns, but not masc coded language otherwise?"

"That's right." I nod.

"Well, it's nice to meet Connor's date. He's told us a lot about you." Viv grins at me.

She's not the only one to approach. Cameron is there too, and as soon as his sister finishes her greeting, he comes in with an exaggerated bro-style handshake and claps me on the back. "Good to meet you, Jax, right?"

"Yep, and you must be Cameron?"

"Guilty as charged." Cameron gives me an appraising glance, then looks behind me at Gia. "Oh, does your dog need to get out? Is she okay with kids and other pets?" Cameron raises his voice and calls to his brother over the car. "Hey, Connor, did you tell the rents you were bringing your bo-I mean date's, sorry Jax, dog to visit?"

Meanwhile, the three tweens who were playing with the younger kids on the swing set are leading Connor's older two niblings over to us.

"Uh, no, I thought it would be fun to spring a surprise furbaby on them." Connor rolls his eyes and sticks his tongue out at his brother.

"He told us," their modaddy interrupts. "Since you're so concerned, Cameron, why don't you offer to walk Gia while your brother and his date bring their things inside and get settled?"

"Sure thing, she's leash trained?" Cameron steps toward the

back seat.

"She is." I get there first, clipping Gia's leash into place before I unfasten her car harness. It's not that I think she'd get into any real trouble. But this is a new and overwhelming environment. I'm not about to abandon my best girl to a stranger. Even if he is my boyfriend's brother. Gia jumps out and immediately bellies up to the closest person for pats. Viv obliges with much cooing praise for my girl. "But I can walk her."

Cameron steps back and gives me a chagrined smile. "Why don't I help Connor with the bags instead while you get her used to the kiddos and the dogs? Harvey's off leash, by the way."

Cameron turns to the trunk as Connor pops it open with the button on his key fob. "I'll be back in a sec. You good with her here?" Connor asks me as he scratches Gia's ears on his way around to get our overnight bags and Gia's dog bed out of the car. The camping gear might as well stay stowed, but I want a shower and fresh clothing in the morning before we set off into the great outdoors.

"I'm fine. Thanks, doll." I smile at him. Connor smiles back, glowing and happy to be home, even if he is still nervous about my reactions to everyone. I'm used to meeting and charming tons of people on shoots; I can handle my beloved's family.

"Hi, I'm Gretchen, this one's better half." Gretchen nudges Viv with her elbow and passes over a toddler who appears to be covered in tomato sauce. "And Harvey is Prescott's old lab. He's napping under the slide, the kids tired him out." She points.

"They're exhausting," Viv chimes in with a twinkle in her eye as she bounces the small child she is holding. "This little goober is Edie, and our eldest is Chuck, on the slide with his cousin. Connor says Gia loves kids?"

"Usually. It might be good to let her meet the kids after she's had a minute to sniff around and calm down after the drive, though."

"Sure. Modaddy and Pop have two little yappy dogs on the porch. They were having trouble keeping up with all the tiny terrors. My pug is at home tonight, since we just stopped by to drop off some extra cinnamon rolls Gretchen made. Noa likes them."

Meanwhile, the tweens join us.

"What do I like?" Noa asks.

"Gretch's rolls." Viv gestures to her partner.

"Oh, yeah, I do. Not as much as you like them, though. Can we pet your dog?" Noa hits me with puppy dog eyes that remind me far too much of her brother.

"Sure, she loves people." I agree.

Noa crouches down to Gia's level to give her a thorough scratch. Gia licks her face, making her laugh. "She's even cuter in person!"

It doesn't surprise me that Connor shared the dog pictures I sent to him with his family. He adores my dog. Almost as much as I adore him. More of his family gathers around to introduce themselves.

Marietta, Chuck, Camile, and Eli join Noa crouched down to give Gia belly rubs. My girl is in seventh heaven, soaking up the attention and cooing praise while I'm subjected to a barrage of questions about myself and how Connor and I got together. I answer gamely, trying to keep up when several of his siblings and their partners are talking at once.

At some point, the three youngest siblings ask to walk Gia around the yard. Gia seems enamored with them after a thorough belly rub. Connor has been walking her for me for months without trouble, and these kids must have had a similar upbringing around dogs, so I agree. I'll be able to see them the whole time, anyway. I hand over her leash and they lead her to a patch of lawn to relieve herself.

Our eyes meet as Connor comes back outside. He and Cameron have their heads tipped together as they talk, and Cameron has an arm slung around Connor's shoulders. Connor smiles and raises a hand to wave at me, almost shyly. I tune out all the noise and just grin at seeing him happy and surrounded by people who love him.

Connor rejoins me, grabbing my arm and kissing my cheek. "Quit interrogating him, you lot." Connor complains. "Come eat, Jax. Pop cooked."

"Oh, if you think food is going to stop the questioning, you've clearly not been paying attention." Cameron teases.

"Enough, don't scare Jax off." Viv shoves Cameron in rebuke. Cameron looks ready to retort, but then his wife tugs him aside for a whispered conversation, and he keeps his voice down.

Connor leads me toward the house, and his family follows.

***

When we're finally alone in the guest room hours later, Connor turns to me and smiles. "So, you survived first contact."

"I did." I agree, squeezing him tight. Everything went well. So far, I like his family and they seem to like me. Cameron's brash questions notwithstanding. He doesn't seem like a bad guy, just that he likes to stir up trouble. I hit it off with Prescott and Matt, which is good, since they are bringing their kids along for the first few days of our camping excursion. Harvey is staying with Connor's folks.

They offered to watch Gia for us, too. Both of us. The delighted smile on Connor's face at being part of an 'us' was one of my favorite parts of tonight. The way his eyes shone and his foot pressed against mine under the table. And I'd be lying if I denied

235

loving the implication that Connor adores my dog as much as I do.

I'm still on the fence about accepting, but leaning toward leaving her here for the next few days. Considering Gia's penchant for getting into things she shouldn't. She's a burdock magnet. And she's sampled more than her fair share of the poisonous mushrooms outside the dog park. That racked up quite the emergency vet bill last summer. And then there's her history of nosing at skunks and porcupines that are better left unsniffed when given half a chance.

I checked that the provincial park where we're camping allows leashed dogs. But why risk taking her into the wilderness when she could stay here with people who will care for her like she's their own? I can tell that about them already. Connor's modaddy even joked about Gia's existence adding another grand-dog to the family. The beaming grin on Connor's face at that remark filled me with warm, fuzzy feelings.

Gia seems to like it here well enough. She had a blast chasing the kids and other dogs around the yard after dinner, playing fetch, and running amok. She is curled up on her own bed beside ours, exhausted from all the new friends she met tonight.

I'm too wired to sleep, even with Connor snuggly and warm in my arms.

"And it was okay?" He bites his lip.

I thumb his lip out from between his teeth and kiss him softly. "Better than okay. They all seem lovely."

"Not too much?"

"No. I mean, I won't lie, they can be overwhelming. Especially when half of them were gauging whether I'm good enough for you, but I had fun tonight, Connor. I love you and they all obviously love you, so, yeah. Worth being overwhelmed."

"You know…we could have *more* fun." Connor walks his fingers over my belly, toward my dick. "This is probably our last night with any real privacy until we get back."

"We'll manage without sex for a week, doll." I grab his wrist to stop him from pawing at my dick.

"No fair." Connor pouts. Or is there a bit of Con in his reaction?

I bring his hand up to my lips for a chaste kiss. "Consider it a game for me, little fairy. Guppy wants you to see how many days you can go sleeping next to me without coming."

He licks his lips, a calculating glimmer in his eyes. "Do I get a prize if I win?"

"Sure." I kiss his nose, suppressing a laugh. "How about, if you can go until we get home without asking for sex, I'll set up another ovipositor scene for you? *And* you can guess what I've added to each of the eggs as I stuff them inside of you."

"What sort of additives?" He narrows his eyes at me. "Is this going to be the figging scene all over again?"

"You'll have to be my very good boy if you want to find out." I shrug nonchalantly. I'd never do anything that might harm him, and I'm sure he knows that. But I have zero qualms about playing along when he wants to scare himself by leaving that tiny thread of doubt.

"Do oral and hand jobs count?" Connor asks.

"Yes." I cup his cheek and kiss him. "Any shared orgasms count."

"Only if I ask for them." Connor counters.

I nod. "Only if you ask for them."

"It's a deal." Connor promptly rolls over and plasters his ass against my groin. He stops short of rubbing against me in a blatant attempt to take advantage of the perceived loophole in the rules by getting me to initiate sex. If we weren't on the other side of a thin wall from his parents, I might give in to his lust.

"Not happening, doll. But just think how good I'll feel inside you when we get home next weekend? My big fat cock filling you up while you beg for me."

Connor groans and rolls away from me. "I think I've made a terrible mistake."

"Yeah?"

"Uh, huh." He turns to face me. "You're going to tease me like that all week to make me lose, aren't you?"

"Only when your siblings aren't close enough to overhear." I agree blithely.

"That settles it; my date is an evil person." Connor pokes my belly.

"I have to maintain my Domly-Dom cred somehow." I tease him.

"Fair enough. Hold me, oh evil one?"

"Sure." I open my arms to him. "Get some rest, now. We've got a busy week ahead of us."

"A busy week of not getting busy." He grumps as he settles into my arms. Con presses his ear to my chest, sighing in contentment. "Like listening to your heartbeat, Guppy."

"Sleep, little fairy." I stroke his hair. I consider saying something totally sappy. Like that it's beating for him, or that I love him more with every beat of my heart. I discard both options as too over the top and go with the simple truth. "Guppy loves you."

"Love you, too." Con nuzzles into my chest. He yawns, and adds in a sleepy mumble, "love you forever."

It's been a long, eventful day. Connor might not mean anything by that. We're a long way from making any sort of formal lifetime commitments to each other. No matter how deeply I already care for him and how compatible we've proven in and out of the bedroom. But I hope that's what this trip together is; the beginning of our forever.

***

Thanks for reading! If you enjoyed Connor and Jax's story please leave a review to help other readers find them. For more kinky adventures, be sure to grab the next book in the series, Quent and Kylee's story, Puppy Love: www.amzn.com/B09YFBWCKV or check out the entire series at: https://www.amazon.com/dp/B09D627KGK

And for all the latest news on my writing, be sure to sign up for my newsletter: https://landing.mailerlite.com/webforms/landing/i2w6l7

ABOUT THE AUTHOR

Alex Silver (he/them) grew up mostly in Northern Maine and is now living in Canada with one spouse, two kids, and a lovebird. Alex is a trans guy who started writing fiction as a child and never stopped. Although there were detours through assisting on a farm and being a pharmacist along the way.

Visit me online at:
http://alexsilverauthor.wordpress.com/

Browse my entire book catalog at:
https://www.amazon.com/Alex-Silver/e/B07NPBW615

Join my Facebook group at:
https://www.facebook.com/groups/alexsalcove

Follow me on BookBub at:
https://www.bookbub.com/profile/alex-silver

Follow me on Twitter:
https://twitter.com/asilverauthor

Sign up for my newsletter for a free short story at: https://landing.mailerlite.com/webforms/landing/i2w6l7

And as always, consider leaving a review on Amazon or Goodreads if you enjoyed this book, reviews are of vital importance to independent authors, thanks!

OTHER WORKS BY ALEX SILVER
Summer of Adventures
Kinky Contemporary Romance

Dungeon Master (M/M)
Knotty Boy (M/M)
Service Call (M/M)
Picture Perfect (M/M)
Puppy Love (F/X)
Stud Muffin (M/M/M)

Table Topped
Contemporary Romance

Roll for Initiative (M/M) Book 1
Charisma Check (M/M) Book 2
Saving Throw (M/X) Book 3
Plus One Bonus (M/X) Book 4
Dump Stat (F/F) Book 5
Party of Three (M/M/X) Book 6

Shift Work
Omegaverse MPreg Romance

Papa Bear (M/X)
Squirrel Trouble (M/M) (expanded edition)
Trash Panda (M/M)

Hauntastic Haunts
M/M Paranormal Romance

Dan's Hauntastic Haunts Investigates:
Goodman Dairy (*Book 1*)
Hawk Lake (*Book 2*)

Ivarsson School (*Book 3*)
Joliet Asylum (*Book 4*)

Free download links to the shorts are available in my FB group: https://www.facebook.com/groups/alexsalcove
Drew's Haunted Hangout (*A Hauntastic Haunts Short Story 1*)
Rafael's Haunted Halloween (*A Hauntastic Haunts Short Story 2*)
Lee's Haunted Holiday (*A Hauntastic Haunts Short Story 3*)

Psions of SPIRE
Urban Fantasy

Shelter (M/M) Novella 0.5
Bright Spark (MMMM) Book 1
Bold Move (MMMM) Novella 1.5
Keen Sense (M/M) Book 2
Weak Link (M/M) Novella 2.5
Quick Fire (M/X) Book 3
Clear Sight (M/M) Book 4
New Look (M/M) Novella 4.5

A SPIREverse daddy kink standalone
New Ground (M/M/X)

Shared Universe Series
Super U - Superhero Romance
Super U: Rising Storm (M/X)

Final Days - Zombie Romance
The Willows (M/M GNC)

Anthologies
Listen: The Sound of Fear
Haunt (M/M trans gothic horror)

Fix the World
Upgrade (gay trans cyberpunk)

SUMMER OF ADVENTURES CHARACTER GUIDE

Martin: Owner of Adventures, MC in Dungeon Master who discovers a kinky boy in the cafe where he's forced to work when his office gets flooded.

Bobby: A barista who first appears in my contemporary series, Table Topped, and finds love with a regular at the cafe where he works. Martin sweeps him off his feet with a whole new world of kink after a misunderstanding about just what sort of dungeon Martin runs draws them together in Dungeon Master.

Monty: One of Connor's closest friends. Tate's best friend. A pudgy boy with ADHD who discovers that his best friend's brother is his perfect Daddy in Knotty Boy.

Luke: Tate's step-brother and Monty's Daddy. He specializes in ropes and suspension bondage and gives workshops on the topic. He and Tate are also business partners. Realizes his brother's best friend is the perfect boy for him in Knotty Boy.

Tate: One of Connor's closest friends. A plumber who owns his own business along with his step-brother, Luke. He is dyslexic and into age play/ABDL. Finds his Daddy after a chance encounter leads to more in Service Call.

Rory: Tate's Daddy. A trans man who moves to Vancouver for his career as a voice actor and rediscovers his kinks as Tate's Daddy. Finds love after a one-night stand in Service Call.

Connor: Quent's best friend. A shy, pierced, Jewish, trans boy looking for his perfect caregiver who can also be his partner. Finds love when his kinky friend with benefits grants all his wishes in Picture Perfect.

Jackson: A kink photographer who offers Connor a kinky friends with benefits relationship the turns into so much more in Picture Perfect.

Quent: Also goes by Q. A fun loving nonbinary pup who uses they/them pronouns. Connor's best friend. They are in a long-term relationship with their Mommy, Kylee. The pair has an ethically nonmonogamous relationship that is open for sex and kink, but closed romantically. Quent and Kylee struggle to deepen their relationship when Quent offers to be a surrogate for their brother in Puppy Love.

Kylee: Quent's Mommy. She is a trans woman who is a motherly figure to all of Quent's little friends, particularly Monty, Tate, and Connor. Her story is told in Puppy Love.

Harry: A contractor who is kink positive. Harry met Quent when he helped with renovating Quent and Kylee's home playroom. He is Connor's friend group's DM for their regular D&D sessions. He also handles the renovations at Adventures for Martin.

Clark: A pup handler who appears in multiple books along with his partner. Niko is his pup and husband. They have an open relationship. His story is coming soon in Stud Muffin.

Niko/Nicholas: Clark's pup. One of the friends pup Q enjoys playing with. He is married to his handler, Clark and dating his boyfriend, Ethan. His story is coming soon in Stud Muffin.

Ethan: Nicholas's boyfriend who sometimes plays with Clark and Niko together. His story is coming soon in Stud Muffin.

Hope: Angel's Domme and partner. They have a teenage daughter, Bethany.

Angel: Hope's sub and one of Luke's go-to rope models for demonstrations and workshops. They are married to Hope and Bethany's parent. The pair appears in several books as members at Adventures.

CONNOR'S FAMILY

Since Connor comes from a large family, here's a little information on all of them to refer to if needed:

Dad: Connor's father who died when he was 2.

Modaddy: Connor's gestational parent who is non-binary, widowed and remarried to Connor's step-father when Connor was ten.

Pop: Connor's step-dad, who is Jewish and bisexual

Prescott: The oldest child in Connor's family, full brother to Connor. Married to Matt.

Matt: Prescott's husband, the boy next door when they were growing up

Carl: Matt and Prescott's 6-year-old.

Camile: Matt and Prescott's 4-year-old.

Cameron: Second oldest, Connor's step-brother. Married to Gail.

Gail: Cameron's wife who is currently pregnant with her and Cameron's first child.

Viv: Third oldest child. Connor's step-sister who was in the same grade as him in school. Married to Gretchen and currently on maternity leave with her youngest and contemplating having more kids.

Gretchen: Viv's wife.

Chuck: Viv and Gretchen's 3-year-old

Edie: Viv and Gretchen's youngest, still an infant.

Connor: Fourth child in his family. Trans man who is looking for love like the other members of his family have found.

Marietta: Fifth youngest child, born after Connor's modaddy remarries. Connor's half-sister. Oldest of the 'little kids.'

Eli: Sixth child in Connor's family. His half-brother and Noa's twin. One of the 'little kids.'

Noa: Connor's youngest sibling and half-sister. Eli's twin. One of the 'little kids.'

www.ingramcontent.com/pod-product-compliance
Lightning Source LLC
Chambersburg PA
CBHW022004170626
46808CB00001B/281